Spiral of Hooves

Roland Clarke

For Michael,
With thanks for everything.
Thrill to the read & enjoy the rides.

August 30th 2017

ISBN-13:978-1548508418

ISBN-10:1548508411

Cover design by Jonathan Temples
Cover photo by Nick Perry

Originally published by Spectacle Publishing Media Group in 2013
Second edition by Createspace Independent Publishing Platform 2017

For Carrie,
the daughter I discovered too late but
who gave me a precious gift
&
For all those who died too young, for
their country and for their sport.

ACKNOWLEDGEMENTS

Spiral of Hooves was a long journey of over 13 years from conception to completion, and I am grateful to the patience of family, friends and colleagues.

Many people, from riders to medics and beyond, shared their experience and wisdom as I attempted to learn more about horses and other topics than my career as an equestrian journalist revealed. There are too many to credit here, but I need to mention with special thanks, Tony Warr, Michael Whitlock, Jenny Dutton, and Fiona Fouracre. Some kept asking which Olympics I would finish the novel by—the answer was London of course, for the first edition published in 2013.

All the errors, and failures to understand the shared knowledge are mine.

My thanks to my colleagues from the Tunbridge Wells Writers Circle who critiqued my work, and to my editors, including Yen Ooi, and to Lin White without whose extensive help this new edition of the novel would not have been possible.

I am also grateful to my friends Jane & Nick

Perry for supplying his photo of my other friend Sarah-Jane Brown of Shoestring Eventing and to my cover designer Jonathan Temples for turning that image into a great cover. I am also grateful to Kristina Stanley for the excellent endorsement on the paperback cover, and for all her encouragement.

Finally, and most importantly, I want to thank with all my heart the person that inspired me to keep writing despite life's adversities: my precious wife Juanita.

You helped me to fly when my wings were clipped.

PROLOGUE

QUÉBEC, CANADA – December 2011

The chair spun across the floor as Lina Jardero stood, fists punching the air.

"Caramba, the coward has emailed more ridiculous demands," she said, and then paused as if expecting answers. "Why does everyone interfere in my work? Doesn't anyone realise that I'm the scientist? There has to be an end to this."

Armand Sabatier swivelled in his chair and gestured towards the snow-covered fields outside the cabin. "It's the Boissard way. This is their stud and they'll continue to fight each other for control—whichever way we try to improve the situation." He was reluctant to abandon the only family he had left, but withdrawal might be the sensible option. "We'll be better off once we leave and start afresh."

Her hands pierced the air again. "Someone may act sooner. Nothing has changed, although the last two years were okay—we can't let one person destroy everything we've struggled for."

As her anger wavered, she broke from his native

French into American. He had seen the explosion coming, but her vitriol, when delivered in choicest Mexican, could be implacable. He was accustomed to the raven-haired Chicana's passion and glad she restrained her vehemence this time. Lina's research at Du Noroît Stud was crucial, and she could not afford to abandon the work.

He stood and put his arms around her, knowing that a friend's embrace should calm the professional fury.

Her wolfdog, Mistico, nuzzled between them, drawing her affection and breaking the fragile link.

"So you'll arrange everything today, Lina?"

They needed a resolution, but Armand was concerned she took risks, even though she was capable of standing up for herself. One of the reasons he had given her Mistico had been his past failure to protect someone precious and accomplished.

"Tackling anyone would be useless. Anyway, I've things I can do 'round here. It's more peaceful than at the office where they're meeting, and probably arguing." She walked over to her chair, pushed it back and sat down, fingers poised on the keyboard. "And you?"

"I want to stay, but I must see someone—about my environmental survey. I need to justify my position at Du Noroît somehow."

"You're always too willing and anxious to please.

Sometimes I think you're not tough enough, Loup. I fear that nickname is inappropriate, despite your wolf pendant."

Armand smiled and said, "I'm happier in the lone wolf role with no need to be macho. We're at the stud as friends, as support."

He had told them enough; his past had been buried forever along with his old Loup identity. He just wanted to concentrate on his current life working at the stud, helping care for the horses, assisting where he could with the breeding programmes.

He kissed Lina on both cheeks before putting on his skiing gear. The flurries outside were tapping the double-glazing at the front of the timber cabin. Any delay was risking the worst of the encroaching storm.

"You should take the Skidoo. This weather may get worse before you're finished."

"I must take some exercise and skis are quieter. I'll manage. My meeting's only along the river trail where we exercise the horses. So I'll be back for lunch. Will you be okay?"

She pointed at her attentive companion. "Totally, I've Mistico, and you always say he's my real wolf. Please be careful, Loup—it's treacherous out there."

Savouring the tranquillity of the frozen world, Armand glided into the snow-laden trees. The first falls of the winter had buried the stud's paddocks, although the top rails of the fences marked them out. Passable tracks had been cut into the snow and curved up to the horse barns nestled around the distant farm buildings. Despite the signs of hibernation, stud life at Du Noroît never ceased and any of the winter chores or the demanding workload could explain the head groom's insistence on the urgent rendezvous.

Odette must have a good reason. We trust each other—no one else. She alone can help me end the pain; heal the past.

The wind picked up, dampening any other sounds. Glancing at the foreboding sky, Armand quickened the pace, his cross-country skis and sticks moving in unison.

If I had any sense, I would've heeded Lina's warning and played my un-athletic role. An inept nonentity. But I can always be mistaken for reckless—and Odette sounded desperate to meet.

At least he could cope with sub-zero conditions. He was frustrated that this new life had been dragged down by one man's callous disregard for everyone.

The Frenchman gritted his teeth and lowered his head against the gusts. He pushed for a rise and crested it, turning as Odette cantered along the cleared trail below on a young stallion. Focused on where the trees crushed the narrowing track towards the rocky bank and the turbulent water, she was oblivious of

Armand, who traversed the steep slope past a ruined cabin towards the trail. He skied nearer, intending to meet her as arranged.

The stallion reared suddenly as if bitten by an angry insect, and Odette fought to control the bucking animal. Clumps of snow dropped from the overhanging branches, splattering the woman's burgundy jacket. White snow merged with the red, creating a vision too much like seeping blood. Armand's head reeled.

A confusion of images hit him: an unseen force thrusting the rider towards the torrent; the horse bolting for home in a whirl of hooves; a white-clad figure with a crossbow dissolving into the blizzard.

The howl of a wolf echoed in his head.

The snow swept in and whipped around Armand as he fought against the storm in his brain, forcing back the terrors the cyclone might resurrect from his past. He struggled down the slope to reach Odette, but she had vanished.

The whiteout descended, blanketing any evidence that might have remained, leaving Armand bewildered and uncertain as to what he had witnessed. Now his panic was building, reawakening the haunting memory that had never faded from his heart. He was back in another country, helpless, as he watched a broken body struggle for life, and the blood on his hands spilt on trampled snow.

The storm in his head swept over him, and he collapsed.

GREAT BRITAIN AND FRANCE - 2012

ONE

The pale sun strove to reach through the mist to the frozen ground. In the dawn light, Carly Tanner rode her horse down the track and through the gate in the blackthorn hedge. Their breath sent out tendrils of steam as the pace quickened down the first pasture towards the fields beyond. The crunch of frost mingled with the squeak from the well-polished saddle.

The home-bred grey mare responded to every subtle request from Carly, whose heart was beating to the rhythm of the hooves. Around her, the sounds of birds mingled in a tapestry of trills and melodies, with the call of a cock pheasant rising above the other songs. At times like this, Hazelmead was more like home than a workplace.

On the lower pastures, she slowed Sylvan Torc to a halt and peered into the mist that rose in swirls from the stream flowing under the wooden bridge. She eased the horse into a walk along the banks of reeds, searching the gloom ahead.

A distinctive scent drifted on the air before the vixen appeared, majestic in her long coat and thick brush with black hairs streaking the tip. Dead rabbit in her jaws, the vixen stared at Carly and the horse with piercing eyes. Then, as though deciding they were no threat, the silent hunter turned away, trotted across the bridge, and vanished into the veil of white.

For a while, Carly considered how this devoted mother could become the quarry. Deserved perhaps if she had killed prized lambs and prolific egg-layers, but she dreaded the vixen's taste for forbidden flesh inviting either the jaws of hounds or the teeth of a gun. The vixen haunted these mists, a reminder of life's intricacies and cruelty.

Death was too close, although it had always been part of her life growing up on a farm. Her mother's death was still hard to bear, even after two years. Finding Marguerite face down in the mud had been a traumatic warning that their shared disorder killed if uncontrolled. So, Carly controlled her diabetes, trying to accept it as normal, even if there were frustrating restrictions. Still, her loss remained, and tears too often escaped.

She cast a bouquet of winter aconites into the water and watched the flowers drift downstream like a Japanese lantern. This ritual soothed the pain, but before the memories overwhelmed her, she pressed Torc into a trot, concentrating on staying firm in the saddle.

As they passed the bramble-smothered gate on the edge of a copse, she remembered the chores that lay ahead. At least she had fed all the horses and cleaned the yard. For now, she would enjoy this short hour of freedom. She broke into a canter, blood racing and red hair streaming from under her hat.

Maybe the post would bring a letter from the French Equestrian Federation granting her mother's last wish, that Carly ride for France. Would her application succeed on just the maternal nationality? Or would she need to produce more prolific results to prove her credentials? Not that those were imminent.

At least on Sunday, she would be show jumping Torc. Perhaps an elusive win would end their run of poor performances. The mare had an incredible jump, but Carly's shortcomings as a rider held the partnership back.

Approaching the farm buildings, she reined Torc back and walked the mare past the tractor shed, and the cattle shed, where the farmer had overwintered slaughterhouse-destined bullocks—that was up until 2001 and Foot and Mouth, the darkest time for farming. The buildings were now abandoned, left for grass and wildlife to reclaim.

As his groom, she had pleaded with the farmer for

more horses to be brought on and sold to keep the yard going. If the liveries paid something, the farmer was deaf to any diversification that yielded anything but instant cash. But soon, he would find that all the liveries would be moving to better places, despite all her efforts.

She turned past the barn where the old horsebox was parked beside the dwindling stack of straw and hay. In the tidy yard decorated with hanging baskets and ringed on three sides by twelve covered stables—some with names on their doors—she untacked Torc. Eight of the stables were empty, as most of the horses were outside, rugged up for protection from the weather. Three liveries had already left, and nobody was clamouring to move in.

With a competition imminent, Carly had brought her mare in from the fields. She led her into the end stable, labelled TORC, and then checked that she had remembered to replenish the hay while re-doing the stable's straw bedding. Inside the next-door box was Torc's four-year-old daughter, Dido; known as Queen of Carthage when Carly entered her in any competitions. So far she had shown little of her dam's flair.

Outside, her flat-coated retriever, Guinness, emerged from his siesta, exuberant again after his earlier exertions, helping Carly hack out horses for owners who required the full livery service. Guinness had been a twenty-first birthday present from her parents, arriving as a furry ball. Now five, he was the companion she could always depend on.

As she glanced around the refuge that she had claimed amidst the decay, she realised that this ordered home for the horses held most of the remnants of her life.

TWO

The cobblestones sparkled with the remnants of morning rain fading in the sunlight. Change of country, change of weather, and change of job. Armand had learned to adapt and move on. Another day and having checked the horses in his charge, he collected the feed barrow and walked out of the yard under the clock tower. He gazed down the poplar-lined drive, past the white-railed paddocks, and across the flat landscape, looking for some pleasure in the black fields. The new Boissard acquisition, Fenburgh Stud, appeared tranquil, but experience had taught him otherwise. England could hide danger as much as Canada.

Back on Du Noroît, death had been lurking in the whiteness. Something had stirred just out of sight, yet his rational mind had called it a paranoid delusion. The accident had not been suspicious, according to the police, but an unfortunate tragedy.

I must always remain alert to danger. I sense it, but who can I trust? Lina? Her work comes first. Gilles craves thrills. Can I find some peace here in England? I could end this all. I can find life in the dikes, hedges and windbreaks, but home will always be in the forests of the Cévennes... tangled in memories.

Yet he had chosen to disconnect from that world to survive. He had tried to connect with his ancestral roots in Québec, but that had only ended in more tragedy. This new existence was another chance to rebuild his life, although this time, he must remain aloof.

A throaty roar echoed across the paddocks, bringing Armand's attention back from the past. A red Subaru Cosworth Impreza swept into the drive, fish-tailing as if the driver were rallying, not coming back late from a night in the city. Gilles Boissard pulled the car to a stop, jumped out from behind the wheel, stretched his lanky frame, and then smoothed back his dark hair before walking around the limited-edition car. He took the hand of a sleek blonde as she slid out from the passenger seat, and then draped a fur coat over his intended conquest's shoulders as he kissed her dark pink lips. She patted his cheek then followed him inside the pseudo-Georgian mansion. The butler would be sent out for the luggage.

Armand turned away. Gilles might not show his face in the yard for a few hours, and by then, someone else would have exercised most of the horses—apart from the stallion, Dragon Du Noroît. With rare exceptions, no one but Gilles rode the twelve-year-old, known by the stable name Drac.

Heading past the mirrored indoor school, Armand wondered if Gilles's blonde catch rode, or was just another admirer devoted enough to watch from the tiered seating. Frustration at Gilles welled inside of Armand and pulled at the threads of their friendship.

Back in the modernised Victorian stable yard, the cooing doves and the contented horses calmed him, but the sounds did not alleviate the exasperation at how much Gilles ignored his work. Not just his efforts at ensuring a spotless yard, but also in hacking out the horses he was permitted to ride. But Armand would bend to every whim and errand now that they had moved to Fenburgh Stud and created a new direction.

Could he ignore the return of the old nightmares when they plagued his sleep? The doctors had warned that they would, but drugs were not an option that Armand was willing to try. Therapy had taught him to recognize that guilt and suspicion only fed his perception of normal situations. However, that was all in the past, in France.

Closing his eyes, he saw forests and a blue sky, heard birds and waterfalls, smelt flowers and the earth. Nature, experienced or remembered, that was the key to his self-therapy—along with the power and grace of the horses.

However, sometimes, snowstorms invaded his

waking day, thrusting him back into his memories of Canada, of a day confused by rumours.

On that day, when he woke in his bed, he had thought a wolf was howling his name, but it was only Mistico licking his face. Lina had explained that she was concerned when the flurries had built into a blizzard. Supposedly, Mistico proved invaluable in helping her find Armand, who had fallen in a snow-drift on his way to work. She said his insistence on independence could have proved fatal. Did he need reminding?

Should I accept that by cheating death I defer an end to my guilt? What price will I pay for my failure? Is this the burden of surviving when I'm responsible?

Tragically, the storm had spared him, but at a price. Odette Fédon's horse had returned—rider-less. After a fruitless search for the head groom, the Québec Provincial Police declared it another winter misadventure that must wait until the spring thaw for resolution. Another loss in the snow. Tears choked inside.

Everyone at Du Noroît Stud had been unnerved at losing such a popular member of the team; all except Gilles's father Roman, who remained unmoved by the tragedy. Gilles distracted himself with a spate of parties and long weekends away, while Lina locked herself into work, as did Armand. The others never knew about his personal connection with Odette, but it added to his distress and tormented him, even now.

I've lost the only person I could share my pain with. Why her?

But he was grateful for the support of Lina and Gilles when they persuaded him to move with them to England and make a new start, out of reach of Roman. Until a more suitable replacement could be employed, Armand was given Odette's grooming job. He found that the extra work distracted him from his mental anguish as the horses gave a noble purpose to life. His temporary role meant more duties, and the horses proved soothing companions, healing for his troubled mind. He was sometimes relieved if Lina, the team's nutritionist, helped, even when Gilles exerted his authority as stud owner and deemed that Armand lacked the appropriate expertise.

Armand's desire for simplicity and normality allowed him to accept this situation, but in moments of paranoia, the troubled faces of his friends made him imagine a new crisis, even in tranquil England, far away from the snow. Could he trust them to resolve the problem if there was one beyond his imaginings?

Yet, two months after the accident, he had no basis for these irrational fears. Problems existed but nothing sinister, just the usual dynamics plaguing a family with money like the Boissards. After arriving in England, everything settled down without any interference from Gilles's father Roman—who was back in Canada—even Lina's nutrition programme. If her problems had continued, Armand wondered about checking out the stud's genetically modified feed trials, which Lina and Gilles had rejected. Perhaps Roman's obsession piqued Lina's professional pride, which was understandable as she was the one amongst them who held the Animal Biology degree with Honours.

She'd be the first to challenge any feed issues. I'll let her judgement guide me, for now. I have to trust her. My hallucinations are false demons deluding me and feeding my suspicions. The medics in France insisted recovery would be gradual—and ongoing.

Half-an-hour later, Armand had put three horses into the walker, a horizontal wheel-like machine that exercised them as it slowly turned. He was in the tack room cleaning saddles and bridles when he heard Gilles and the blonde stroll into the yard, so he went outside to receive the expected order.

"Can you get Drac ready and—"

"Willow hasn't been ridden yet," said Armand.

"No way, I need something classier than her."

Gilles walked towards a stallion that was watching them.

"Pin is amazingly laid back but moves like a dream. He'll be perfect. You'll find he has beautiful paces, Tara chérie."

Armand agreed since Gilles rode Pin at the intermediary level in pure dressage. The blonde's nod indicated she knew what she liked. As the groom, Armand was expected to ready both horses while Gilles continued his seduction to one side.

Mounted, the couple rode out towards the back drive, then Gilles stopped and turned towards Armand who standing by the empty stables, expecting more instructions.

"Oh, and you can ride the Witch. She won't mind if you just hack her out. Keep to the field verges in case she rears."

Once again, Gilles was maligning the poor mare that had never attempted to buck Armand off. She reserved her rebellion purely for Gilles in a bad mood. Once, she had leant over her stable door and nipped Gilles, after he had sworn at her.

Armand put a bridle on the mare, and she nuzzled him. He had tried to get the stud staff to call her Willow, instead of the derogatory stable-name Gilles deemed appropriate. Gilles dismissed the alternative name, even though it was also derived from her competition name of Sorcière des Saules—Sorceress of the Willows in French.

Should he remind Gilles that he had bought the mare believing she had great potential? It would be difficult because Odette Fédon helped find Willow, and contact with the French breeders resurrected too many memories for Armand. He had detached himself from those who were back in France, those who had lived with his failure. Distance might even have healed the wounds he had inflicted; yet, the bond would never be broken. At least at Fenburgh, everyone was unaware of his past, and nobody ever needed to know.

An hour later, Armand was untacking Willow when Gilles and the blonde returned, straw-tangled hair betraying them. Gilles handed him the reins of the two stallions and then reached into his breeches' pocket, pulling out a sheet of paper.

"Nearly forgot, here are the events I have to do. Can you send the entries? Not sure when the closing dates are, but find out." He turned away, put an arm around Tara, and sauntered off towards Fenburgh Hall.

Merde, why does he always risk leaving his entries until the last moment? He presumes he won't be balloted out.

Odette had once said that Gilles forever depended on the goodwill of long-suffering entry secretaries and the presumption that his late entries would always be squeezed in. Glancing at the list, Armand smiled. He had already second-guessed his pleasure-distracted friend and entered the correct four horses in the season opener at Isleham. However, Gilles wanted to compete two more a week later at

Poplar Park, another nearby venue that should favour local runners. Once again, the Canadian's organisational inefficiency would go unpunished, as entries remained open for another two days.

Once inside the yard office, Armand took three minutes to access the entries websites and complete the two forms for the later events, which left time to check through Fenburgh's extensive computerised records. Any files that would simplify his environmental impact assessment of proposed improvements to the equestrian facilities would be invaluable since a visit to the local council had yielded basic plans but no more.

Scrolling through the morass, he noticed documents on a dozen Boissard horses placed in a "transit" folder, which all related to Canada. Curiosity kindled, he opened a few files and studied them. He struggled to find any irregularities, but the obsessive detail of the records could be obscuring the obvious. He hesitated and resisted re-filing the documents as re-organisations annoyed Gilles, who needed to remain in control. Obsessive like Roman, their common trait fed one area of their business feud.

Perhaps the jumble is intentional. Is Gilles's ongoing search for new bloodstock or Lina's attempt to improve the horses' nutrition post-GM behind this?

Although nothing seemed illegal, Armand had learnt to suspect anything secreted or camouflaged, except this appeared more akin to a filing error and was probably best ignored.

Gilles would deal with the mistake, as he was integral to the Boissard Équestre's setup and was determined for the enterprise to succeed. The year they had all met, Gilles had discovered Fenburgh as a potential UK base when he competed in Europe with Odette Fédon. She had only been employed as Gilles's groom for a few months when she was promoted and allowed to attend the international events.

She should be here with us. England was part of her dream. Another tragedy.

Three years later, the move to the stud in Suffolk was proving an invaluable chance to regroup beyond Roman's tyranny.

Armand glanced again at the documents and noticed some Du Noroît records. Had someone created a computer link to Du Noroît that allowed Roman to monitor the new stud in England? Roman was vindictive and irrational enough to undermine his own son's share of the business using any information gleaned. Any agreement that each stud would be independent of the other must have been ignored. Perhaps Gilles was hacking into his father's records instead?

Before his assumptions diverted him, Armand pulled back, forcing rational deductions to pull him free. Now was the time for careful surveillance;

observations and hard facts were required, not gut reactions. Experience taught him to be prepared for all eventualities, but first, the horses required his commitment as the proxy groom.

THREE

The next morning, Armand headed into the hay barn with its regimented storage areas and tossed some bales off the end stack. Remaining invisible behind the academic image was no longer an option, even if he could hide his muscles. When Gilles and Lina had first met him on a university field trip, Armand had just recovered from his injuries, so the inept bookish image had deterred any awkward questions. It was simpler to continue to foster this persona and allow his new friends to believe they had introduced him to new outdoor challenges. Oblivious to the truth, they had helped rebuild his life, so the researcher emerged and now this role as a groom.

He loaded the wheelbarrow with five bales and eased it up. He strained as he turned back towards the courtyard and Gilles stumbled around the far corner. Nine in the morning and the Canadian was either already exhausted or hadn't slept at all the night prior.

"Criss—women. I can't make them out. I gave her a great time." He caught Armand's shaking head.

"Not just in bed, although that was real wild."

"So, what did you do wrong?"

"No idea. She was up early demanding breakfast, refusing my needs and now she's in the Orangery reading. Says she'll stay the weekend, but that's all. No way are we taking her anywhere. You finished with the horses?"

"Most of them, but I left you Drac and Pin, as my research is suffering and overdue." Armand continued as he swept the yard. "You know I'll always stand by you... like at university when your father didn't believe in you." Armand added in a lowered voice, "You did help me find my feet..."

"Papa never has, though he sounds convinced Drac is ready. Says he'll let him service more mares this season. Even claims he'll support me at the major events."

Armand grimaced at the idea of Roman agreeing to Gilles's intentions. "No doubt your father has other plans, which we'll all regret." He stifled his doubts as he said, "You still want to go to the dance this weekend? Even without your guest?"

"Sure thing. The butler will deal with her, and the stud grooms can do the horses once we've left. I'll take Lina—we must celebrate her birthday." Gilles saw Armand's expression and said, "No excuses this time, you're coming too, and no argument. Think of the women—the guys say some real hot ones come to this dance."

Armand let his friend weave the dream while they carried more hay into the feed room.

"Hey Loup, let's take some horses to Sussex so I can showjump on Sunday. It gets boring competing at our local centres too many times," said Gilles. "This way, I'll face different competition, and I can assess new horses for potential. Might even find that elusive head groom—time for a real one, sorry Loup."

Glancing around at the heads peering over their shiny wooden doors, Gilles added without waiting for a response from Armand, "I'll ride Drac and... " hands on his brow, he stared at a grey head, "... I suppose the Witch. *Joualvert*, I wish I'd bought another stallion."

Two months after they had met, Gilles had competed at Le Lion d'Angers, France's premier Six and Seven-Year-Old Championships. He was also checking out new stock to buy, as the show was perfect for talent spotting. Gilles had no doubt overlooked the horses for girls, even with Odette there to keep him in order. As Armand had history in France, he'd taken a lead from Lina and pleaded that he had too much studying to do, so Gilles and Odette had found the mare together, as they had Fenburgh.

Armand didn't want to remind his friend about the trip to France, but he said, "Are you forgetting Gilles, what you told me after Le Lion?"

"No, of course not. For eventing, a horse must be good at three phases, a tri-athlete. Sorcière has the paces for dressage; stamina, speed and scope on the cross-country; plus, accuracy in the show-jumping."

"You came home saying she had star potential, perhaps in her genes, so you had to buy her whatever the price. So why this reversal in thinking only weeks before the season?"

"Well, second place three years ago at Le Lion as a seven-year-old proved she had ability, but she's changed. Now she gets so moody, just like a woman, I never know what scheme she's brewing. I must show her that I'm calling the shots or she'll continue to be a problem horse. Her results are erratic and—"

"She might need a subtler approach, like with women. They can respond to what you're feeling, even if you say nothing." Armand's suggestion might work, but unless Gilles changed his attitude to those he misunderstood, he would attract more obstacles.

"I'd better school Drac, and I suppose the Witch as well. So, Loup, you get the truck loaded while I do some flat work... oh and drop by the lab. Tell Lina she's coming to the dance. She's not working all weekend." Gilles mounted the stallion and rode out through the archway towards the school, hooves ringing on the cobbles.

Like his father, expecting everyone to concede to his plans. Armand was sure that business manoeuvres had to be behind this willingness to complicate their 425 kilometres round trip to a dance, which meant Lina would not be there as mere decoration. Gilles must be on a mission to find horses worth buying, and she had more appropriate expertise, having trained in animal biology.

He walked over to the far side of the complex and entered the secure compound that was guarded by CCTV cameras and alarms. Although fewer than at some racing yards, the surveillance was enough to deter Armand from prying. Reviewing his mental notes on the security as he loaded the horsebox, he wondered whether the phials of semen, laboratory equipment, and bespoke saddles were valuable enough to justify this surveillance, even with the level of yard thefts in the area. One day, the complete 3D visualisation of this target area, down to the idiosyncratic way the security lights flickered when the alarms were switched off, might prove crucial. Maybe something else lurked at Fenburgh Stud—or perhaps paranoia was stalking him again?

I escaped the oppression of Du Noroît, so why hasn't my anxiety lifted? What did I forget? Or did I bury too much?

The thought flashed painful images and he clung to a wall, controlling his breathing until the blood and the snow dissolved from his vision.

FOUR

Tempted eyes and jealous glances followed the shimmering vision as the redhead walked into the room. The dress, with its angled hemline, showcased her body, and her curls of auburn hair were piled high and fastened with a silver clasp. Unabashed by the attention, the young woman greeted a group at the bar.

Gilles turned to one of his local mates. "Now that's one pure dream. Bet those legs are perfect to wrap around a horse or me. She's amazing. Who is she?"

"Not sure," replied a friend. "They all look different out of jodhpurs, can't always tell. But those guys are showjumpers. Perhaps she isn't even a rider, just here for the evening and—"

"Whatever, she's perfect." He nudged Armand. "So, Lina's all yours. She's here to enjoy herself. Time to use that charm we all keep expecting."

Armand sighed. *I'm not ready. The memory of her is too raw. I'm only here for the meal and the wine.* One dance with a friend didn't mean anything, so he would make an effort, for Lina's sake.

The oak-beamed room with the dance floor at its centre was filling up with people of all ages. Everyone had come dressed in their smartest clothes for the event. The women were bedecked in a myriad of dresses and even the men sported a little diversity with colourful waistcoats and the odd kilt.

At their table, the hors d'oeuvre of melon and Parma ham waited along with the bottles of Burgundy Pinot Noir and Alsatian Riesling that Gilles had ordered for their group.

Invigorated by the main chicken dish, Carly was enjoying the chance to chill with friends. She talked and toyed with her Pavlova when she noticed a guy at another table staring at her. While her neighbour kept chatting, her replies became murmurs of inattention. The guy was handsome, although maybe the flowery waistcoat under his dinner jacket was a bit flash. As he tried to flick a stray hair away from his eyes, she realised the thick hair, boyish dark looks and knowing grin had drawn her attention. She hesitated. A bad time to be thinking about another guy, when horses were the real priority. A new boyfriend was inviting trouble.

She was managing to ignore him when one of her friends leant over. "Have you noticed that really fit one eyeing me? If I wave him over, will you dance with his mate, the other foreign-looking one? Please,

Carly? He's okay, a bit dull though. Don't misunderstand me. Probably a great dancer with all the right moves, which means..."

As her friend babbled on and the waiters served coffee, people milled around the room and the band started playing. The fit guy came straight over towards Carly, having pushed his cute friend onto the dance floor with a dark-haired woman who moved like a panther.

"Bon soir chérie. Tu sais je suis ton destin."

He gestured at the dance floor. Carly was cornered, intrigued by the stranger. His movements were purposeful and elegant, and the French words tempted her. She considered what he said—perhaps he was her destiny?

"Oui, allons danser," she replied.

He smiled, eyebrows raised, and then took her hand. At first, they swayed in unison, then the beat washed over them, and their movements became more extravagant. Weaving across the floor, they rode the rhythm of seamless songs.

When the band stopped, he guided her back to his table. The panther woman was still dancing with wild enthusiasm. Their poor friend was sitting alone, sipping his wine. His face was drawn, and the sorrow in his eyes was too familiar. She wondered if he had lost someone precious. He registered enough to pour her glasses of water and wine. Her tempter sat close beside her, gazing at her face and stroking her hair.

She stared back and said, "In case you're interested, I'm Carly. Sorry, I don't know your names or anything about you."

"Gilles. Oh, and this misery is Armand. We met through university, in Canada. When he's not so morose, we call him Loup."

She was about to ask which university when Gilles continued, "He's the old one in our group. He was doing a late Ph.D. at Québec à Montréal. I graduated in business studies from McGill. My family are in pharmaceuticals, and breeding horses. I'm down for the weekend from one of our studs and jumping at a local show tomorrow, so maybe I'll buy some more. Can never have enough..."

She let him talk more about himself, amused that here was the rich guy her friends joked about catching. The words drifted past Carly unheeded, because of his caress on her knee. She was tempted to brush it away. Like a butterfly beating its wings against her, the touch wove patterns along her thigh. Her skin tingled, and the feeling spread, making every nerve-ending twitch in anticipation. Her breathing sharpened, and her heart beat faster. She needed to shut him out, close her eyes. As he loosened his bow tie and took off his jacket, she wanted to ignore the line of his broad shoulders and the flex of the muscles under the shirt. The rise of his chest matched her breathing.

Escape was imperative, but as she stood up, Gilles swept her into his arms and back onto the dance floor. The music slowed and she moulded herself against him, evading his kiss-stealing lips.

When the music ended, he was caressing her, and she couldn't let go. She was losing control. Her head was swimming, and she clung to him not in passion, but in fatigue. Her legs were giving way, and she finally broke from his grasp, collapsing onto the nearest chair.

"Are you alright?" Gilles asked, concern rising in his voice.

"Yes, it'll pass... I just need a moment." Embarrassed and feeling a little foolish, she tried to calm herself down. What would he think? Some guys could be so insensitive and stupid if they discovered she had diabetes as if it was catching. "Don't worry, I'll be okay. I don't know what came over me—maybe it was something I ate."

She smiled and slipped away to the ladies' room, her whole body shaking. She found that she was sweating, and her pulse was racing. For a second, she feared the worst and dug around in her purse, unsure whether to take a tablet or inject. She needed to check her blood sugar. Something was wrong.

She had forgotten to adjust for the evening, unlike at competitions where she had a fixed regime to control her insulin levels. She laughed, feeling stupid. Dancing with Gilles had done this, and the emergency snack bar in her purse was the solution. She needed to end the situation before it went too far.

When she returned, the band was playing a slow number, but Carly never reached Gilles. Her past waylaid her in the form of her cheating ex-boyfriend, Mick Roper, arriving to spoil the party. Despite her desire not to confront him, Mick knew how to sweet-talk her, and had soon steered her back into the throng. At times, she detested him after their messy break-up, but found it impossible when he turned on the charm. His pleading eyes and soft words had warmed her life, while he was more than happy to indulge her with gifts and thrills. Even though she had walked out on Mick, she retained some of her feelings for him, and they had remained friends. How could she refuse him?

Mick took her in his arms, but she could never forgive his betrayal, even if his passion tempted her. She knew that it was a moment to be elsewhere, yet for once, the familiar embrace was safer than the headlong thrill. As the song ended, she slipped away, confused.

When she reached the Canadian's table, she said, "Sorry Gilles, I must drive home now as I have an early start—" she glanced at her watch, "—in five hours. Perhaps I'll see you jumping at the show."

She gave him a quick hug and, guided by her French inheritance, kissed him on both cheeks. She then said goodbye to Armand with the same gesture.

Instead of chasing after her, Gilles sat at the table stunned, staring at the glass of wine in his hand.

"Losing your touch? Twice in two days, that's bad," said Armand.

"Don't see you with anyone. Lina deserted you fast. At least mine actually wanted to dance with me, and tomorrow she'll come looking for me. Wonder how good she is at riding?"

"Well, if we find out, please ensure you concentrate on the horses."

He was beginning to worry about Gilles finding a new distraction just when focusing on the future competitions should be his priority.

"Cool it. Carly's a perfect challenge. It's fun charming a showjumper groom for a change."

"You're being reckless. Why waste time seducing her when your horses need you? Anyway, I'm going as well—to sleep. I'm taking the Impreza. You're not fit to drive, nor is Lina. I'm sorry but you'll be safer in a taxi."

Gilles dropped the keys on the floor. "Great friend, chasing after my girl, you've no chance." He finished his glass of wine and stood up. "The night's young so I'm going to rock. I'll get a lift and a bed, no problem.

You've struck out big time, you know. Lina has some real admirers. Just go."

Armand wanted to say, "Carly means nothing to me. Why would I chase after one of your women?" But the Canadian was already with another female on the dance floor.

Outside, the night was cold, and a corona ringed the moon, glistening on the treetops. On the slope above were shadows that gave the venue its name, High Rocks; yet another cruel echo of the towering crags of the Cevennes.

No one realises how desperate I am to escape this half-life that chains me to the past.

He had been shaken by Lina's comment before they danced, "You lost your soul in Canada. Why don't you enjoy yourself for once?"

This space is my lifeline. Can I find peace when I can't stop reliving my guilt? Odette, my precious Cygne, you're the one I'll hold close, forever. I welcome the warm memories, even soaked by grief. Beyond resolution and redemption, you are all I live for.

FIVE

"Câlice. That's all I need, a horse that can't jump the simplest poles."

His perfect dismount didn't disguise Gilles's mood as he lit a cigarette. The collecting ring inside the showground's indoor arena was busy with riders and grooms preparing their horses for the next class. It was going to be a long day of indoor jumping, particularly for any revellers from the previous evening's dance.

Gilles had tried to convince everyone in earshot that Willow was at fault for fences down in both classes and the failure to make either jump-off. He inhaled the smoke in short gasps, snorting it out towards the ground.

"Maybe you tried too hard," said Armand, although his opinion would go ignored as usual.

Gilles always blamed the mare, especially when the odds against winning even a rosette increased when competing against sizeable fields that included many riders preparing for the eventing season that was only a fortnight away.

The cigarette was discarded and ground underfoot, and Gilles thrust the reins into Armand's hand.

"Just get this Witch to the box. She's the one that always lets me down. Thank God I brought Drac. Make sure he's ready for the next class. I've work to do."

"Can I help?"

"Don't worry, it's only stud business—so if you see Lina, send her over."

Frustrated at being cut out of all the horse dealings, Armand shook his head, but Gilles had already turned away. Did it matter that Armand hadn't seen Lina since they arrived five hours earlier? He had last noted her wandering off talking to Gilles.

Will Gilles wait for Lina? Does he even need her guidance? She's here for a purpose, though, as the stud's nutritionist.

He noticed a familiar redhead beside a blonde woman on a black gelding. Carly was checking the tack over and gesturing at the fences. He tried to read her body language. Was she the groom or the instructor? He guessed groom, but he only had time to acknowledge her with a raised hand.

Outside, the sun gave some warmth and relief from the foot-numbing sand of the indoor arena. If the day yielded anything valuable, then Armand could put up with the minor discomforts. Extreme cold and wet were among the many occupational hazards he had long ago learnt to ignore.

Armand had taken Willow to the horsebox and was on his way to the collecting ring with Drac when he saw a knot of people watching some horses warming up in the outdoor arena. He stopped and watched the riders, which a female journalist was taking photos of and scribbling in her notebook.

Joining the spectators, he found Lina leaning on the railings.

"So, if Willow is not right for Boissard Équestre what are we searching for?" he asked her.

She gave a good imitation of a Gallic shrug and embellished it, tossing her head, making her raven ponytail flick like a whip.

"Well, I was convinced she was. But I'm not sure even Gilles knows when he's distracted by the riders, especially today. He's really looking for that redhead."

"Carly."

He hoped this was professional concern and not female rivalry.

"Better to ignore him. Carly means nothing. He'll move on and find another and then another—always does. Anyway, I've noticed a few horses that I liked—a mare and two stallions—right build and length for breeding, performance potential and all the signs of good care and nutrition. But then I feel

Sorcière is good, as you do. Not sure if Gilles makes the final decision anyway."

"Roman?"

"*Exactamente.* I can handle Gilles with his flirting while working and even his attitude to mares—"

"And demands on his friends," said Armand.

"*Si,* but Roman meddles and tries to thrust his ideas and advisors on us." She stopped, her face darkening. "Being here won't thwart him, Loup. Gilles is wasting time. He has to tough up and tackle his father."

The vehement edge to her voice concerned Armand, but an innocent smile washed away her Latin intensity. Her laughter warmed the day.

"We're paranoid. Gilles is shrewd and will make this move work. Even if he has to flirt with every woman pretending they're his next groom."

"Even you, Lina?"

"Hell no, I've more sense than to be taken in by him. Anyway, he needs me professionally—in the lab—not chasing him."

They led Drac towards the indoor arena and near the entrance they saw Gilles talking to a large man with a moustache and gesturing towards a black stallion.

"That's one of the horses and he made the Newcomers class look easy," said Lina. "Bueno. I am right as usual, so I will continue checking out the horses.

Hasta luego."

Resisting the urge to follow and sound Lina out more, he walked Drac towards the entrance into the arena. Gilles and the owner were making a deal inside the door, so he melted into the background, asking someone for the time.

Gilles examined the stallion. By the Canadian's gesticulations, a price was negotiated, although it would be subject to a vet's thorough inspection of the horse. Armand turned away as the parties shook hands and exchanged business cards. He hovered unnoticed, as his friend made a call on his mobile.

"I have one... yes... I'll check tonight and confirm. Possibly another one... the usual arrangements. Bury him... yes, today."

The word 'bury' reverberated like a rifle crack in Armand's head and the glistening snow blinded him. At his feet, her body was dying, blood smeared against white. Then, the pain—he stumbled and tried to clutch at life. A hand grabbed him and the snow dissolved along with her body and her blood.

"*Criss* Loup, I thought you could hold your drink. You look terrible."

"I'm okay, Gilles, probably my cooking. I've brought Drac, have you sorted your business?"

"Oh sure, checked out the Newcomers winner, a Hanoverian with a fast time too. Not convinced he's quite right for Papa. The owner might have others, and says he'll stay in touch."

Armand was glad Gilles had forgotten the near collapse, as any explanation would be awkward. First, the nightmares had returned, and now another flashback had almost exposed him.

I'm not ready for this. Did Gilles's dealings trigger it? I need to make sense of his call.

The French-speaker on the other end had not been Roman. The casual tone had suggested a very different relationship and Gilles had instigated the arrangements. Is Roman being cheated by his son, or is this part of the family intrigues? Was the voice another partner in Boissard Équestre? Armand wasn't desperate to trawl through the chaotic computer records on a vague suspicion. There were authorities to deal with infractions - if anything illegal existed.

"I've found the person I want as my groom," said Gilles.

"Person, that means Carly. So you've talked to her?"

"Sort of, a blonde was fourth in the Newcomers and Carly's grooming for her. Two horses in her charge, so she's perfect. Carly, for our head groom I mean."

"Don't rush into this. Okay, Carly may be brilliant but check her out first. What do we know about her?"

"Well," said Gilles chewing his lip. "Just look at the gelding: beautifully plaited mane, oiled hooves, shining coat, immaculate saddle, and smart tack. That takes a conscientious groom. It's obvious. She's the one."

Armand agreed, but there were other criteria, even if Gilles was already satisfied that Carly was his target. *I'm willing to be convinced if we learn more.*

Gilles pointed to where Carly was heading out into the arena to walk around the fences with the blonde rider. "Time to check her out, and the course, naturally."

Pacing out the distances between the jumps and assessing her options on approaches, Carly realised how much she missed her mother's guidance. Her friend Beth might be a rider, but her good advice was limited, and not just over jumping.

Beth nudged her. "There's your guy and that weird bloke. Are you trying to ignore him? Good technique for keeping his attention."

Carly had noticed Gilles earlier, jumping a beautiful grey mare that to a casual onlooker would resemble a young Torc.

"I don't have time to worry about him, not now when—"

"Shame, I understand you chucking Mick out your life, but you're totally stupid if you lose this one. You can't afford to."

Carly ignored her friend, even if she was the boss

today, and instead focused on walking the course. Only when they were in the food queue, ten minutes later, did she explain.

"I don't need any distractions when I'm riding Torc. I can't rely on her always sorting me out, or so you all keep reminding me."

"You're an idiot, Carly Tanner. This guy is your break, your chance to avoid being an itinerant groom forever. Okay, you're good, but you deserve more than a yard on a failing farm."

Carly concentrated on ordering a cup of home-made soup, plus a bottle of water for later. "I'm not chasing him, especially here. It's not my style, even if it worked for you. Sorry, your husband's brill but–"

"Still, I say you're crazy. That's one fit hunk, and you say he's loaded. Don't blame me if someone else steals him from under your nose. Just take my advice, go for him, Vix."

"No, not until I've won the class." The perfect riposte silenced her friend. Winning was unlikely, and for regular riders, the hard graft was the only way to progress.

SIX

Armand suppressed his amusement at his confused friend. "So, you thought she was a groom and now she's riding. You might have to offer her more than the grooming job."

"Working pupil then, and she'll cover all the work you do," said Gilles. "It's brilliant. Thanks."

"If she's interested. She seems pretty single-minded today."

"Then I'll just have to beat her, prove that I can offer the best deal in town."

Armand was not optimistic that the situation could be resolved. He had noticed a British flag on the jacket underneath Carly's fleece. "Wait, impress Carly another time. Please pay attention to the horses, you need results."

Gilles walked up to Carly, ignoring Armand. "Bonjour chérie. Clever, you not saying you competed. That's a fine mare you're riding. Selle Français?"

"Selle Français cross Arab, but she's not for sale. She's out of my mum's jumper so very special. But this lady –" said Carly, placing a hand on the blonde's arm, "– owns a superb gelding you can buy, at the right price."

"Ah, except he's no use to a stud," said Gilles. " Then again, nor is my mare on today's performance."

"She's fab—Anglo-Arab I'd guess. Home-bred?"

"Only the stallion – he was bred at Du Noroît, our Canadian stud. I run the one in Suffolk, so I'm talent-spotting potential."

Armand rolled his eyes and sighed. Locked into the gameplay, Gilles ignored Carly's polite smile. She noticed Armand and blushed, then glanced away before asking, "So you want just proven competition horses to breed from?"

Before Gilles could reply, the loudspeaker called for the first competitor in the Foxhunters.

"I so need to concentrate on this, but you never know, we might see each other later."

She was moving towards the arena when Gilles took her right hand. "Please, we're both in this class, so why not make a bet? If I beat you, I'll treat you to a meal, and you tell me why you speak French. Otherwise, I'll leave you alone. Deal?"

Carly grinned, pursing her lips and nodding before she kissed him on each cheek. "Sealed. Better watch out, I thrive on challenges."

The day was getting colder with the weakening winter sun and encroaching darkness. It ate into

Carly, feeding the diabetes that only activity was keeping controlled. A few brief moments of jumping weren't worth suffering for another freezing hour. A chance to beat the cocky Canadian, with his strange half-French, half-American accent was motivation enough, but what mattered was giving Torc an opportunity to shine. The mare had the speed and the turns for the shorter jump-off track. His stallion might be fast, but Gilles was over-confident.

She focused, talking through the course with her more experienced colleagues.

An Olympic team rider set a tight time that would be tough to best. The next three attempted to beat him with fast and wild rounds but dropped poles. The only ones that jumped clear were slower.

Carly was second from last to go, right after the former double European three-day-event Champion, who proved how she could hold her own in show-jumping. Her smooth, confident clear took the lead as Carly, adrenaline pumping, entered the arena.

"Go for it, Vix. You can still do it," said Beth, putting friendship before the bet.

She heard her mother's reminder echoing in her head, "Relax, and it'll happen. Torc can do it if you don't chase her; just let her flow."

She rechecked her course, knowing one tight turn remained that nobody had tried. With Torc in a rhythmical collected canter, the energy flowed as they flew round. Knowing the mare's ability, she went for the tight turn after the second parallel, risking a sharp angle into the first part of the double. But they were clear, then over the last and through the finish. The whoops of delight from the crowd made her realise she had done it. She'd taken the lead. Her heart was pumping even faster as she returned to the collecting ring. But she couldn't relax yet, as Gilles was the last one to tackle the course, with all the advantages learnt from watching others fail or go clear.

He studied the fences, checking his route before he went for his winning attempt. He shaved even more off the corners than Carly, and as he cleared the parallel at the end of the arena, he went for the turn like she had. Heart thumping, her breath quickened, yet time slowed. He could have made it, but his stallion slid, clipping the first part of the double. The fastest round, but four faults.

Carly beamed from ear to ear.

Beth, who was holding Guinness, said, "Thought you weren't bothered about impressing that guy, so what happened?"

"I don't like losing, especially when some guy thinks he can bribe me with a meal, that's all. He's so not my type. Call me crazy, but we're leaving."

SEVEN

A smile from Armand was never going to salve his friend's wounded pride, but Gilles had the strength to say, "*Maudit*, she's awesome. Not surprising—she's one hundred percent a showjumper—look at those guys congratulating her. Plus, I suspect that flag means she jumped for Britain as a Young Rider."

"Which means she's good at this game, so we're done. She won't want to be a working pupil for an eventer. Forget her, please," said Armand.

He hoped Gilles would stop letting passion rule his judgement, an irrational approach to choosing an employee. Finding a head groom was important, but surely they were not this desperate.

Why not Carly? What am I scared of? Is it my failure to protect Odette Fédon? I can't handle another fatality, and yet there's no danger.

"Loup, she's a chick okay but that's not my reason. Guys are good too, even you're okay, but well, we need the best, male or female. Someone as perfect as...." Gilles closed his eyes and swallowed the name.

Armand nodded, unable to say her name either.

He could not express his real emotions, as they were churned up. For him, nobody could ever replace Odette.

"Don't undermine my decisions, Loup. I'm not giving Carly up that easily. She's the one I want as my head groom and working pupil. She is now a real challenge, and I'm sure she wants me."

"Perhaps, except you lost the bet. It's over."

"No way. I'll even offer her the Witch to ride. She liked her and –"

"Finish it, now. You had a deal. She lives hundreds of kilometres from Fenburgh, and she's a show-jumper. Find someone on the eventing circuit that knows the sport."

Armand smiled as Lina appeared from the horse lines.

"*Vamos,* we've a long drive home. Congratulate Carly and say goodbye, *rápido.*"

However, as they approached Carly, the photo-journalist came up to her, wielding a notebook and pen.

"Can I have a quick word please?"

"Well, okay, but I'll have to leave shortly, as I've horses to muck out and feed at home," replied Carly.

"Thanks. I'll be quick. I'm Fay, and I write for a regional magazine. That was a fantastic performance. Where are you from?"

Armand and Lina were unsure about staying, but

Gilles waved them onto a bench within earshot.

"Oh, I live a mile up the road at Hazelmead, a livery yard, well, sort of a farm."

"How long have you had Sylvan Torc?"

"My parents bred her fifteen years ago, on their farm. She was fab today. She always knows what I want before I ask. Got a real mature head, but flies round like a youngster."

The Open had now started, and Carly started watching, dividing her attention between the interview and the competition.

"So, she's got a lot more wins in her. What are you aiming her for, second round Foxhunters?"

"Well, I suppose she's proved she's ready, but I'll only showjump her between events once the season starts next month. I won't be able to fit many runs in around work."

"And I thought she was a bloody showjumper," said Gilles pointing at Armand, "and you encouraged me to think that. *Sacre,* why haven't I seen her before?"

"*Silencio,* then you might find out," said Lina.

Fay stared at Carly then said, "Uh, how long have you evented? We've talked before, haven't we?"

"Yes, nearly six years ago, when I was in the Young Rider team at the Europeans."

"Sorry I haven't covered your results since. Been tied up riding myself as well. I just do this part time."

"Not much money in horses, either. You didn't miss anything to write about, as my other rides were only so-so or filled with amateurish rider mistakes that kept us out of the prize-money. Torc's been off with an injured hoof and having a foal, and I moved to my new job at Hazelmead."

"No time for competitions then?"

"Well, last year I did two three-day events and managed to finish fifth at Bramham and sixteenth at Blenheim. My dressage lets us down, so I've been concentrating on the flat work. It's my weak phase."

"I could sort that out," said Gilles, his voice making Carly glance over.

"So where are you aiming Torc? Badminton?"

Carly shook her head, "I did some senior winter training but soon realised Badminton's beyond us." She paused as the final rider's effortless but fast clear round won the Open class. "Torc's fantastic and owes me nothing. If it wasn't for her injury, we might have gone. Without a top horse, Badminton's just a dream."

"But you'll do some other three-day?"

"She might cope with the three star at Bramham again, maybe the 'Under Twenty-Five' section."

"Remind me, how old are you?"

"I'll be twenty-six in March."

Armand shivered at the revelation. The same age as Odette. Gilles can't take her. The burden will be too much. Who will protect her? I can't. Twenty-six is too young to die. He closed his eyes and prayed he could fight off another assault. Focusing on the distracting words, he let them banish his dangerous thoughts.

This reaction is illogical. This interview is just about horses.

Fay finished scribbling and put a hand on her head. Glancing over at the Open prize giving for her next interviewee, she said, "One final thing, am I right that your parents train you?"

"Mum did, but..." the tears flowed as Carly continued, "she died two years ago, a stupid accident. Dad still… supports me, when he can."

"I'm so sorry." The journalist put a comforting arm around her.

Armand's concern went out to Carly, and yet he couldn't help her. Death was too close to him already, a part of his past that he could never bury. Each time he ran away, something emerged to re-awaken the nightmare memories.

Anyway, she was braver than him. She had faced up to her loss and was fighting back, rebuilding her shattered life. Under those tears, he recognised fire and strength, and knew he was wrong to doubt her abilities.

Fay handed Carly a clean tissue, then said, "Be strong, you'll keep winning. I just hope we talk again soon, thanks."

As the journalist hurried over to the winner of the

Open, Carly turned to the Fenburgh team and said, "Sorry guys, guess you want to say goodbye. That was so embarrassing. Challenging enough being interviewed, without then bursting into tears."

"I'm the one who needs to apologise," said Gilles, putting his arm around her waist as if comforting her. "That was ace jumping. Glad an eventer won. Wish I'd known about your situation. I'm gutted for you and want to help–"

"It's not that rough. Anyway, you're the one having problems!"

Gilles furrowed his brow and gaped.

How much does she know about Fenburgh? Armand pulled back from suspicion and smiled, impressed by her gutsy style as she added, "Perhaps I should be giving you jumping lessons."

"Agreed, but I can offer you a job as my event groom in our competition yard. I've plenty of horses that would benefit from your touch, and I can provide a better wage than you're probably getting—in fact, way higher, plus better hours and the best accommodation for you and your horses."

The silence and Carly's purposeful pace, as she walked out towards the horseboxes prompted Gilles to stride after her, continuing his desperate sell. "And I'll throw in those flat lessons you need, as my working pupil. Perhaps share the ride on the Wit... on my mare."

She stopped and turned. "Hang on. I was just joking around. I've commitments and friends, so I'm fine, honest."

Armand wondered if Gilles would be as slick in closing this deal as the covert horse-trading earlier.

"We need more of the feminine touch," Gilles said, then noticed Lina, fingers tapping her face, "on the riding front. The science is all down to Lina, but you're perfect for the team."

Armand nodded his agreement, realising Carly could be the ideal successor to Odette. If her CV was as impressive as her practical credentials, she would be perfect as the head groom.

My paranoia has made me apprehensive about Carly, but she's the one. I mustn't compare her to Odette, even if Carly keeps Gilles from focusing on the horses.

Carly shook her head. "I'm real flattered guys, but it's not so simple. I need to make this decision in my own time. There's too much at stake. I'll let you know later this week, but I'm not promising anything. So, if you give it to someone else—well, I'll see you around at some event perhaps."

Gilles reached out and took her hand. "Look, here's my card. Give it some thought. I'm sure you won't get a better offer."

EIGHT

The dead-end job, or the tainted dream? The dilemma plagued her all day, along with Gilles's grinning face. If just the liveries had guided her, then she would have called him before midday. A chance of a lifetime, they persisted in saying; the guy with the money to realise any dream. A tempting grooming position on a stud that boasted superb facilities and a good team, including great rides. Plus, Gilles was offering an incredible wage with a home for her and her horses. But she wasn't willing to pay his price—his hands groping her and his lips straying from her cheeks.

The moon failed to melt the darkness, and she was exhausted from work and the mental turmoil. She thought she had made her decision, but why was she apprehensive? She was tempted to close her eyes, but she staggered up and gazed out through the bungalow's open curtains at the woods behind. Hunting owls flickered like ghosts in the moonlight, their quavering hoots spurring her to prioritise her aching body.

A while later, she was sitting at the kitchen table

with Guinness curled up asleep at her feet, his appetite sated. Injecting her third dose of insulin and eating some reheated beef stew had given her the final lift. She was tempted to join Guinness, with another predawn start ahead, but she had to do at least some of the accounts before succumbing. Grabbing a glass of water and some bananas, she went to the desk that doubled as the yard office. Amidst the copies of 'Eventing' and 'Horse & Hound' magazines, she cleared a space by putting some books—including her well-thumbed Pippa Funnell and Lucinda Green biographies—back into the bookcase.

Guinness padded over and laid his head on her leg, hoping she would give in to sleep. Bed was tempting, but not until she'd finished some office work. She glanced at the photos above the fireplace, remembering Marguerite, supporting her through long days. They were memories not to indulge in, but to give her encouragement and strength. At their heart, the hard lesson in living and rising above her diabetes, the condition her mother too often ignored. Her mother's recklessness had invited tragedy. Marguerite could have avoided the heart attack, if only she had stuck to the regime prescribed for her diabetes and related hypertension.

"I need to feed the mares in the river pasture," was Marguerite's twice-daily cue in any weather, and her final words, after asking Carly, "Have you checked your sugar levels?"

Why not her own? Her mother had put horses before her health and her family. Was that why her father Peter buried himself in his work? Did building designs offer an escape from horses?

Carly held back the tears and switched on the desktop, then waited while it struggled awake. She prioritised the bills to settle by the due date and dealt with them, but Gilles's face slipped back into her mind.

She coaxed the computer online and searched for Boissard, the word throwing up a dozen options. As she scanned the search results, Carly dismissed the ones offering information on the 16th-century antiquary and poet. She went straight to Gilles's eventing results, which were mixed, although with enough success to put him in the Top 100 of the World Eventing Rider rankings. No three-day-event wins, but even some of the best had missed out there.

Standing up and stretching, she forced away the sleep that pressed at her eyes. She had to make the decision. Looking at her computer, she saw a link that echoed something Gilles had said—Boissard Chimique, the family firm's website showed where the money was, but Gilles did not seem connected to the business. Perhaps he was a minor relation living in the fallout of their success, and not the rich kid he played at being.

However, a link tucked away like an afterthought, gestured at the family playing with horses—Boissard Équestre. The stud site had the usual detailed and impressive pedigrees, plus photos of sires, dams, and foals in white-railed paddocks. Everything he had expounded; except for the menu button at the side saying GMO Feed & Fertility. It triggered something as her past reared up and threw her off.

She drank all her water and ate a banana, unsure whether she should delve more. The past was reason enough to stop.

However, it could be pure coincidence. She went into the kitchen. Cool water from the tap splashed the sink and her tired face, revitalising her. She drank, then refilled her glass before returning to her desktop. Succumbing to curiosity, she clicked on the GMO link.

As if reluctant to destroy the dream job offer, the web page emerged line by teasing line. The feed regime using GM rice bran was familiar from her college work. Even now, the industry-revolutionising claims challenged her beliefs that there were safer, more natural alternatives.

She forced herself to read more. For at least ten years, Du Noroît Stud in Canada had fed their horses on a diet supplemented with oil from genetically modified rice bran. The aim was to enhance the oil's natural steroidal effects without causing any side effects. By the stud's figures, it had increased the number of successful inseminations, indicated by photos of the brood mares with their progeny.

The youngstock appeared promising, but the parents were nothing special, lacking the lean muscle mass and overall body condition that the feed promised. Her college research had shown that the significant side effects included loss of appetite and increased stress and agitation.

A wet nose nudged her hand, and she stroked Guinness as she leant back in her chair. The desire to escape to bed was growing, so she stood.

However, scanning the shelves, she saw a maroon folder, her old college project on 'Comparative Analysis of Feed Production Regimes'. She removed it, blushing at the tutor's pencilled 'A++ Excellent work—provocative' on the cover. Eyes closed, she wanted to relive the first time she read the words then punched the air. Enough now to sink into the sofa so Guinness could lick her.

As she flicked through the pages, it felt strange that Gilles's family was involved in GMO feed. Synchronicity, her mother would have said. Carly wondered if the studs had completed their trials or whether the results had forced a change of regime.

When she saw Gilles again, she could ask him about the results; to get a sort of closure on the project. College had been great and had taught her so much, but the project had challenged everything she believed, fanning her commitment to the organic approach and her opposition to GM. Despite the unproven claims that GM was the future, non-GM stabilised rice bran was now an accepted equine supplement. Organic was still the way forward in her line of thinking.

The Du Noroît link was enough to reassure her that re-awakening the past now was crazy. No job was worth that, even if it paid well. No way was she taking the grooming job, however amazing the opportunity. Getting back into the heart of the sport was not a sensible reason to accept the job. Gilles would be a dangerous distraction, or even frustrate her real priorities.

The last banana and the rest of the water fuelled her struggling mind, and she hibernated the computer. Guinness was relieved when she switched off the office light and trudged down the corridor to her bedroom, the workday and the dilemma driving her exhaustion. Although, she still had enough energy to fold her clothes. What would the morning bring?

She could not ignore the stark reality of her position on a failing farm. She had no future at Hazelmead, however hard she worked. The place deserved an owner who believed in it. Could she continue to juggle her life to keep the income trickling in? Trying to fit in the liveries, teaching, backing horses, and then long nights of pub work and waitressing? Maybe she should resort to a nine-to-five office job, become a weekend rider? That wasn't her. Despite the long, often dirty and wet hours, horses ruled.

The rich guy who would give her everything she desired was a pipedream. Better her simple existence, however wet and cold it could be. Wealth and prestige scared her anyway. She told herself Gilles wasn't the man of her dreams; he was pretentious and would make too many demands.

There were too many unknowns, as well as her shortcomings, which would always count against her. Serious employers would never take on a head groom with no license to drive a large horsebox, and they could misunderstand her dependence on medication. Even her sport had restrictions on the use of insulin, although her medical card, worn on her arm while competing, should inform any paramedics that she had diabetes.

Gilles would never relate; his expectations and presumptions were too high. He would never understand that she had to measure her sugar levels before and after exertion.

Far simpler to say no and let him go. She might see him at events, but no more than that. As she slipped into bed, it was clear: Hazelmead was home.

NINE

Carly sat on Torc and gazed across the patchwork quilt of greens and browns that melted into the haze of the distant downs. The musky sweat of other stamping horses stirred her. Their riders tried to keep warm as breath misted in the cold, and the chomp of bits and the creak of saddles filled the air. Just below in the copse at the slope's end, hounds were working, the Huntsman drawing yet another covert.

Then a shout came as a fox broke from the trees. The hounds gave throat, music to the ear. Brown, black, and white shapes poured through the undergrowth as the Huntsman's horn echoed.

Then the field moved off, gathering pace as the hounds streamed out in pursuit of the quarry. Hooves beating rhythm as the first obstacle loomed, Carly and Torc found their line and leapt the hedge, clearing the ditch behind. The speed continued to build towards the next obstacle, and Carly checked Torc's power and loosed it, sailing over, their mutual excitement building.

Others had fallen, their skill not matching their

recklessness, and some followed more cautiously as the hounds kept hunting and the fox kept drawing them on.

Their route twisted and turned towards a road snaking away to where fingers of urban growth encroached into the rural quilt.

They slowed to a walk as they approached a gate opening onto the road. Carly saw crowds of people jeering, placards, and blue lights. Words of abuse preceded figures breaking from the throng, rushing into the next field, flailing at horses while avoiding whips; but the riders moved off again.

She focused and concentrated on the jumping, the exhilaration rising inside. The countryside was rushing by with the wind. Hooves and heart pounded as the baying of the pack stirred her blood. This sensation was the thrill of the chase; an urge, natural, uncontrollable, although checked from being wild. A primal need to hunt down prey, to feed, and to live.

They had now closed on the Huntsman and the hounds. The figure was in sight, determined and cunning, looking for an escape. It needed to lose them and dodged from side to side, then disappeared down a culvert.

Had it outwitted them? There was a long pause as the hounds worked, seeking scent. Human eyes were watching, as they waited.

Then, the hounds spotted a glimmer of red diving

for sanctuary in a covert and the cry went up. The pursuit continued, and the wood held no escape; that bolt-hole had been blocked hours before. There was only time for one final ploy.

The shape broke from cover. It sensed the hounds closing. Its fear was growing, and limbs were tired. Panic had set in. It twisted and swerved in vain.

And then it turned and confronted the pursuers.

Carly was terrified and felt guilty. The quarry was calm and still, tall and indistinct. Legs apart, arms at its side. The hounds moved so slowly, leaping towards the figure as it raised a long shaft, levelled straight at her.

Before she could understand how the fox had become a man with a gun, a flash of light pierced her, and she tumbled down with Torc into the mire. Lying in a heap, she tried to lift the mare's head out of the mist that swirled around them. She struggled, unable to feel her own limbs. Scarlet spume spattered across white. She clutched at the threads keeping her conscious, but a presence fought to deny Carly of her life.

She jerked awake from her nightmare, shivering, sweat pouring, and heart pumping. Her head swam, and she grappled for some focus in the darkness of an unfamiliar room. She could hear a distant, wailing call outside, totally unlike Hazelmead's soothing sounds. She heard horses, and she regained some of her shattered senses, but her head throbbed.

She scrabbled at the bedside table for the blood glucose tester; too low. She fumbled for some dextrose tablets, chewed them, and then devoured two bananas with a glass of orange juice.

Awareness stirred. This was Fenburgh Stud, and her new home. Hazelmead was a part of the past now. Although the eerie cry had faded, the nightmare echoed, and she stumbled over its significance. Did it mean anything? Why was she the prey? Who was the hunter, and would she regret changing jobs? Did her mind perceive a threat to her organic ideals from Fenburgh's GM connection? It was more likely the ease with which Gilles had seduced her.

That had freaked her out. At least she had resisted calling Gilles until her friends had persuaded her that Fenburgh was a job to die for.

Before she could dwell on her paranoia, Guinness bounced her out of bed. She had another day of acclimatisation ahead, so she showered and dressed. She re-checked her levels and injected the first of her two daily doses of insulin before heading down for breakfast.

"*Hola* Carly. Sleep okay? You'll need it today. Plenty to do, but Armand will help, as you know. He's a real amigo."

"Slept a bit restless but good enough. Just—"

"—Strange new place, strange sounds," said Lina,

adding, "after a hectic move."

It made sense—all her friends were left behind at Hazelmead. Gilles had collected her, the two horses, Guinness, and her life's possessions on Thursday from the event at Tweseldown, where Carly had needed to do the Open Intermediate class on Torc. Her third place should have impressed him. From there, it had been a quick turnaround to get Gilles's four rides ready for his local event at the weekend. Luckily, he had not blamed her grooming when he had failed to get a single prize on them.

For Carly, it had been an intensive introduction to her job, with a dozen horses in her charge, even though Armand's help and guidance had been invaluable. Sharing a cottage with the stud's nutritionist, Lina was a bonus, which made the move so much easier. She realised that it was time to build a new friendship while learning what made Fenburgh life run smoothly.

Lina glanced at her watch, "Time to leave. The horses will get restless."

"Like our boys." Carly pointed to where their dogs were both standing by the back door. She grabbed her jacket as Lina let them out. "So, what is he, wolf or a—?"

"Czechoslovakian Wolfdog. Armand gave him to me, as my protector."

Carly had to ask, "So you're both... sort of..."

Lina laughed. "Nah. He's sweet, but just a friend. I sometimes wish he wasn't so shy."

Carly said, "Perhaps he needs encouragement, unlike Gilles."

Carly's head was awash with information. She had questions, but Gilles had been determined to give her the full tour of his domain. Probing was unnecessary, as she was sure Lina would have more exact answers for her later.

Armand had offered to muck out the rest of the boxes, insisting on Carly going home, as he was aware of how many horses she had ridden, not all with Gilles's help. He had his favourites to ride, mainly his stallion, Drac. The others were ignored, like the two unproven youngsters that were called Huginn and Muninn. Armand insisted this was normal, so another day of mucking out boxes didn't matter. Was he as trapped in his drudgery as she had been at Hazelmead? And again, when they spoke, there was that sadness in his eyes. As Gilles was the alpha male, she wondered why Armand was called Loup, the wolf.

Lina was busy at her laptop on the kitchen table when Carly walked in. The running suit suggested she would be a match for Carly in the exercise stakes; pretty necessary if she was to keep her dog so fit. Mistico was sitting patiently by the door, a snow-white watcher studying his new houseguests. Guinness's black body quivered, tail wagging.

"Sorry I didn't get back for lunch. Gilles had me riding all day and insisted on lunch."

"*En el palacio*?" She registered Carly's nod and said, "He's real serious. Watch out..."

"...said he had too much to tell me so—"

"—that's how it starts. Not that I minded." She caught Carly's look. "Don't worry; ours was a stupid fling. I can't let such feelings cloud my work, so it's over, he's all yours if you can hang on to him."

"That bad?"

"He's not the Flying Canuck for nothing. Good at flying changes and not just the dressage moves."

"I appreciate the warning, but he's as expected. Thanks, though. Not that I'm ready to get involved."

"Loup, though, is entirely the opposite."

Carly grabbed at the opening. "So why that nickname? Not a Gilles joke, I hope."

"No, it's the wolf pendant he wears. And he was so alone when we met him, trapped by books. Now he's a little better, but still our intellectual."

Carly remembered noting the pendant, on a chain with some old ring. The nickname was appropriate to him as a lone wolf lost in his sadness, but had someone rejected him, or was this a self-imposed exile?

TEN

The night crept into the attic room on moonbeams that explored the patterns in the rug. Cries of nocturnal inhabitants gave Armand some companionship and reassurance that all was well. Now engrossed in the environmental assessment, he had perspective on his suspicions, and he was grateful to Carly for freeing him from his old chores. Approval for the scheme to re-use much of their grey water and to compost the manure was his next hurdle, although a minor one.

Gilles would agree to anything Carly suggested, especially as she was resisting his advances. She had used this to get him to accept a new stable name for Sorcière even though the mare was still proving to be Gilles's nemesis. Carly had beaten him again at the weekend's show-jumping event.

On Sunday, she had asked Gilles, "Why are you always calling her that name? No wonder you can't get an understanding with her."

"Guys here had trouble saying her French name, so it's Witch as she can be one."

"That's mean. I find her real magic, bewitching.

Okay, sometimes she seems to be dreaming, or her mind's wandering, but I'd call her Wanda, like a witch's wand."

Now Gilles was calling her Scheming Wanda; maybe that was the only plot stirring at Fenburgh.

A diesel engine broke the illusion. Armand turned off the lights and went to the window, night binoculars at hand. Old habits die hard, even if spying on others felt wrong, but with suspicions gnawing at his mind, he needed to know more. If he was better prepared, he could protect without failing again, so any detail noted might save a life.

The silver Jeep Compass Sport+ slid around the house, heading for Lina and Carly's cottage. As the security lights flickered on, Armand registered the personalised registration plate; someone with money or out to make an impression.

He hoped the dogs would be deterrent enough, but he was prepared for a possible confrontation. The Jeep stopped outside the garden gate, and a short-haired blond man stepped out, the lights sparkling on his polished leather boots. The trousers, waxed jacket, designer stubble and smooth smile said salesman, but at this hour?

I've seen him before. Not here—at The High Rocks dance.

The dogs barked furiously, but the salesman walked up the path. The cottage door opened and

Guinness leapt out, only to be called back by Carly. She greeted the visitor with kisses to the cheeks then showed him inside.

Guinness stopped barking, but the hair rose along his hunched spine, and his teeth glinted. The flatcoat seemed to share Armand's suspicions, even if Carly had danced with the man.

ELEVEN

Once the horses had their morning feed, Carly dropped in to see Lina. The ultra-modern office and the high-tech lab had sparked off Carly's questions, and Lina was ever the obliging friend.

"Not definitive proof, but it was enough to end that phase of the GM trials."

"So, instead you're exploring this new regime?"

"*Exactamente.* I gave Roman everything I could. Everything to show there was no benefit to his horses at Du Noroît—"

"So, the trials ended there? And here?" asked Carly, praying for closure.

"Here, the strategy is my choice and Gilles can make it work. Concentrate on the horses, and nothing will go wrong."

"It's just like, so weird. My research project back in college and now here. Plus, you guys are making that move away from GM, which is great. So, you convinced Gilles this is the correct direction for Boissard Équestre?"

Lina stroked Mistico, who was snoring quietly

beside her in a duet with Guinness. "It was easy. I have ways with Gilles. Just trust me, I know the way he operates when it comes to the family business."

"Ah ha, so it was more than a fling then."

The hum of computers filled the pause. Had she pushed too hard?

But Lina said, "We were students, which gave me time to understand him. But Gilles is straightforward—if everything falls into place."

The team dynamics seemed to be growing more complicated, but Lina was an invaluable guide.

"So, what should I do about Gilles? He's the boss and...very persuasive."

"Playing games is his style. Just concentrate on the horses. On my side, he wants this feed change, especially as his father hates our regime. But Fenburgh is not Roman's. We've started re-building here, despite him."

"And Loup supports you, I know. It fits his work and–"

"—He listens to you. Perfecto. Perhaps you fancy him, instead of Gilles?"

"No way. Although Loup's sweet." Carly didn't see Armand in that way, although an intellectual didn't worry her; but the work was the priority, as Lina told her.

"*Vamos,* we must find them now."

The dogs sensed this decision involved them and

led the way to the door. Lina locked the one to her lab and set the alarm.

Gilles and Armand were standing beside the manure heap. "...Mick's the new rep for Vidarranj, but it's a bit odd, his visiting so late," said Gilles.

His words drifted over on a green mist, and his presumption riled Carly. "Lina, I think we have two jealous guys..."

"...who we didn't invite to last night's party. *Trágico!*"

The boys' expressions, imitating gasping fish, invited more bait. "A dishy lover you didn't know about."

"Carly's, as she danced with him, except Lina orders our supplements," said Gilles. "Why wasn't I told either way?"

"Mick's just a friend from Kent that goes way back."

A string of horses and jockeys went past, and Gilles pretended to study the mounts and nodded at their lads. He was perplexed, and the accusation was as inevitable and sharp as frost. "He's your...you conned me, played with me, just for the job."

"Why not? If he's not my boyfriend, then what?" She walked towards the yard, where she had pressing work.

"Please, Vix. You're not serious. This is a wind-up. You mean so much—well, to Fenburgh."

"Don't worry Gilles, it's over..." she paused to play with his feelings, his chosen game, "...between Mick and me. There's only one guy now."

She could hear him behind her, his breath a breeze stirring her hair. She was ready to turn and kiss him; except not this way, and not here. "I meant Guinness, sorry. Look, Mick heard I was here and just brought me a present for my birthday next Saturday. That's all. Anyhow, everyone knows Mick! Time I did some work."

"Okay whatever, Vix. Let's all celebrate your birthday—a foursome. Armand, you book us a table somewhere real special."

The drizzle had developed into a downpour that had sent Gilles and Lina off to discuss the progress of her feed regime inside. Armand was in his room updating his report, and only Carly had stayed outside exercising horses, saying, "They need the speed work and the field's best for that with its all-weather track. I need them ready for the weekend."

Remembering his outstanding task, Armand checked the restaurant details in his notebook and booked the table for Carly's birthday celebration. However, he was more concerned about the salesman, her ex-boyfriend Mick Roper. Guinness was wary of him, and he worked for Vidarranj, one of the feed supplement companies that Boissard Équestre had dealt with in Canada, although Gilles had claimed he would stop dealing with the company in England.

Grabbing his laptop, Armand decided to go online, logging on via a non-commercial secure server in France. It had been a while, but his comrades would note his re-emergence. Searching for Vidarranj, he found their website, a straightforward marketing tool promoting their products. Mick must need Boissard Équestre back with his company.

Does Mick think he can use Carly as a lever to inveigle himself into the setup? Or is he already entrenched?

However, one glance at the range of products reassured Armand that Carly and Lina would have no use for them. Vidarranj was biotechnology at its most zealous, claiming to belong to an alliance tackling poverty and helping humanity through scientific advances.

He clicked the SALES button, and the website produced a map. Mick Roper's smiling face and mobile number were the sole information for Suffolk. He noted the UK main office was in Sussex, about ten miles from where Carly had worked.

He stretched doing some Tai Chi exercises while letting his mind still. The slow, deliberate movements were integral to his self-help treatment, and a chance to regain skills.

The nightmare lurks in the shadows, and I must fight it. Sleep is no escape; I must keep the memories at bay.

Somehow, the past has to be faced.

With the images restrained, he kept exploring for other information on Vidarranj. His first search led to an article outlining the main concerns about some GM rice bran. Vidarranj was a major player in both the trials and the promotion of the related products. The primary problem seemed to be their failure to produce an effective 'super' feed that would have had any scientifically provable nutritional advantage over the less expensive conventional brands of rice bran.

Armand stood and paced the room. The mournful cry of the stone curlew echoed in a distant field, and for the first time, it filled him with dread. A chilling thought was creeping into his head, and he forced it back where it belonged. Something was making his mind churn up the unthinkable. When GM rice bran had been the basis of the horses' diet, Odette Fédon had been the one required to implement the feeding.

Was her death really an accident? Did she discover something? It's my duty to our family to find out why she died.

Was someone contracted to remove an obstacle to the commercial plans Vidarranj had devised for Boissard Équestre? Blinding white light threatened to overwhelm him, so he buried his head in his hands, squeezing his temples and shutting his eyes, as he saw blood seep onto snow. He grasped for some logical release.

If anyone had opposed the GM regime, it was Lina, and she was still alive. If Vidarranj had a lever like Mick Roper, then they need not resort to murder. The salesman knew Carly, who held the influential head groom's job. There was no evidence of murder, but there must be a motive for the new arrival and her slick ex-boyfriend.

TWELVE

The breeze and sunshine were a welcome arrival after the overnight rain. The broad and flat expanse of grass beyond the start was as inviting as the first few fences. From there, the course curved away towards the line of trees in the distance. Behind was the bustle of other riders warming up their horses. The mare was on her toes, anticipating the thrill. Their dressage test, plus one of the few clears in the influential showjumping had set them up perfectly for this final cross-country phase. In the start box, as the starter counted Carly down, her nervous nausea vanished.

He said, "Good luck," as Carly headed towards the inviting first fence. She increased the pace, and determination set in as they settled into a rhythm, adrenaline coursing through her. The knots of cold but ardent supporters dotted around the course whipped past. She kept the flow, jumping the straightforward fences out of the mare's stride. Wanda was economical over the jumps, wasting no time in the air and needing little encouragement. Carly eased the responsive mare back to a controlled canter on the approach to tougher fences, like the steps, but kept the horse's impulsion going to jump the arrowhead beyond. After seven minutes of high-energy concentration, they sailed through the finish, her grin telling her friends how pleased she was with the round.

When she had dismounted, loosened the girth and finished hugging Wanda, she reassured Gilles saying, "She was amazing, never looked twice at anything. We had one anxious moment when I got her in too close on a roll-top, but she saved me."

She gasped out the last part as the pangs of dependency stirred. Completing her first event on Gilles's bête noir was great. There had been some apprehension earlier while walking the cross-country course with Gilles, as it had been a while since she had tackled a course this substantial on Torc. He had encouraged her to rise to the challenge, although the mare had been the real star. Now, time with Gilles took precedence over time to deal with other priorities on her mind than this event, but she still worried that he had his own agenda.

Armand handed her Guinness's leash and began leading Wanda back to the horsebox where he and Carly untacked her. They washed down the mare, as Gilles filled another bucket, adding electrolytes to the water so the horse could drink.

"Did you jump through the river crossing as I suggested?"

"Sort of, but Wanda improvised coming over the Boat. Saved time—she's real clever like that." He tilted his head and stared at her silently, so she continued, "I felt I could trust her. Like Torc, she's not stupid, and like you asked I didn't push her, although she still has a lot more to give."

"Never made me feel confident. She's temperamental. Hope her foals don't inherit her worse traits. We had high expectations of them—well, Lina still does. If you're saying she's more responsible after the second foal, I suppose..."

"I can keep the ride, you mean?' Carly abandoned discussing the breeding programme to embrace the Wanda dream.

"Well, you seem to have forged an understanding with each other. *Batêche*, hope Papa accepts my decision. He's never keen on grooms competing."

"Why not? It's your horse and your stud, right?"

Gilles started to enlighten her when her mobile beeped.

She scanned the message and tried to make sense of it. Any missive from Mick was typically cryptic. "Grt 2 c u & L. Hpe probs buried. M xxx" He had signed it with the usual devilish smiley face. She presumed 'probs' referred to the day she threw him out when she found the furry handcuffs and recognised the perfume. Bloody bitch with her pink sports car and her shady business—he was welcome to her. Carly had forgiven him if he could remain just a friend.

Gilles was still talking, "...so that's how the arrangement works. Papa will have to be okay. Over these horses, I'm the boss."

Carly glanced at Armand, who had started putting on Wanda's travel bandages, as he said, "In Canada, it was Roman who ruled one hundred percent. Perhaps he'll be more accepting of Gilles's decisions now that we're here."

"He will. Trust me."

Armand shrugged and continued working. Carly nodded and helped him finish, thanking Gilles for his confidence in her.

Once the mare was bandaged and settled in the horsebox, Gilles glanced between the two vehicles and gave Armand the keys to the 4x4. "So we don't hold you up. There are the others to work on at home. I'll bring the truck. We'll have lunch and check if Vix has won anything."

"So, you and your Papa don't share or...?"

As Gilles heated the broccoli and Stilton soup, Carly encouraged him to talk more while she tested her levels and injected.

"My dream has to be out of his grasp, as he has a way of destroying them."

As she gazed into his eyes, she saw darkness and loss. Should she comfort him? She needed to know more. "You have to tell me, now. Your father, can he stop you? Can he wreck Fenburgh and take the horses—and Wanda? Because I will stand by you, just as Armand and Lina would."

The Canadian sighed as he put two soup bowls down.

"No, we are building something different, without any interference from him or anyone. Now that I've found you, the past is at rest, and we can put the incident behind us."

She remembered Mick's text and the words 'Hpe probs buried'. "Incident?" she asked.

"Oh sorry, a winter riding accident in which we lost our... head groom."

The news should have scared her, although risk and danger were part of her sport, maybe part of the thrill even, but that didn't explain her fears and churning stomach.

"Armand was the most upset. There were rumours that he was...seeing her."

The soup seemed cold now as she sipped it before saying, "That's why he looks so lost and hurt, so withdrawn. It's not just his intellectual manner then?"

"No, we pulled him out of his books and encouraged him to go outside more. Even introduced him to skiing, though he's like a clown on skis."

"To be a clown, you have to be skilful."

"Yes, but there's good, and there's lucky. We

helped Armand a lot, but then...well, he stopped after the..."

His words were choked back and lost, like the details of a tragedy that must have hit him hard. Maybe later, Carly would learn more, but for now, she embraced Gilles and let him kiss her. He buried his head on her shoulder and then nuzzled her hair, muffling his sobs. He kissed her again. "Your hair reminds me of a maple grove... I will show you one day, in Canada."

He fondled her hair, teasing it with his fingers, and stroking her cheeks and neck. He reached down and eased her boots off. For a moment, she wanted him to stop. He had tried wearing her resistance down over the weeks, pursuing his selfish goal.

Could she let him continue on her terms—to satisfy her own desires? Or was that a mistake? She must pull away before it was too late.

Her fingers began caressing a passage into his shirt, teasing the buttons undone. She allowed his hands to work their way into her jodhpurs, both probing, seeking entrance. She lifted her hips as he slid everything off, and then gently kissed her from the toes upwards, savouring every inch.

Why couldn't she just accept the tragedy? The memories of the afternoon offered a warm escape. Instead, the incident ate away at Carly, forcing her online to find an article from the Montreal Gazette, dated December 21st, just three months earlier.

> *RIDER MISSING FROM EASTERN TOWNSHIPS STUD*
> *MONTREAL—Odette Fédon, 26, head groom at the Du Noroît Stud near Bromont is now feared dead after she disappeared while out exercising a horse last Friday. The horse returned riderless but uninjured. Roman Boissard, Du Noroît's owner, said, "Mlle. Fédon is an excellent rider, but conditions were bad that day, and the horse is young."*
> *Initially, the Quebec provincial police believed Fédon might have returned to her family in Les Trois-Ponts near Chicoutimi. A friend said, "Odette was close to her family and, even when away at shows abroad, always kept in touch." However, Fédon's family has not heard from her.*
> *The police do not suspect foul play, although further investigations are pending until the spring thaw.*

Horses could be dangerous, but death was always unacceptable, and Carly could never forget the tragic year when five top eventing riders were killed in accidents while competing, prompting safety changes. Somehow, this incident in Canada seemed more chilling. She was filling a dead rider's boots, and tomorrow, she would be the same age as Odette

Fédon. Was that what Mick had been warning her about, or was he taking pleasure from digging up the past?

She switched off the computer, and with tears running down her face walked to the open window. They flowed for the faceless Odette and for all those taken before their time. Alone, she screamed at the wind, "Why?"

From the darkness, the wind howled an eerie reply—or was it a warning?

THIRTEEN

The French landscape would have re-awoken his nightmares once, but the paintings on the subtle cream walls only released warm memories. The company and the food added to the ambience that Armand had aimed for.

Lina reached into her handbag and took out a neat parcel, which she handed to Carly. "Happy Birthday," she said with a smile.

"Oh, you shouldn't have! Should I wait?"

"No way," said Gilles. "I've been waiting all day. You can start with Lina's, but then open my envelope."

The package was dark red, and Armand was trying to ignore it where it rested against the white tablecloth. He sighed with relief as Carly carefully unwrapped the present and the wrapping paper fell open revealing a beautiful shawl, which she ran across her blushing cheeks.

"So amazingly soft!" She stretched to embrace the Latina.

"Vicuna, an animal similar to llamas, knew it was a good choice. Let's see what Gilles has thought up," said Lina, looking as mystified as Armand.

Carly opened the envelope and cocked her head. "Typically mysterious. I have an appointment at 3 pm on Monday in the yard. What's up, Gilles?"

"It's a surprise, so you just have to wait and see. No guessing." He grinned and hid behind the menu, leaving them all wondering.

"Well, it can't be a ring," said Lina.

"Or a horse," said Armand. Although with Gilles that might be exactly it.

The shape of Armand's present gave it away.

"Trying to turn the poor girl into a bookworm too!"

He ignored Gilles's remark and ordered his dessert as Carly unwrapped the book. Her face reassured him that he had chosen right.

"Worried that you might have it, but..."

"I couldn't afford it when the book came out, but the college library had it. So, this is fab." She gave him an appreciative kiss, then handed 'The Organic Horse' to Lina. "You'll find this valuable too."

Even Gilles delved into the book, and it seemed as if the quartet were united in their cause. For the first time in months, Armand was at peace and part of a strong unit.

"So Vix, you get anything else then, like from your dad?"

Carly elbowed Gilles gently.

"Of course, because he's worried about your high expectations, he's given me the perfect gift..." Gilles's face dropped as if his intentions were being questioned, so Carly took another spoon of Crème Brûlée, savoured it, and then continued. "...Some armour, which after yesterday, I might need in bed." She took another mouthful, then said, "One of those shaped Kan body protectors."

"Hey, no way. I'm not that... rough."

"El Caballero. Watch out for his spurs—or maybe that's Mick. You've looked in the box, Vix?" Lina asked, pointing at the package that Mick had brought over the other night.

Carly flinched. It was okay for Lina to know about Mick's habits, but not the others. She took out the threatening present, hoping it wasn't anything so provocative.

She unwrapped it, suppressing her shaking hands. Inside the box was another, and another, like a Russian doll, but the final jewellery case reassured her. The vixen pendant was perfect, although belated, as Mick had promised her one when they were together.

Gilles hesitated, but put it on for her, stroking her hair as he closed the clasp and kissed the nape of her neck. No sign of jealousy, just a sense of approval and claim.

"You don't mind then?"

"He's your friend, and Vix is your nickname, so

why not? He's not exactly chasing after you like some stalker."

The words betrayed him, so she kissed him.

Still, his words ate into her mind, and the nightmare echoed; a chase, and she was the prey. She tried to focus on her friends.

"You okay, *amiga*?"

"Stupid, it's just well..." She should forget it, but it was like an infection. "Do you guys ever have recurring fears? Sort of ones you can't lose? Bad dreams?"

The blank expressions dragged on until Armand rescued her. "Dreams carry truths but don't worry about everything in them. Usually, the mind plays tricks with memories."

Gilles had persuaded Carly to relate the dream to disperse her worries. As he listened, Armand tried to ignore the echoes.

When Carly had finished, she said, "I don't understand, I became the prey."

Lina stared at Gilles and said, "Like most women."

"Yeah, but I'm not, well, like that, and as Armand says, it's just memories. Carly's been hunting all winter, and with our sport always under strict controls, we're all victims."

"Yes, that could be it. With the bloodhounds, we chase people, runners."

Armand asked her, "So, you haven't seen foxes killed?"

"Well, not for ages and–"

"*Madre de Dios*, such an inefficient way to control vermin."

"At least it gives them some chance. You can't be saying gassing or shooting them is better, Lina?"

"Maybe not, but destructive vermin that serves no purpose needs to be controlled."

"Hunting's barbaric. Why make killing a sport? Is that civilised?" Armand said.

"Sorry Loup, it's been part of the Brit's tradition for centuries, doing no harm. The fox lives by killing and wits, so what better way to die? Hunting them is justified when you've seen a chicken house after a fox has broken in—feathers, bodies and blood."

The image made Armand flinch, but forced him to ask, "Does that justify the foxes being chased and torn apart?"

"At least it's a quick death," said Gilles. "A few seconds of fear as they realise they're going to get caught. The rest's just adrenaline."

"But whose life are we concerned for?" asked Carly. "Foxes that take the lives of lambs and chickens to live, or thousands of hounds that will have to be cared for, if not culled? I'm unsure now. They all have a right to life."

There must be a solution that unites us. I need to abate

the fire, not feed the flames that will consume us.

"Your sport doesn't have to be cruel. Drag hunt or chase a hunt follower. Those who care so much can still keep the hounds that can't learn new tricks."

"But what about farmers?" asked Carly. "They'll still want the foxes culled."

"You can still shoot them. A trained–"

"Don't you know anything, Loup?" interrupted Gilles. "That's far worse. Can you imagine lying wounded, cold and bleeding—dying slowly from gangrene?"

Armand winced as the words came as a blow, triggering visions of blood splattered across the snow. He knew all too well, but he forced himself to speak, cutting out the memory that was stirring.

"A skilled marksman with a rifle and infrared sights could do it, waiting for the right shot, but I agree—not a farmer with a shotgun."

Lina stared at him and then said, "Makes sense. The fox is a predator—out of control, but we must ensure enough vermin die, cleanly. When an animal threatens another's existence–" She glanced at Gilles then continued, "–like a fox with chickens or even a wolf with caribou, then it needs to be culled."

As Carly and Gilles agreed, Armand sat holding back the past, fearing what he was going to say. "Except man is the most dangerous predator. Are we condoning man killing man, like in Carly's dream?

Are we that ruthless? Or maybe nature will turn on us?"

His friends stared at him, and he wished he had kept quiet and played his meek self. Carly diverted their attention, saying, "Suppose that's sort of what my dream said. Well, the man as predator problem, but how do we weigh up lives when the balance has already gone?"

Nobody answered, letting her continue.

"Do we save all the threatened creatures first? What about the research that uses animals to save lives—the lives of children? No, don't answer, just change the subject." Carly put her arm around Gilles and rested her head on his shoulder. He enfolded her in his arms like a cocoon of safety.

Are we all killers in some way? Are we all hiding from the knowledge that others die to keep us alive? Am I running away from my guilt?

FOURTEEN

The alarm on his laptop had woken Armand early. The network sniffer, which he had set to monitor any Vidarranj activities on the Boissard system, had detected an email.

Re: Explain!

From: mroper@vidarranj.com

To: Boissard@boissardequestre.ca

Boissard. Goods stoppage. Explain and rectify.

Roper.

Having accessed the message and read it, he marked it as unread, leaving no trace of his incursion. The email must be addressed to Roman in Canada, but was Gilles still a part of Boissard Équestre? With Gilles and Carly at a weekend show, he dealt with the remaining horses as he mulled over the cryptic message. Although Mick would be the one supplying supplements, Boissard Équestre could only provide horses, but none had been exchanged—unless they had never passed through Fenburgh.

Chores done, he checked the computer records in the yard office. There were no acquisitions recorded since they had arrived in the UK, not even Gilles's dealings, like the stallion bought at Ardingly.

He scanned the list for other omissions and noted that neither of Wanda's embryo transplant foals was recorded. Was Gilles hiding information from his father, or from Vidarranj? Were they a partner in Boissard Équestre? Rumours of a new partner had been implied in Canada, but not since.

Was Vidarranj meant to be receiving horses, or something else?

He had no time to delve as he heard a voice barking in Québécois French. He realised with shock that it was Roman, whose arrival was rolling across the yard like a storm cloud and disturbing the horses settled in their stables.

Outside, a tall man with oiled black hair strode across the yard pointing a swagger stick at Armand.

"Plane was late, then nobody met me at the airport, and now nobody's here. I had to take a taxi, which is coming out of your wages, Sabatier. Should have guessed you were behind this mess. You're useless, but think you're so damned clever with your books. Army discipline would sort out your sloppy ideas. Get rid of that hair for a start." The decibels continued as he targeted a new victim. "Don't expect that new *salope* is any better. One goes, and he finds another."

Armand weathered the storm and looked busy. "Many apologies, sir, we were never told to expect you. What can I do for you?"

The glower and the stick poking at the cobbles suggested he should grovel, but he knew Roman's type too well. No more dangerous than a regimental mascot, he was all parade-ground bark and no real guts in his rigid manner or stance. Major Boissard might have retired, but he still needed everyone to know how important he was.

"We've finished the horses for the afternoon. I was preparing for your son's return."

"I see. My son gets the service, and my emails go unanswered. You knew when I was coming. I even had to ring the butler to have the master bedroom cleared. So, is my son still letting that useless groom ride? He never learns—grooms are only good for one thing."

Armand pointed at Torc, who was in her box. "That's her mare. Carly is grooming for Gilles, and he's riding the two stallions and resting the mare Sorcière."

"The one whose foal was born last Sunday to the surrogate? That's another idiotic thing, calling it Poisson d'Avril." He shook his head and muttered some curse about his stupid son. The tapping stick intensified as he asked, "So, where is the foal? I need to see it if it really exists."

Armand led Roman to a stable with its own paddock, where the foal was suckling an Irish draught mare. A week old, the colt stood on firm legs and nudged his surrogate mother as he drank.

For a moment, Armand saw another side of Roman. He was genuinely captivated, especially when the colt gambled around the old mare, demonstrating his breeding with turns, dinks, and bursts of speed, which was a beautiful echo of Wanda.

"The sire's genes will make up for that disappointing Witch mare." Like son, the same insult, except more. "*Tabernac,* Gilles has no judgement. First, he buys a useless horse, and now he thinks the groom can get results on her." He stared at Armand. "Don't lie to me, Sabatier. She's still riding that Witch—not today but other times, I know."

The eyes burned into him with the intensity of a sergeant-major, but Armand could handle such men.

"Don't think for a moment I admire this misplaced loyalty to my son. Be warned that it will cost you, and at a time of my choosing."

Roman strode back to the yard and began a thorough inspection, moving anything he deemed out of place and running a finger across every surface.

"Sloppy, not good enough. Tomorrow it has to be spotless and ordered."

Armand was made to feel personally responsible by Roman. In Canada, he had envisaged upending the larger man onto the ground as the move was so simple, but pointless even now. Better to defer the moment.

"By the morning, Sabatier, I expect to see my face in these stones."

Armand half-expected to be told to use a toothbrush like a raw recruit, but the stick was tucked back under an arm, and the strut echoed out of the yard leaving some barked clues. "Roper said the stud was in incompetent hands, but not now that I'm here. Plus, that foal goes to Du Noroît."

Armand had believed Roman's incompetence was a key factor in the studs' problems. Now he realised that appearances could be deceptive and dangerous. Roman's military record needed exposure. Bombastic outbursts could disguise military precision.

It had been so easy at Du Noroît to be lulled by the stud staff talking behind Roman's back, suggesting, "The nearest that the major came to combat was with a potato peeler. Command promoted him, so the troops didn't starve."

Armand had searched the Canadian Army list and discovered Roman had served in a combat service support regiment, but details on the nature of the postings were missing. A thorough investigation into Roman's career was imperative and could indicate whether the Boissard activities masked something illegal.

FIFTEEN

It had been a pre-dawn start so the four friends could all pitch in to ensure that once they had fed the horses, mucked out their stables, and polished all the tack until it gleamed, they had time to clean the yard until it was spotless in every cranny for the dreaded inspection.

However, by midday, the horses were restless and noisy amidst the tension that Roman stirred up. He was everywhere, finding invisible dirt or fault, shouting orders and insisting that everyone update him about their work. His foul mood grew as the morning progressed and the quartet stood firm; that didn't stop him from taking out his frustration on everyone.

As Carly trudged back to the cottage with Lina for lunch, she said, "My position as Head Groom is under threat."

"Why?" Lina had stopped outside the house, looking concerned.

"He's as controlling as you said. He feels the horses are in poor condition and unfit. That it's my fault, even the results, and I can't even get their training regime right. Damn the bastard!"

"Ridiculous. Only Pin has had bad results, and after lunch, I want to test him, before we have to call the vet."

"Roman will still insist I get my priorities right. He says Wanda is useless and he wants her sold. And I'm not to ride her or any of the horses competitively. I can't even ride Torc if it affects my job. Damn, I could kill him."

"Typical, he ignores the facts and demands what he wants. We will find a way to stop him. Fenburgh is Gilles's domain, and his father knows that. Roman is only provoking him."

"Which is why Roman claims I'll be judged by Gilles's results. Plus, I must provide a progress report on the exercise schedule today and every day. Should I refuse?"

"No. There is another way. I'll help you after lunch. He will demand one from each of us. He's obsessed with paperwork, so we blind him with reports, as we did in Canada, for a while."

"Oh, for a while? What happened?" Carly remembered the accident, which must have been connected.

Lina said nothing as she buttered her toast and added some peanut butter, seemingly reluctant to remember such a horrendous event. But she finally answered.

"It was like now, with Roman abusive and irrational in his demands. Gilles started making plans to move out."

"Planned with you or with Odette?" asked Carly.

"With Odette. She was with him when he found Fenburgh. I wondered back then if she was..." Lina hesitated and wiped the hair from her face.

"Gilles was having an affair with her? Not Loup? What were the rumours saying? They hardly talk about her. You're the first one to share."

Lina looked at her toast then said, "It was the way she kissed Loup, too familiar. But he just backed off, which was sensible since she was Gilles's head groom–"

"So, Gilles seduced her?"

"They travelled a lot together. I think she may have fallen for Gilles and expected him to... well, it was never like you. You'll never be like Odette, *gracias a Dios*. But then..."

"...she was killed?"

"*Si*—it was a tragedy that affected us all at Du Noroît. Well, all except Roman, who callously said she was *une salope* and he could never understand–"

Carly had to interrupt. The situation was horribly familiar, and she shuddered, saying, "...what Gilles saw in her, as she was so incompetent, except just one repulsive thing."

"Exactamente." Lina was staring at Carly, who tried not to shake as she finished her juice. "So, he told you the same today?"

"Yes, and now I'm worried. Was the accident as reported?"

Lina went as white as snow and turned her head away. "Yes, she disappeared in a blizzard. The same one nearly killed Armand, but with the shock, I think he has forgotten... gracias a Dios." She crossed herself then stood up, glancing at her watch. "We are going to be late if we don't leave. Bring Pin to the lab as soon as you can."

"There are signs that he's not right, but nothing points to the feed or exercise regime."

Lina was carefully studying the data on her laptop, after an extensive half hour of tests using the equipment in Fenburgh's lab. Carly had rarely seen such an array of high-tech gear, from the treadmill and bio-sign monitors to the latest capnograph and pulse oximeter.

"So, what next?" asked Carly pointing to the stallion hitched next to Drac. Pin looked anxious, unsure if they would subject him to more tests.

"I have to tell Gilles he needs to call the clinic. Probably a virus but the vet will know."

"Infectious?"

"Unlikely. None of the others show these symptoms and certainly not Drac. He's been the perfect comparison."

"Proof your feeding regime and my exercise schedule are working. But, will Roman accept your findings?"

"I will give the results to Gilles as he's the one who has to ride Pin at Kentucky, not Roman. But if the vet says it's a virus then he won't fly Stateside or go anywhere. Rest and then slow work, maybe even the aquatred."

Lina gestured at some smaller electrodes and monitors. "Okay, you're next *amiga,* not that I doubt your fitness."

Earlier, during one of Pin's treadmill runs, Carly was taken aback when Lina mentioned the athlete performance tests, so she asked, "Aren't humans outside your remit?"

"Not when they're athletes as well," Lina had reassured her.

Carly was still chuffed at being thought of in those terms, even with diabetes.

"These should show what you can do, and I've personally tested the equipment," said Lina. "I needed to know if my euphorbia allergy slowed me down. The effect seems to vary per species."

"Is it bad like say, a nut allergy?"

Lina laughed. "Don't aim to eat the plants. Anyhow, we have to get on. I need to know about you."

Carly built up a steady pace on the treadmill, and her heart beat rose, while Lina noted down figures for her pulse and breath. Despite tiny beads of sweat she was breathing with minimum effort, so Lina told her to increase her speed.

"*Fantástico*. You are *magnifica.* No way is your ability troubled, but can I have a blood and sugar sample, please? We must ensure you stay at your best. After that, please run again."

Carly was beginning to feel like the two stallions. Like the horses, she trusted the Latina, who was placing the labelled samples into her metal briefcase.

"One final time, please."

Again, she built her walk up to a steady jog then found her normal focus so she could maximise her performance.

"What the hell is that *salope* doing on there? She's not even a horse."

Roman filled the door to the offices. Carly jumped but managed to slow down with the treadmill.

"I have tested the stallions and now have to check the riders. It's no good if they aren't fit, and competing at this level is demanding. All the top teams do this."

"Ridiculous. She isn't the jockey and might not be a groom for long. That boy is an idiot for employing another useless one. Back to work girl, you have lots to do—now."

As Carly headed towards Pin and Drac, to take them back to their stables, she noticed Roman was looming over Lina and staring at her laptop.

"So, do these results prove anything, other than the fact that you are wasting time, too?"

SIXTEEN

Everything was unravelling again like a constant nightmare. Armand was concerned, even though Lina was preparing a report to prove her case. Gilles was reassuring his friends that everything was under his control.

Why do I sense a third force at work undermining Boissard Équestre? Who can I trust if the past replays itself?

As he exercised and stretched, he unravelled the facts from his negative fears. Roman's arrival had upset the new beginning at Fenburgh. Mick must have been reporting to both Vidarranj and Roman. Maybe Gilles's behaviour had made them suspicious of his horse dealings. From a rational standpoint, the envisaged threat was just a regular business manoeuvre and the adversaries would eventually withdraw.

Yet, parallels with the last two months at Du Noroît were unavoidable. Back then, Lina had tried to use science to combat Roman, while Gilles had insisted he could deal with the problems and ensure the move to Fenburgh would happen.

Armand replayed his conversations with Lina at

the cabin in Canada, and the fear crept back. Odette's death had followed the plotting against Roman. If that was repeated, then Carly was under threat. But, why? She was the head groom, but not as outspoken as Odette, nor was she involved in Gilles's scheming.

Climbing into bed, Armand calmed his overactive brain, shutting out his anxieties—but sleep kept slipping from his grasp. The walls glared white in the moonlight and swirled into a snowstorm, which whirled around him and tried lifting him off his feet. Then through the blizzard, he saw a woman grappling with an invisible assailant. She staggered and then crumpled—a mannequin dissolving into the mist as he tried to reach her.

He woke sweating, his heart pounding as he gasped out a name—Odette. Someone had killed her; he was sure of that. But he was confused about everything.

Didn't I bury Cygne? Or is that my guilt and my memories?

No, Odette Fédon—they had never found his cousin. Lina and Mistico had rescued him—from the same storm that Odette had vanished in.

Was I there when she disappeared?

The snow buried her along with the truth.

Reality slipped into his periphery.

Did I see her killed?

The questions tumbled like an avalanche.

Why was she killed? Why was I there? Why have I so

easily forgotten? Did the killer see me?

He held his head in his hands and sought for a ray of light.

Then his wife was there, reassuring her soul mate that he was not to blame for her death and she would be waiting for him forever.

My precious Cygne. I laid your body to rest in France. My mind has used the past as a barrier to protect me from new horrors. Except now I remember something hurling my cousin Odette into the river in Québec. Somebody murdered her.

SEVENTEEN

Carly tried ignoring them, but Gilles was being too friendly with Lina. Why was his arm around her? He had no reason.

She circled the start box again, concentrating on the starter who was saying "Two minutes."

Ever since Roman's tirade, the others had left her out of all the counter-plotting, which was understandable, but annoying.

"One minute."

She turned the six-year-old back towards the railed start box. After a neat dressage and a clear show-jumping earlier in the day, this was the final test of the bay gelding Huginn's first intermediate. Gilles only wanted to compete his stallions, Drac and Pin, so Carly was taking on his discarded rides. She welcomed the challenge, and riding three horses over two days at Burnham Market was straightforward.

"Ten seconds—ready—go. Good luck."

They set off at a steady pace, dismissing the distractions. The gelding took everything in his stride and seemed keen. At the corner combination, on the far end of the course, Carly had to hold Huginn back slightly. Then, his enthusiasm carried them across the ridge along the field margin.

She found her focus slipping; an image of Gilles with Lina that made her shudder.

Huginn was too fast. The light dimmed as they entered the wood with the first water. She tried to give Huginn time to adjust to the dark and shadows. The gelding clipped the fence hard and stumbled on landing. She attempted to sit back as he dropped into the water, but he skewed again, and she was pitched off the saddle.

The water dulled the pain but not the humiliation as she lay there in her inflated air jacket like a beached whale. A fence judge ran to help her to her feet, and she saw a black shape bounding up through the water. She clutched at names. Guinness? He should be with Arnold. No, Armand. This wasn't good. Confusion was dangerous. She had to focus on her breathing; slowly, deeply; and the shaking, she needed to control it and ignore the pounding in her head. She needed to concentrate and focus on priorities.

"My horse?" she asked. Her breathing was still erratic, and she was made to sit on the bank by the attentive judge.

"The young man with the dog ran to catch it. He was fast so it won't get far."

Two vehicles pulled up, and two people leapt out

and asked how she was. This situation was getting difficult. She had two more horses to ride, but would they let her? She had to cover up any signs of injury. Her sodden state might explain the shivering, but she knew that she needed glucose or her low blood sugar would bring on a hypoglycaemic reaction. This was not the moment to collapse.

The sprint had ensured that Armand could head off the loose horse before it ran into an obstacle, like a rope. Leading the gelding back to the horsebox, he was relieved that the horse had no serious injury from the fall, although there was a slight swelling that would need monitoring. He wasn't so sure about Carly.

While an event vet had checked the horse, Gilles had rung to say he and Lina were with Carly. She blamed herself for the fall but insisted she was fine. Gilles had been sure something was wrong, but the doctor, taken in by her fitness demonstration, had permitted her to continue to ride. Lina, unconvinced by the display, had warned she could still face suspension.

Armand led the horse across the natural amphitheatre in which the show jumping arena was set. Flanked by an array of marquees and trade stands, people sat along the banks overlooking the fences, enjoying the jumping and the spring day.

For a moment, he glimpsed a figure in the crowd who looked like Mick Roper, but the figure vanished. Entering the lorry park, the pungent mix of horses and cooking assailed his nostrils. In the sea of boxes, people were getting horses ready, while riders in smart top hats and tails for international dressage passed by those wearing a pallet of cross-country colours.

He noticed some vets challenge a rider, then perform tests on her horse, storing the samples in a metal briefcase. They seemed to be checking horses competing in the advanced and international classes, which meant Torc and Wanda—the next ones he had to get ready.

Two tested riders were debating the issue.

"Blasted vets and their spot tests. They seemed more interested in blood than urine."

"Well, drawing blood is easier than expecting them to pee to order."

"When they flashed those IDs, my heart sank even though I know Scrub is clean. I so hate officials."

At the box, Armand rubbed the gelding down, and then he rang Gilles. "Salut, Gilles. How is Carly? Is she riding?"

He suspected the answer, although he worried about the outcome, as an injury to a person with diabetes would take longer to heal; but she knew that.

"We tried to persuade her to withdraw, but she's

determined. I even offered to ride the Wi... Wanda. I think..."

There was some muffled scrabbling as the other phone changed hands, then Carly said, "I'm perfectly okay, and the doctor agrees. I'm riding Torc, and then I'm riding Wanda. It's my damn decision, and no one is stopping me. Hell, Roman would love for me to fail now."

EIGHTEEN

"Badminton! You're crazy. There's no way."

"Lina and I feel it's the right moment, Vix. You're ready for the challenge," said Gilles. "And it's what you've always dreamed of doing."

Carly was completely against this, even if it was her dream. It was why they had been talking at Burnham.

"The ultimate test—isn't that what riders say?" said Armand, pausing in his yard sweeping.

"Well, in eventing, yes. Ever since pony club I've wanted to ride there, but–"

"But nothing," said Gilles. "You're riding there. It's just one level above what you've been doing for years, not some strange new discipline."

"I can't groom for you at a four star and ride. You and Drac have to be my priority."

Gilles stared into her eyes, so she turned away and continued mucking out the stall. "Babe, you've proved that you can ride and groom, at Burnham. Forget your fall, we all make mistakes. Most importantly, you jumped double clears on Wanda and Torc."

Third and seventh in the Advanced had been a timely confidence boost. "Thanks to your birthday present—the surprise Devoucoux saddle..."

"And your ability. The saddle was just an aid. Plus, I love you."

"Don't forget us," said Lina. "Loup and I'll help at Badminton, *amiga*. We've discussed it."

Armand nodded. Her friends were right, but she said, "No way Roman will accept this."

"Papa treats you like a groom, but I took you on as my working rider as well."

"You have talent, and we believe in you. Ignore Roman and go for what you're best at," said Lina.

The world's most prestigious three-day was daunting, and she should have done it, but she had never risked even attempting to get there. She knew deep down that now was the right moment to live her dream. Maybe her father would find time to support her. As she gave into the others, she rationalised her decision to herself, and said, "Okay. Torc and I have done a few three stars, so we need a challenge."

"Don't worry, Vix. You can both handle it. I have faith in you," said Gilles, putting his arm around her waist.

"Well, Torc's usually consistent, even out of the field. For Badminton, she needs another advanced run, so okay. But, there's a problem." She paused and shut the stable door. "Even though that double clear qualifies us, entries have closed."

Silence.

Then Gilles grinned in his enigmatic way. "And yours was accepted just after Great Witchingham as soon as–"

"Damn you. You used my rider and horse info—how dare you! You bastard, you used me."

She stormed across the yard fighting back the tears. "You had no right. That's it, I quit—now."

Gilles followed, with his friends in tow. Were they his moral support or witnesses? Carly didn't care. Gilles's deceptions stopped today.

"Hey hang on, please, Vix! I only did it because you're the most talented rider I've met, ever—except when you lose it, like now."

Carly knew she was being impetuous and stupid, but she didn't want to stop herself.

"...and I love you to bits, babe."

She turned, and he was there, behind her. She flung her arms round him and kissed him. "I hope that's the last time you make decisions behind my back and... what else you planned for me?"

Gilles shuffled and chewed his bottom lip.

Lina said, "We think, as a wannabe French rider, you should do Saumur, on Wanda."

Her stomach flipped. France's elite three-star, at the renowned cavalry school? She gulped. Her mother would have been so impressed with Carly competing there.

"Well, you said you're okay at that level. So, why not, *amiga*? You and Wanda are a perfect combo. Third in your first advanced—that rocks."

Their smiles inspired her self-belief, although Armand's face bore a furrowed concern he was unable to hide.

"So we all agree, then. Armand, do the Saumur entry, now, before anyone upsets this."

"Okay, Gilles, but I may not be able to make France. I've work to do around here. The place needs a lot done."

"You're coming. We need you, and that's final."

Dark clouds heralded Roman's arrival, although he wore an air of beatitude. He began his inspection by checking the horses and talking to them softly. If only humans had hooves, he might respond to them better, thought Armand.

"So, did you win yesterday, boy?"

It was unlikely he didn't know the answer.

Gilles continued sharpening the plaiting scissors before answering. "Bottom line: obtained the qualifications in the advanced we needed to do spring three-days."

"We? You let that slut ride again when I–"

"Yes, and she was third on Sorcière des Saules. Cut her some slack. She's better than me."

"Not difficult, as you're useless, and that's no excuse for disobeying me. Don't think I am blind to what you and your *salope* are trying to do. It won't work."

Armand saw Gilles breathe in deeply and square his shoulders before saying, "These horses are mine to compete with as this team sees fit. Du Noroît is your stud, Fenburgh is mine."

"And next week you'll be back home riding to my orders. You and Serac D'Or need to prove yourselves at Kentucky."

"He's not ready, Papa."

"I want you in the Canadian Team. It's the only thing that stallion's good for." He turned to Lina as he said, "Your useless feeding regime has ensured he's firing blanks."

Gilles said nothing.

"Señor Boissard. You forget I ran extensive tests when he was here, and he was performing - until he contracted the virus. The vet confirmed my findings."

The two Boissards glared at each other.

"Papa, you ignored our vet who said that he shouldn't fly, so now this has happened when Pin reaches Du Noroît. I am not wasting my time competing him until he is one hundred percent fit. He will do Saumur like Sorcière des Saules."

Roman strode towards his son. "Don't tell me, she's riding, as you're incapable. While you're denying that, what about Badminton? You've failed to tell me she's riding there too."

"Sir, it's my choice," said Carly, stepping forwards. "Torc needed a challenge. If I mess up as a groom because of it, then you have every right to sack me."

"Tanner, don't worry I will—maybe before you get there. My son may protect you now, but not forever."

Gilles continued sharpening the scissors. Then he turned to his father. "Papa, these are my friends, and I have a share in this business—unless you want to buy me out?"

Roman tossed his head and marched towards the archway out of the yard. "Watch it, boy, don't think I won't. I know your weakness. Let sex blind you in business, and you will fail. I think it's time you moved out before I end this... at your expense."

The scissors whistled through the air and embedded themselves in a post, having narrowly missed Roman's head. He wheeled round and pointed at Gilles. "I can deliver a messy resolution." He strode out, swearing.

It was either a lucky throw, or Armand had another suspect.

"Did you mean to miss your father?" Lina asked jabbing an imaginary dagger. "If not, let me take the next shot."

Perhaps I have two more suspects.

"If I meant to hit him, I would have. Next time

he pushes me too far, he'll regret it. Karma is a bad kickass. Period."

"Hang on guys. This is not the way. Okay, the idiot insulted me, us, but you don't mean kill—do you, honey?" Carly stared at Gilles and Lina, eyebrows raised.

"Don't worry, babe. I will deal with this, but we may have to be ready to move. Papa has friends who may force our hand—unless I can talk to them too."

Armand tried to find reassurance in the words, but there was none if unpredictable allies were involved.

Does Gilles mean Vidarranj or someone else? Who's making the decisions? Neither of my friends is a killer, yet someone murdered Odette.

NINETEEN

"Fantastic Lina, you'll so love it there," said Carly. "Well, it needs work, but–"

"Perdón, I have to stay here, where the research facilities are, for now."

The fork hovered in front of Carly's open mouth, the chunk of chicken ignored.

"Damn. I so wanted you there. Hazelmead is like my dream place."

She had been so stupid to suspect Gilles and Lina when all they had been doing was talk about the spring three-days.

"I'll come at weekends to be with the team, and so Mistico can spend time with Guinness. Vecheech, the company that bought Hazelmead, asked me to stay on here at Fenburgh, so Gilles agreed."

"I thought this was a simple move until he started explaining it. He's never mentioned Vecheech before. Who are they?"

"Amiga, it's just typical Gilles, straightforward until challenged... by Roman. All I know is that the owner of Vecheech knows the family and wants to help. No doubt make a profit too—they're rumoured to be that type of company, but we keep our jobs."

"Well, let's hope Gilles is right in agreeing to manage Hazelmead for them."

Carly took their plates to the sink and started counting back the weeks. "Damn him, he's done it again. He told Vecheech the farm was in trouble soon after we met."

"Surely that's good? It's special, so he's ensured it survives."

"Yes, but for all the money he... the family has, he doesn't buy it, just lets someone else." Her mind jumped to a troubling conclusion. "Shit, you don't think he's been spending too much? He mentioned the horsebox being extravagant, but it's his pride and joy."

"Wouldn't be the first time he ditched a toy or ran out of money."

Carly remembered the Devoucoux saddle he had bought for her birthday and his comment, "You can never have too many," as he showed her the tack room for the first time. The list went on, from the state-of-art lab equipment to his car, but she wondered if this was a flying change or a U-turn.

"Well, let's make the most of the next few days when I'm here. Although, Gilles has plans to take me to the beach and teach me to jet ski. But we can still fit in some quality time with the dogs."

*

Armand sat on his bed reflecting on the relocation. This decision was strange, as somehow, Vecheech Enterprises had engineered a solution that, on the surface seemed to satisfy both father and son; it was too contrived.

Roman gained control of Fenburgh, while Gilles had a new base to compete from. Yet neither of them had total control of Boissard Équestre or their individual futures. Armand suspected Gilles was still a partner, although Roman must have retained the majority share.

Vecheech—were they the shadow that he sensed lurking out of sight? They were reputed to be a corporate raider, so what had they gained? Hazelmead was theirs outright, with Gilles managing it. *Can Vecheech keep Gilles's excesses in check?* They must have some financial hold over him. Could the mysterious horse dealings be for them?

Armand stood up and paced the room.

Lina's actions should be beyond question. She had agreed to stay at Fenburgh and continue her research until they could install the equipment at Hazelmead, although she would stay at Hazelmead before driving to Badminton.

Vecheech—Lina wasn't working for Gilles or Roman. She was working for a company with a ruthless business reputation, headed by a shadowy figure,

Patrick Harfang—a man that was so rarely seen that even the paparazzi had never photographed him close-up.

TWENTY

The ke-wick twoo of owls and the scent of jasmine drifted on the night air. Guinness's snoring mingled with the sound of Gilles's breathing, and his arms cocooned her, just as the sounds and smells of Hazelmead had enveloped her, welcoming her home.

She was back, and the dream was alive—alive with the man she loved. She stroked his hair, not wishing to wake him, but desperate to savour all of him. Everything had been enhanced, including their lovemaking, the climax to the day.

After the four-hour drive from Fenburgh, she had mixed emotions coming up the rutted farm track past fields that were idle and empty. Sadness at the feeling of abandonment, but not quite dejection as the yard was as spotless as when she had left it, thanks to the liveries. They had jumped at the chance to return and had already painted and varnished the stables, festooning them with flowers in boxes and hanging baskets.

Although the sporty 4x4 and the luxury horse-box with its satellite dish would have looked out of place at Hazelmead, she was worried about Gilles's finances when he so willingly sold them and a few horses. However, the four-horse lorry, which Armand had driven down, was more appropriate to the stud of her dreams; and it was cosier.

Guinness leapt out of the second-hand 4x4 station waggon and bounded around checking everything. He was so busy rediscovering his domain that he was nearly left behind when they had to leave for the showground. At least the event was on familiar territory, and once again home-turf for Carly. She intended to withdraw Torc before the cross-country, but the course tempted her with a mix of new tests and old favourites, so she notched up a confidence-boosting win.

Gilles secured sixth in the Advanced Intermediate on Drac but seemed devastated by her return to Ardingly form. "Lost again and here. There's no beating you on home ground."

"Maybe next time... if I let you."

"Don't think I stand a chance. There are days when I wonder where the dressage hater went."

"Well it's your fault' honey, you created this dressage fiend."

He still swept her up in his arms after her victory, until she forced herself free to add a steady double clear on the other youngster, Muninn, who might be ready to stake a better intermediate claim than his injured stablemate, Huginn.

It was bliss to drive just a couple of miles home and settle the horses into the yard that she had done so much for.

Sadly, too many of the horses had remained at Fenburgh or had been sold. This move was a new beginning, and Gilles had said that in time, Vecheech would buy more horses to compete and breed from. For now, there was a lot to do at Hazelmead, and although Gilles said Vecheech would expect them—meaning Armand—to do most of the restoration work, she made one crucial call. Sprawled on a sofa in the familiar bungalow after Armand cooked them a meal, she rang her father, who had done architectural designs for a building firm with expertise in equestrian properties.

"It's so good to be back, Dad, but there are repairs, and I was wondering if you had time..." He remembered exactly what its dilapidated state had been, so he had teased her about the hopelessness before giving in, "...okay, we really need a lot of help, but you're the best. We can't use the farmhouse as it is."

As Gilles's antique clock struck one in the morning, she closed her eyes on the homecoming memories, feeling inspired again and ready for Hazelmead's new dawn.

*

As he returned to the yard where Carly and Armand were starting the afternoon feed, she saw Gilles's face was drained, so she moved to hold him. A kiss might stop the dreaded words.

Too late.

"I've just rung Canada... the Québec police. They've found Odette—her body. In the St. Lawrence, on a beach."

Carly shuddered and noticed Armand wince. They had little time to absorb the half-expected shock when Gilles continued.

"They're doing a post-mortem, but initial thoughts are that a branch knocked her into the river, the blizzard you see..."

Carly did a frantic map search in her head. "But your place is inland, so how?"

"Our river feeds it, so possibly the body was trapped in the ice until the thaw—happens in Québec. Must have been carried downstream—fisherman found the body."

Armand was silent. His morose expression had returned and weighed upon his face. Carly could see tears forming.

He asked, "The funeral, Gilles? When are they... burying her?"

He turned away and picked up a tin of saddle soap. Carly joined in the pain displacement, finding a bridle that needed cleaning.

"Not sure, probably immediately after the post-mortem. The Fédons will ring me. I'll have to go, since Papa won't. He won't even ring the police...or the family."

Carly put her arms around Gilles, and then pulled in Armand; they needed each other through this.

"*Maudit*, this should never have happened. Odette was..."

"...so special," said Armand, eyes closed and shaking his head.

"Yes, totally. I must ring Lina before my father tells her—his way. I need to phone her anyway, about Wanda's foal going to Canada."

TWENTY-ONE

The sun pouring into Hazelmead should have eased the despondency, but Lina's arrival had given fresh blood to the dejection.

However, Carly was glad Lina planned to stay for a week, until after Badminton. It had lifted everyone's spirits, and the Latina was relaxing into the life that the farm offered. As Carly led her friend down to the water meadows, the pheasants called in the woods. Trees were awash with fresh green, white blossom dotted the hedges, and wild flowers were emerging in the pastures. Scudding clouds chasing shadows made Carly wonder whether it would be another evening with rain.

At the bridge over the stream, they paused to watch the swirls. Carly remembered her mother and closed her eyes.

"You can't hide it either, *chica,* even though you never knew her."

Carly let the misunderstanding go. She was after all upset about Odette as well. "I feel I knew her, through the way you all talk about her."

"Te Dios vayas bien," said Lina and crossed herself. "Life will be better when she is buried."

True, although the emptiness would never leave, as with her mother. "It can't be easy for you, not going. No closure. Loup seems torn up."

Leading the way for Lina and Muninn, the uninjured six-year-old, she rode Torc over the bridge and along the river.

"Simple *amiga,* Armand has a swan tattoo on his right arm."

"Hang on, swan? Like Swan Lake? Isn't the heroine...?"

"Called Odette, yes. Poor Loup, I must be there for him. I'm worried. He has a nasty scar on his shoulder."

"Scar?"

"Let's just say I saw injuries like that... growing up—street violence. I think someone attacked Loup. He's not strong, or wasn't, so he must have lost."

"Over Odette? Why? Did he love her?"

"Probably just a distant fantasy or the scar was from when he was younger. They have gang problems too, in France."

Carly was uneasy. Gilles would have reacted badly if his friend and his groom were having an affair. Or, had someone else having a relationship with Odette attacked Loup? Maybe that person had killed Odette? Lina was concentrating on her horse, so didn't notice

Carly's anxiety.

They rode onto a lane that crossed the stream, and then they turned left by a black barn down a cinder track. Carly shivered. Was she cold in the trees' shadows, or in fear of what had happened? This was crazy; she was creating a conspiracy— murder. She felt as though she was losing her mind.

But she remembered the scissors flying towards Roman's back.

The trees shuddered, and their branches whipped the air. Snow tumbled as the blizzard tried to wipe everything out. Odette stood no chance. Helmet shattered, she laid lifeless on the ground, blood oozing into the snow cocoon that buried her.

But there had been a flash from the farmhouse, and there was a shadowy figure in the swirling snow.

Armand struggled out of the storm in his head, knowing it for what it was. A jumbled mass of memories fighting to bury the truth; two memories merged.

My soulmate is dead. My cousin was murdered. And I saw someone: a murderer. My memories were locked like a mental safe. Trauma induced amnesia. I was warned by the doctors about the condition. I never thought it was possible, but now I have to unravel the tangle. I must stop running away. It's time to confront the nightmares.

He slipped off his bed trying not to wake Lina in the spare bedroom next door. Fortunately, the violence of his nightmare and his cries hadn't woken her. She must have been exhausted by everything, including the stress at Fenburgh.

Earlier, he had tried to convince her to end the unrecognised work, saying, "You should leave Fenburgh. Why remain there? The lab is nearly ready here. We need you at Hazelmead."

"Don't worry, Loup. I need to finish at the stud. I'll survive. I've lived through worse."

She hadn't elaborated, and delving wasn't the right move.

He slipped down the corridor, past the main bedroom that Gilles had claimed, then into the kitchen where he retrieved his notebook diary from behind the food cupboard. He had to unravel the twisted strands to make sense of recent events, but without his guilt and pain overwhelming him again.

He recorded his mental profile of his cousin's assassin:

(i) Adept at moving quickly and invisibly in the snow;

(ii) Proficient with weapons—E.g. crossbow;

(iii) Appraised of Odette's movements;

(iv) Knew where to strike so river would remove her body;

(v) Access to area of murder;

(vi) Although pre-meditated, didn't need to know the victim.

With the profile, he analysed his suspects logically,

listing their names, plus: (a) Possible motives; (b) Opportunity; (c) Profile comparison; and (d) Overall evaluation.

ROMAN:

(a) Motives: Open dislike of Odette—threat to dealings &/or GM trials

(b) Opportunity: None—all day meeting with Gilles, BUT could have hired assassin

(c) Profile: Military and hunting background; home patch; access to details of staff movements

(d) Evaluation: Motive strong. Profile match 4/6

The obvious suspect as far as Armand's gut felt, but he had to follow this task through to its conclusion. Eliminate the outsiders, as far as he could—if there were any.

GILLES:

(a) Motives: Threat to his dealings and activities

(b) Opportunity: None—all day meeting with Roman, BUT could have hired assassin

(c) Profile: Hunting background and extreme sports/ athletic including skiing. Home patch—knew Odette's movements

(d) Evaluation: Motive medium/strong. Profile match 5/6

Armand rubbed his neck, feeling the tension knotting up his muscles. He was ready to abandon his approach as it seemed flawed, especially if Gilles was more suspicious than Roman. There had to be others, so he added one of Roman's associates.

MICK:

(a) Motives: Odette openly opposed to Vidarranj & GM

(b) Opportunity: No evidence in Canada—except Vidarranj active there;

(c) Profile: No evidence

(d) Evaluation: No opportunity. Motive medium. Profile match 1/6

If not Mick, then who had been in Canada? An unknown assailant, even one paid by Roman, or Gilles, could not be followed up—for now.

A sigh from the nearby bedroom made him pause, and he closed his notebook.

Standing up, he remembered waking after the blizzard. Lina had been searching for him and found him in the snow. He sat down and opened the notebook, then added another entry.

LINA:

(a) Motives: Possible jealousy of Odette's influence as head groom

(b) Opportunity: Outside in blizzard around the time of the murder

(c) Profile: Athletic & fit, including skiing. Knew location; knew movements

(d) Evaluation: Motive poor. Profile match 4/6

Armand stood up. Outside, the owls called, and he wondered if he had lied to achieve the results.

The notes pointed to a hired killer, and he, or she, was still unidentified. There were still reasons to suspect everyone, even Mick, whose past relationship with Carly couldn't be ignored. Although she held Odette's post, a groom job was no motive. However, in France, she would be guilty until proven innocent.

Passing over thoughts of Carly as suspect, Armand realised that there was another. One he wanted to ignore as it was the hardest to address, but he added the name:

ARMAND:

(a) Motives: None

(b) Opportunity: Outside at time of the murder. Witnessed Odette's murder

Was he right? Was it her murder that had invaded his old nightmares? What was he covering up, burying in his trauma?

(c) Profile: Trained to kill. Knew location, knew exactly where to find Odette and possibly when.

If only I could remember more before the blizzard blasted my mind into confusion.

(d) Evaluation: Motive none unless hired. If so, profile match 6/6

He winced, realising he was the prime suspect, especially if the police found any incriminating evidence, now that the body was being examined. The word *trained* condemned him, even if that training had let him down when it mattered. He could so easily have killed Odette if he had been made to forget the family tie. Any motive was buried by his memory loss, which was a convenient alibi for a murderer—a hired killer who knew Gilles and Roman.

Did they use me? How could they bury so much unless they doctored my mind? Guilty as charged until I can prove otherwise. I must expose the other suspects.

Someone was capable of devising a means to kill without leaving a trace. Who could disguise murder to seem like misadventure? It could have been someone with technical or scientific skills, perhaps. Or, someone with access to weapon technology—like a high-spec crossbow.

A shadowy figure stepped from the nightmares and into his head. Memories were trickling back. Odette's killer in the snow was too real now. A custom-made crossbow bolt could be designed to knock a rider into an icy river, leaving traces that forensics could explain away as a tree bough tossed by a blizzard.

A padding noise made him close the book.

It was only Guinness coming for a drink. The flatcoat lapped, then came and rested his head on Armand's lap. He stroked Guinness's soft fur and relaxed again, until his focus slipped onto Carly. She didn't match the killer's profile, but she fitted the victim's: head groom, championed by Gilles, opposed to GM and hated by Roman.

TWENTY-TWO

"So, tell me again what we're going to do here." Carly stood in front of the lake fences. The dawn light glittered on the water and across the majesty of Badminton House behind. Crowds were already gathering to watch the crucial cross-country, some walking the course, others choosing the best vantage point for the action to come. Some riders, like Carly and Gilles, were putting the final resolve on their chosen strategy.

Carly was gesturing at the substantial brush fence into the lake, knowing the crowds would be massed along the banks, some waiting for a faller in the water.

Gilles pointed across to the narrow fence in the water and the bullfinch on the bank directly opposite.

"Well, I intended to take that route, but the brush comes up a bit sharpish after the Mitsubishi Pickups. You know Drac's a little bold."

"So, you're considering taking the alternative. There's a similar fence into the lake, then a wade through, followed by a bullfinch out. I don't understand—almost identical fences, just a longer, more time-consuming route. It's no easier."

"After failing to do Kentucky I need to go well. Twenty-eighth after the dressage, I can't afford a mistake but..."

"Your father wants you to be among the leading challengers. Does he expect you to ignore common sense today? Ridiculous. Most people will take a few alternatives, to reduce the risk of mistakes at the really tough fences. Not this one, though, where there are as many potential errors as on the short direct route."

"But I could make the Canadian squad if I do well by playing safe here, then go direct everywhere else, and make up time."

"That's not you talking, that's Roman's pride. He doesn't care about the means or the cost, just the result."

Gilles nodded, and Carly slipped her arm around him. "You know what's best, not him. You must ignore him. Have faith in yourself and Drac—just don't take any risks, anywhere, please, promise me."

"Same goes for you. Don't be reckless to prove a point either, trust Torc."

The possibility of rain wasn't putting anyone off, and already there was the promise of a Saturday in the sunshine. Families, gaggles of youngsters, and couples of all ages flowed alongside the course in an ever-growing stream of colours: reds, browns, greens, blues and even some neon beacons; an enthusiastic congregation drawn to the sport's spring celebration. Variety was everywhere in footwear, headgear, dogs and even languages. Television cameras peered at the track in strategic places, expectantly waiting, while their still brethren roamed for the shot that would grace some wordsmith's page or an internet blog.

Gilles and Carly walked along the sacred track between the fences, watched by the fence judges and autograph hunters.

Ahead lay the Village, a combination of house-like fences on the site of a medieval settlement, and the best route wasn't obvious. Whichever way she went, she would have to use Torc's energy, late in the course when the time would be crucial. Carly carefully walked the route she favoured: three jumping efforts all on the angle. She was satisfied with the lines that they had worked out together, fixing an object beyond each one as a marker.

Then Gilles forced himself to walk the 'father' route: one less effort for Drac but one of them was a wide ninety-degree corner. Crazy, as they had already agreed that they didn't like it even though some of the top riders would take that route.

"Come off it, stop confusing yourself. What do you feel is right for you and Drac?"

She could sense him struggling for an answer as the doubts crept back into his head. As at other events, his mind would freeze up, and his stomach begin to churn—except this was too early.

She held his face in her hands and kissed him. "If you can't think clearly for yourself, how about for me? Remind me how I should ride it—but if I was on Drac."

He walked her through their route, pacing it out with her. He relaxed as the 'father' route vanished, exorcised forever, unless Roman interfered again.

For the remaining fences their own conviction replaced confusion, and by the time they returned to the Start-Finish area, they had sealed their strategy for tackling the four and a quarter miles and thirty fences in a few hours' time.

TWENTY-THREE

They all stood willing Gilles on but seeing only what the monitor showed, as it cut between the three riders tackling different parts of the course. This was frustrating, especially with one of the top British riders out on the course getting the attention.

They had watched Gilles clearing the first fence, the Mitsubishi Starter where Armand took a photo. But from there, it was either the commentator or the screen following his steady progress—or neither.

Carly was rigid with worry, and the pounding in her head was worse than any nightmare. Watching was hard, but she had to, whatever happened. The further round the course Gilles and Drac reached, the harder she found looking. Although they were halfway, some of the toughest fences were still to come.

The wait was agonising with the cameras locked onto one of the top New Zealanders, jumping the final five fences and taking the lead on his best horse.

The picture cut back as Gilles tackled the Farmyard, but, clearing the second corner, Drac stumbled on landing. Carly's hand grabbed Armand's for comfort and hung on, even after Gilles had recovered and headed on towards the next obstacle.

"He can't be tiring already," said Roman, "I thought he was fit, Lina!"

"The going's tiring him, but he's okay. Gilles will save some for the last part."

The Hexagon Hedge, with a narrow brush fence set at an angle over a ditch, was coming up too fast. A fall seemed inevitable, but Gilles turned the stallion enough for the right line and scraped over the hedge, Drac finding his legs on landing.

"What an amazing horse!" Carly said, realising her fingernails had dug into Armand's palm. He hadn't flinched, but she could see the marks. "God, I'm sorry." She was confused on whether or not to kiss it. She was stupid, but even if it didn't help, the gesture might.

His eyes were as sad as ever, but he smiled. "Merci, it's better. I was worried as well."

Carly prayed that Gilles would stick to their plan through the final questions remaining, including The Village.

Drac would have made it. As Gilles approached the houses, they were on the right line to take the long option, but he seemed to change his mind and turned right-handed for the quick route. The horse toppled over the first element, cleared it, but there was no way they were going to make the house looming in front.

The stallion jumped it at one edge, but clipped it with his front legs, then twisted in the air, removing the flag. Gilles seemed to jerk off the saddle, and his protective air jacket inflated as they fell, but the cameras had switched to a leading contender about to start at that moment.

Carly clung to Armand, who had his arms around her. "Gilles, Christ. No, roll clear."

Her next concern, voiced by Lina, was the horse, but the screen was still held on the start.

"Crétin. I told him how to ride that turn, but he never listens to me. He will have explaining to do. Idiot boy."

"Worry about your son. It's nobody's fault. Some of the best had problems there." The hold at the start and the air ambulance circling in the air stirred Carly's worst fears.

She dashed out to drown herself in gulps of fresh air. She was fighting the tears, and the pounding was making her dizzy. She had to hang in there—this was not the time for a hypo. She struggled for the glucose tablets. Nobody noticed as she knelt on the grass recovering, oblivious to anything except her breathing and all the worst fears about Gilles and Drac. Her fears about riding this same course were let loose too.

When she looked up, a blue and white cap bobbed

through the crowd and then it was heading for the Mitsubishi Garden, the final fence. Horse and rider were splattered with mud, but they were still alive.

Carly turned towards the tent where a clump of figures stared at the monitor. Roman strode around berating his son. Armand had his arms around Lina.

"Hey, they're okay—they're out here," she said, gesturing towards the finish and then ran towards the pair, as the vet finished checking Drac over.

Gilles was loosening the girth as she threw her arms round the horse's neck and kissed it. At least Drac appreciated it, leaning his head against her for more.

"I see, the horse comes first. Women."

"He brought you back safe and anyway..." she let the sentence drift as she folded herself tightly around him and smothered him with kisses. "...now you're in my arms, I won't let you go. Well, not for an hour or two."

Drac dragged them away from the start, craving the soothing attention he now deserved.

"For a horrible moment, I thought that was the end—Drac stumbling, his legs twisting." Gilles clutched his head. "But he never fell, just gave me the time to stay on."

"So, no fall?"

"Course not, although the jump judges gave me a refusal. Drac was okay, but that's the last time I ride a four star. The road ends here for those personal kicks."

They reached the others, but before Lina could offer Drac some water or Armand could remove the saddle, Roman flew at his son. "You call that professional? Ignoring my orders, taking too many alternatives, tiring the horse and then you mess up. Idiot!"

"I was trying to make up the time. I had to go that way. It was faster—you told me yourself."

"You were about to go your way, and you confused the horse. You're useless."

Gilles knelt and buried his head between his legs. Armand carried the tack away while Lina checked Drac over for any visible injuries to treat, before giving him some water with electrolytes and removing the studs from his hooves.

Carly would have helped but wasn't going to let Gilles suffer anymore, unlike Roman.

"Don't ever let me see riding like that again. First Kentucky, and now here. You're not fit to have a horse. Didn't you learn a thing from me?"

"He knows a damn sight better how to ride across country than you ever will! It's your meddling that nearly killed him—what sort of father are you?"

"How dare you talk to me like that? What do you know or care? You only want our money—like all of them."

"I care a lot more than you, it seems. At least I love

him, and I know he doesn't need your misguided advice."

"Where did you find this vulgar thing? And after all I've given you, it hurts. I taught you everything."

Gilles just looked at Roman's feet.

"That's why your son had to come here, to England, and freedom. You're dictating his life for your glory."

"Boy, I can't abide this slut anymore. She's not a rider and will never be a groom. I've had enough. Again, deal with her."

Gilles was in a heap on the ground unable to challenge his father.

"Stand up for yourself. Please Gilles, or you'll lose everything." Her tears rolled.

He threw up, all over Roman's designer suit and Prada boots. Standing, he took Carly's hand and faced his father. "Papa, I'm afraid I will stick by her whatever you say. She's right—I should never have listened to you. Clean your own boots."

TWENTY-FOUR

An hour later, and Roman persisted with his silent censure, forcing Gilles to say, "I thought you were leaving, Papa. You said she would never be a rider."

"Yes, and I will see her fail as you failed. It's inevitable—*tabernac,* she's not even a groom."

Roman had insisted on watching Carly go cross-country, on the TV in the competitor's area.

"Typical, approaching too fast and the wrong way—just like you, boy."

Carly and Torc were negotiating the fences through Huntsmans Close, and to Armand, she looked in control.

"*Criss,* quiet Papa—you aren't helping us at all."

"*Si,* just watch. Your son was perfect here too."

Gilles chewed his lip and his knuckles. His right hand gripped Lina's, and by his jerking, he was jumping every fence.

"Hope the argument with Papa hasn't thrown Carly's focus."

"It won't—she's a pro," said Armand.

Carly and Torc were setting a good pace, covering

the ground well and up on the clock approaching the Lake fences.

"Walking this, she said she wasn't worried, but I sensed her concern at the crowds, and after Burnham, I didn't know what to say. It's a tough course—one of the sport's ultimate tests."

As she cleared the Pickups, Armand said, "She's doing great. Roman's poison has added to her determination. She'll prove him wrong, you'll see."

"Now, what is the *salope* doing? Only the reckless and stupid take the direct route on their debut."

Except, Torc was fast, making every stride count over the narrow fence into the Lake. The mare seemed to skim across the water and over the island hedge before leaping out and away.

Armand punched his fist. Both Gilles and Lina turned and grinned at him.

Unfortunately, the TV switched to a name rider again, and all they could rely on was the loudspeaker commentary. The minimal information, fence after fence, was frustrating everyone.

"Huh, now for the complex you blew, boy. Don't expect her to learn from your stupidity."

"Wrong, she'll show everyone how it's ridden. She listens to Torc, not me, and not the fears you try to feed."

The TV panned back onto the duo as they arrowed through the tricky direct route of The Village.

"Fantástico. Vaya chica."

"That's my girl. Go for it, babe."

Four more jumping efforts and they would be home safely. Hopefully, they would remain clear and close to the time. It was tight.

Armand prayed and made resolutions. Gilles and Lina had their arms round each other; Armand hoped it was for mutual support.

"She's blown it—*putain stupide*. She's taken too many alternatives. I told you, but you never listen to experience."

Armand turned his back, joining in the Hazelmead team bonding.

As Carly cleared the penultimate fence, her friends rushed out of the competitor's tent to watch her and Torc fly the last. Armand took a perfect photo on his camera as she came through the finish grinning and patting the mare. They were a few seconds over the cross-country time—just 4.5 penalties to add. Going into the last day's show-jumping, they should take a top twenty position.

TWENTY-FIVE

Armand had expected Mick Roper to be at this key event in the equestrian calendar. It was an ideal place for the Vidarranj rep to find new contacts and secure existing ones. However, seeing Mick talking with Roman was intriguing, so Armand zoomed in with his camera and took some pictures. They moved away from the feed stand they were on, and Armand slipped after them. He noted the silver briefcase that they both carried; similar to the ones the vets at Burnham were using. Pure coincidence, as it was very common, or was this suspicious?

He followed them through the trade stands towards the scoreboards. They stopped to point at the scores, which already showed that Gilles and Drac had provisionally finished in thirty-fifth. Not what Roman had demanded; his clenched fist striking his hand confirmed the anger.

Once they had exhausted their argument, the duo continued to the Members Pavilion, which overlooked the main arena. The uniformed doorman nodded as they passed through, and, after hovering, Armand walked in behind a family, showing his rider's guest pass.

The plush marquee was inviting with low chairs and tables arranged along its length, many occupied. Armand glanced to where the bar spread along the back wall beside buffet counters laden with food. No sign of his quarry. Had they noticed him and left by another entrance? He walked through, checking faces and halted. Outside, at a table by the railings overlooking the ring, Mick and Roman were talking.

He slipped outside through the farthest door into the enclosed outdoor area and found a safe observation post. People that had been watching horses in the lower order show-jumping were now milling around. The activity gave him cover as he watched.

The camera recorded the moment when they exchanged the cases. Only Mick checked the contents of the one he received.

An exchange of money for goods? Is Mick supplying Roman with illegal drugs for the horses? Not for the event horses, unless someone at Hazelmead is involved. Racehorses at Fenburgh more likely. Or is this related to the GM feed?

The two men stood up and walked out of the members' pavilion. They were too busy talking to notice Armand tailing them, although he had experience in staying invisible.

Outside, they walked a little way and then stopped to shake hands, before heading down different avenues. Armand followed Mick through the crowd, concealing himself among the shoppers taking advantage of Badminton's wealth of shopping. Mick knew a lot of people either as Vidarranj's rep or in his own right. He accosted a familiar figure at a feed stall and kissed her on both cheeks—Lina.

Who is she working for—Roman, Gilles, or Vecheech? Or is she one of Vidarranj's contacts or scientists?

The encounter became heated with Lina stabbing at the metal case. Mick responded with some hand slashes of his own. The briefcase stayed in Mick's hand, although he gave her some sample packets, then slipped away into the crowd. Armand had run out of free time.

At least that run-in with Mick shows she's not allied to Vidarranj. Well, not willingly.

He looked to see where Lina was heading to, as they needed to help Carly, although Gilles had insisted on being in control.

"What are you doing skulking around here, Loup?"

He stayed calm and casual as he turned. Lina had somehow dodged behind him and was grinning. She threw a hand on his shoulder, then kissed him on both cheeks.

"Tasting the atmosphere, and forgetting about Roman."

"...and your duties I think," she said. "Carly needs us, remember? The afternoon show-jumping is soon."

"I haven't forgotten. Not when her dad has driven up to help, unlike Roman."

"...who demands miracles."

"There weren't many clear rounds this morning, but Gilles proved that the course was jumpable without faults," said Armand. "All down to Carly's coaching."

"Don't tell Gilles that. Their rivalry is getting out of hand."

Carly stared at the saddle, convinced that this had to be a mistake. She was British, but there were others placed higher than her and Torc in thirteenth place, although the commentator was saying something about being Under 25. The Master of the Worshipful Company of Saddlers was smiling as he handed the saddle to her, and the onlookers were cheering. If it were true, this saddle would be as precious as the Devoucoux that Gilles had surprised her with for her birthday.

"And the winner of the Laurence Rook Trophy presented to the highest placed British athlete who has not previously completed this Event, is Carly Tanner on her own Sylvan Torc..."

Sounds and colours blurred, but she was going to hang on and enjoy this moment. Her father beamed with pride, and inside, her mother was with her.

TWENTY-SIX

The rain clouds had passed them by, diverted by a light breeze. The afternoon sun bathed the yard with a yellow sheen as she rode through the gate and down to the stables. Opposite the bungalow, Torc was enjoying her well-deserved rest in the Orchard Paddock. The air was full of birdsong, insects and flower scents. The tapping of Armand's hammer was a distant reminder that Gilles said Hazelmead's owner had accepted her father's designs, although only in part.

However, dark clouds hung around Carly. Gilles hadn't rung for over twenty-four hours, despite all his promises when they said goodbye at Heathrow. He had to meet Odette Fédon's family before the funeral; it was his duty as her employer and the sole Boissard Équestre representative at the funeral.

Damn Roman, surely he could have gone? He was back in Québec, it was easy for him, but he had insisted it had to be Gilles, alone. The blasted head of Vecheech, Patrick Harfang, having agreed to Peter's modified designs, had also decided there was too much to do at Hazelmead, so Gilles had to go without Armand and Lina.

Carly was annoyed with Patrick Harfang. Mr Mysterious, Mr Super Rich, Mr Important. He was as annoying as Roman. Although the name was familiar, she was sure that she had never met him, nor did she ever intend to face such a man.

She dismounted and then untacked Wanda. The mare was reaching her peak fitness. Her regime was crucial and every bit of hill work invaluable. The phone remained dead, and she concentrated on the horse. Wanda was the priority—not a boyfriend who had forgotten to ring. Anyway, the funeral was in a couple of hours. When she was back inside, she must ring her father and discuss her dilemma, since Gilles had insisted on moving into the farmhouse, even though the restoration work was unfinished. Now she had to go back to an empty building while Armand had the warmth and comfort of the bungalow.

Her mobile rang, and she checked the number. Not Gilles, but familiar.

The caller was an official ringing from British Eventing. "Congratulations on your thirteenth with Sylvan Torc at Badminton, an impressive debut. We were very pleased."

Embarrassed, Carly choked her thanks, saying it was all down to Torc. She found a bench.

"It was a marked improvement from Blenheim, so

you must have made the most of the winter training we provided."

"Yes, I'm very grateful for that. The trainers and the advice were very helpful," she said, aware of the benefits of their World Class Programme, for which she had been chosen, on the basis of her supposed potential as a rider. They thought she was a rider capable of winning medals, but that still seemed ridiculous to Carly. However, she was unwilling to admit that Gilles was the primary catalyst for her improvement.

"We're glad to see you're now in a working pupil position. Please note that our comprehensive support network is designed to benefit you as well. We will follow your progress with interest. I see you have another advanced ride."

Carly had visions of a file labelled "Tanner, Carly" and was amused. She managed to say, "Yes, Sorcière des Saules is one of my employer's horses."

"Another mare—an Anglo-Arab. How do you rate her?"

"Well, she's the best horse I've ever ridden, but don't tell Torc." The official laughed, and Carly continued, "If I can get Wanda… Sorcière round Saumur clear, then I'll be thrilled."

"Good luck. We hope you both do well. Anything you need, remember British Eventing is here to help."

"Thank you. I won't forget. Bye."

"Goodbye."

She stared at the phone, stunned to get such encouragement, yet realising it was probably just to ensure she stuck with their training programme and didn't give up, as she had done after Young Riders. She had to achieve more if she expected recognition in more concrete terms, but the key thing was having achieved her dream of riding at Badminton. That was only the beginning, and the price of aiming higher was worth paying, whatever the conditions.

However, she saw a problem looming: the French Equestrian Federation. What happened if they approved her application to ride as French? Adopting her mother's nationality might take time, which meant she couldn't go on accepting British Eventing's training.

She had to talk to someone about her dilemma and went to find Armand, although she guessed he would suggest taking the French option. She trudged round to the outbuilding that Armand was converting, but there was no sign of him, even at the bungalow. He could be anywhere with so much still to do around Hazelmead.

It was after five, so she tried calling her father on his mobile, but he wasn't answering either, only the message service. Typical architect—he must be in another meeting. She needed someone now, except this was getting irrational. Sweat stained her t-shirt. Should she ring Lina? Was her advice good? Was she still a true friend she could trust?

Thirst cramped her mouth, and her stomach ached. She pulled out her glucose meter. Her blood sugar was too high. She cursed as she glanced under her damp shirt—her insulin pump had died. An injection resolved the immediate problem, but she needed to ensure it didn't happen again. If left uncontrolled, hyperglycaemia could cause her serious harm, damaging her body irreversibly. Or as with her mother, kill her.

TWENTY-SEVEN

Armand tried hard to escape, but all he could see was Odette Fédon's face frozen in fear and a figure shrouded by the storm. It was always the same horror, of her untimely death at the hands of an unknown killer.

I couldn't have coped with another burial, but Lina should have gone. She was as close to Odette as Gilles. I don't need any more memories to face; witnessing her murder was hard enough.

It was all he could do to send flowers, Euphorbia fulgens, as they had always been Odette's favourites.

I've a harder anniversary to live with, and France to remember as well. Can I handle going back to Saumur? They will attend the event, especially if Wanda is competing.

First, Canada. The memory of that day in the blizzard and all its echoes haunted him. Could it be that those were just the older memories, trying once again to unhinge him and unleash his guilt?

I need to focus, or the nightmares will return, and I will have to stay hidden from everybody, or just end it. No—concentrate. I can defeat the demons.

He stared at his notes, assessing his suspects again. No bolt of inspiration, but it was an aid to his dilemma.

After working in the fields mending fences and thinking through his observations, he had returned home and re-assessed his list of suspects; two stood out.

The exchange of briefcases had prompted Armand to run a computer search on Mick and Roman.

Mick was an exemplary sales rep for Vidarranj, with previous positions in the industry and a brief career as a jockey. He had no obvious skill with weapons or snow skills, and there was nothing to fault him on, as with Roman.

Roman had set up Du Noroît after leaving the Canadian Army. His posting with a support battalion merely covered the supply of essential equipment. His claim to be an ex-Major had proved unfounded. He was only a corporal who had failed to be promoted. Still, Armand was not ready to ignore Roman's role as a facilitator who could have access to weapons. If Odette Fédon had discovered any underhand dealings, it would be a motive to order her killing. Being in his meeting was merely a convenient alibi.

Armand had to add Patrick Harfang to his list of suspects, although he had so little information about him. Harfang's company Vecheech had a share in Boissard Équestre, which was vulnerable to a takeover. Neither Roman nor Gilles had inherited Grand-père Boissard's business acumen and the means to combat a financial predator. Harfang was friends with Roman, and now Gilles was his employee, although that seemed out of character for the playboy. There must be some debt tying him to Harfang, which he had tried to reduce by selling off his expensive toys and cars. The covert horse deals had to be connected as well. Were they for Vecheech? Or had he been acting independently, perhaps with the assistance of Odette?

He noted what he could about Harfang, although so much remained speculation.

PATRICK HARFANG

(a) Motives: Discovered Odette was involved in misuse or misappropriation of Boissard Équestre resources

(b) Opportunity: Unknown as an invisible recluse

(c) Profile comparison: Being an invisible recluse, masked skills required and his knowledge

(d) Evaluation: Motive medium/high; profile match x/6

According to media knowledge, or perhaps just speculation, Harfang had shown a ruthless business streak and had access to a range of services. He would have the means to hire an assassin for himself or a partner like Roman Boissard.

Did all this suggest that Gilles was the next victim if he was still deceiving his business colleagues? Unless Gilles was working off his arrears, under threat of death. Still, this was all purely supposition.

Find the killer, and I have the motive and the paymaster.

As night closed in around the bungalow, he tuned his mind to those of the night hunters, who were seeking out their prey, as he also had to do with lesser tools.

Now is the time to be Loup, but without my pack—without the Zoos, my trusted friends. Those days must stay buried in the past. I can't ask them to stand beside me again—not when I failed so tragically before.

TWENTY-EIGHT

"Damn, he looks terrible! No way that's jet lag!" said Carly, as she led the horse out of the horsebox.

A crowd of owners and riders gathered by the yard at Hazelmead, studying the horse. Hairy and forlorn, his head hanging low, Pin stared at those surrounding him, feeding their anger and concern.

"It can't be true, yet it's the only reason," said Armand, walking around the horse.

Carly nodded. "The bastard had him castrated—probably when he arrived in Canada. Gilles will be livid! No way did he know when he phoned. Saumur is out, as his muscle is pretty wasted. We won't have time to get him fit."

"*Merde,* what was Roman thinking? It's madness for a stud with so few stallions left."

She glanced at her watch. Gilles should have landed at Gatwick well over an hour ago.

"I should ring and warn Gilles."

The 4x4 appeared and pulled up beside the farmhouse. As the onlookers went back to work, Gilles rushed towards Carly, arms wide.

"I'm so sorry, babe, it's been so hectic. I would've phoned but..."

He froze, letting Carly slip from his grasp.

Tears welled as he noticed Pin.

"Câlice, he'll pay for this." He threw his arms around the horse. "Why punish poor Pin for my decision? It makes no sense unless..."

"...this is him warning you what he can do," said Armand, voicing what Gilles couldn't say.

"He doesn't know what I can do, Loup. I'm going there now, once Lina knows."

Gilles stared hard, his eyebrows furrowed and mouth thinned. He pulled out his phone, took some photos of Pin, texted them and then called Lina. He walked off towards the farmhouse, cursing his psychotic father.

Carly had never seen him so incensed, except when he threw the scissors. She tried to control her panic by settling Pin in a stable and giving him a high vitamin convalescent feed.

As Armand helped her, she sought reassurance.

"Lina will calm him down, won't she?"

"I hope she can. We can't have them both fighting with Roman."

Carly assumed that this meant that Lina would erupt as well, although she couldn't blame her. Inside, she was seething at the injustice and ready to confront the cold-hearted bastard herself.

*

It was half an hour before Gilles emerged from the farmhouse and it was clear that Lina had fuelled Gilles's rage. A measured response had been too much to hope for; her temperament was against the reasoned approach.

"My father is a monster. There's only one way to deal with him," said Gilles, adding a stream of expletives.

Carly held him. "We share your feelings, but don't do anything rash. Please."

Gilles broke free and climbed into the 4x4.

"I'm calm inside. I know what I must do. Roman's ruined the breeding operation. I have to get Lina and the last of my horses out of there, and he won't stand in my way."

"Then we'll all go."

"No, too many. The confrontation can wait. I can deal with this, my way."

He slammed the car door and drove off waving, skidding as he turned past the bungalow.

Carly tried to say, "Please drive carefully," but all that remained was the dust.

"This is totally crazy. At most, four hours tops to get to Fenburgh and three to deal with Roman. He should have answered by now, Loup."

"Maybe Roman made sure he wasn't there at first, or...."

"Or Gilles was hurrying and crashed," said Carly.

She tried to force away the vision of the 4x4 mangled around a tree and Gilles's lifeless body resting inside of it.

"He's too good a driver to crash. I think Roman created problems, like refusing to let Gilles back onto Fenburgh."

She wondered if Roman had forced Gilles to cave into unreasonable demands. Had Gilles given away everything he still owned? Could Roman have physically harmed him?

"He must be there, Loup. Otherwise Lina would have phoned us. Have you tried her again?"

"Yes, and her mobile is off, so I sent a text. I'm sure they'll ring when they can. Don't worry, please, Vix."

Armand helped her measure out the horses' feed, which took her mind off her fears. They had two more buckets to fill when her phone rang.

"Thank God honey, I was worried. You're okay?"

Armand gestured that he would finish the feed so she could talk.

"Babe, I would've called, but it's been really stressed here." His voice was strained and tired. Flat.

"Are you okay, Gilles? What did you tell Roman?"

"We stood up to him, even though he got abusive and suggested I'd be next. Lina showed him."

Carly heard the Latina whisper in the background.

"She has to get out. Roman is making her life hell.

Says Pin's problems were all because of her regime. First, the loss of form, and then him firing blanks."

"No mention then, of his callous decision to fly the horse with a virus?"

"No, but I said I was keeping Pin, and the horse would prove himself—even if Papa and Vecheech want to get rid of him."

"So, you're coming back now, with Lina?" Carly was hopeful but feared more was being unsaid as Gilles went quiet.

Distant whispers broke the pause.

"Well, yes... but we need to make plans. There's lots of valuable junk here...like lab equipment and files, as well as horses. I need to make arrangements with Vecheech—it's theirs mostly."

Her stomach flipped, but this was no hypo—although she could have screamed.

Armand came over and put a supportive arm around her shoulders as she asked Gilles, "So, you'll be back late or tomorrow? What about Chatsworth?"

"You'll have to go with Armand. You'll cope with just two rides, babe. Lina wants a word."

"*Hola, amiga,* we'll try to be there on Sunday. Sorry about this, damn Roman." Lina sounded stressed too. "But don't worry, we can deal with the bastard. He's all bark and hot air."

Carly was reassured in part but stabs of jealousy thrust into her. She needed to be with Gilles. Sleeping alone in the old farmhouse was tough, and the noises kept her awake, even though logic said it was the building and the wind.

TWENTY-NINE

Ageless—she will always be twenty-six, even as I grow old. This photo might fade, but the memories will never dim. Why did she die? It made no sense. The conflict made no sense. It was only duty that took us there.

Armand let the golden face draw him back into their too-brief a time together.

I will always love her, for eternity.

He clutched the ring that bound them forever, wishing she was here, and they could celebrate her birthday today, together.

I must continue to honour Cygne's sacred memory. For her, I must face France?

The old excuses were too easy and too weak. It was Armand's duty to help his friends and to face whatever Saumur threw up from the past. Seeing Odette's parents was overdue.

He dressed and went out into the dawn light, to the welcome chorus, which promised immersion in work to escape his thoughts. If anyone needed him, they would know where to find him.

*

Carly bent down and ran her hand over the stifle, hoping the injury was gone. She smiled, reassured that Huginn would be ready for the Open Novice at Borde Hill. It was her favourite venue since her days with the Pony Club, and her father's builder friend was co-organiser, which was an added reason to support the event.

However, first, there was France. Why did Saumur faze her more than Badminton? Was it the prestige of competing at the home of the Cadre Noir, France's world-renowned cavalry school? Or was it the memory of how her mother had perceived her native country's premier event?

Or is it the nightmare?

She had woken without Gilles noticing. Cross-legged on the bed, Carly had fought to dispel the sensation of falling into a water jump. The nightmare was always the same; she struggled to keep the horse and herself from drowning in a morass of mist and mud. Then she woke sweating and shaking, needing some glucose.

She forced the memory aside, knowing it was a delayed reaction to her Burnham fall. Instead, she crept outside and checked all the horses, noting which ones needed exercise before she left for France. It was unreasonable to leave everything for the yard groom, who Vecheech had hired to help. Task complete, she headed back to the farmhouse with Guinness.

Gilles ended his online call to his contact at Vecheech as she hugged him. "I'll call you back when I know more."

He kissed her, playing with her hair.

"Horses and apricot. Love it. So, you worked out the schedule for the new girl, Vix?"

"All in my head. I'll type it up before we go. What do our bosses need to know now? Don't they know we've a lot to do and need to catch the Channel tunnel?"

"They want my advice on which Boissard Équestre horses they should buy from Roman."

"Buy? Why? At least we know your Papa, however impossible he is, sorry love. We've lost too many already. Now you want to sell more?"

He put an arm around her. "Okay, I'll be honest with you. Vix, I was going to tell you all. After what he did to Pin, I can't trust Papa."

"Nor can I, but this Harfang doesn't sound any better. He's using you and doing what Roman can't—profit from our success."

"I trust him enough now that he's bought Hazelmead. He's annoyed at Papa's reckless actions too." He held her close then continued, "If Vecheech buy Papa's share of the horses that we still have here, plus Wanda's new foal and the broodmare, then I'll sell my share of Fenburgh. It'll secure the eventing side of the business—for us. It makes sense, babe.

Roman gets what Harfang knows he craves—a profitable racehorse enterprise."

Carly swallowed. She had faith in Gilles's judgement, yet this sounded too risky. He could lose everything to Vecheech.

"This isn't right, Gilles. Did you discuss this with anyone? With Lina? Or with Loup? He's suspicious of Vecheech, although I suppose he's down at the moment."

Gilles looked at the floor and stroked his forehead. "Well, Lina has been telling me which horses were needed to keep the stud going. You can check the list, of course."

She wondered if that was all they had discussed, but horses were within the remit of Lina's job, at least on the breeding side.

"As for Armand," said Gilles, "I think he's been away from France too long. He's not been back in four years, but he worries too much about returning."

"Maybe something happened in France, at Saumur. Or in Canada, like..." Carly stopped, worried whether she should ask. Could it be Odette? Gilles must have noticed the wedding ring Armand wore on his wolf pendant.

Gilles chewed his lip then said, "Babe, maybe something happened, somewhere. He'll tell us when he's ready, but he'll be there for us in France, trust me."

He gave her a long kiss and held her tight.

She wondered what he knew about Armand and Odette. She hated it when he shut her out. What was he hiding?

THIRTY

Wanda halted perfectly, and Carly saluted the judges. She tried to contain herself and not punch the air as they left the Saumur arena, knowing the mare had done a great test. Riders often said, "Just 'cos you thought it was great don't mean the judges share that delusion."

The faces of the crowd and their applause told her the marks on the scoreboard were better than she expected. The reaction was fantastic, and as she rode out, she could see Gilles and Lina celebrating, even though this was just the first phase of the competition; and other riders still had to ride their dressage tests.

She dismounted, and Gilles hugged her.

"That was brilliant, Vix. I knew you could be a dressage queen."

As Lina took Wanda and praised the horse, Carly said, "As she says, it's all down to Wanda—and, of course, your training."

They walked the mare out of the practice area towards the stables with Gilles still letting the compliments flow when Carly spotted Armand.

He was talking to an elegantly dressed couple; a slim blonde lady and a tall silver haired man, whose bearing was reminiscent of the cavalry officers of the Cadre Noir. Although he was not wearing the distinctive black uniform, she wondered if he was one of them. Why was Armand in animated conversation with them?

"Hey, honey, who are the couple Loup's talking to?"

Gilles studied them, scratching his chin.

"They look familiar... kind of looks like Wanda's breeders. *Maudit,* it's been a while since I met them. Armand never said he knew them."

"Well, perhaps we should talk to them," said Carly, keen to share with them after Wanda's brilliance.

"After we've untacked her and settled her in the stable. Although I could do that with Lina if you like."

Carly was torn between curiosity and duty. Maybe this was her chance to learn more about Wanda, and perhaps connect with her mother's homeland?

Saumur was everything she had dreamed of, but she wished that her mother was sharing these moments with her. Although the event was in the woodland area outside the city, she had glimpsed the turreted chateau and the cathedral spire, towering over the elegant townhouses along the Loire. At least her father knew what Saumur meant to her, and was making time to come to the event at the weekend.

*

Armand wasn't ready for them all to know, but he could resolve this. He let Gilles and Lina leave with the mare. Armand would face fewer questions without them. He waved to Carly.

"Brilliant, Vix. We thought that was so beautiful to watch. Wanda was floating."

"The crowd and the atmosphere lifted her."

"Carly, these are Wanda's breeders: Natalie and Jean-Pierre Duchesne... friends, like family."

He was relieved when the couple smiled, greeted Carly with kisses on her cheeks and said, "You ride her so softly and effortlessly. I'm sure you will do very well on Saturday."

Carly blushed. "It's all down to Wanda, I mean Sorcière. She is the one with the talent. Like her parents, perhaps?"

"Wanda is a lovely name, so please use it," said Natalie. "Her sire Phénix has tremendous presence and stamina. He was a top-class jumper. And her dam Lune excelled at dressage especially. She had natural paces, which Wanda certainly inherited."

Carly gestured towards the stables and suggested they come and see the mare. Now was the wrong moment, so he looked at his watch; the Duchesnes understood.

"*Merci beaucoup*, but we need to return to our horses at Compiegne," said Jean-Pierre "We are coming here

Saturday. We won't miss her jumping *le cross*."

"I'll walk with you to your car," said Armand.

He had postponed this moment for too long, which was a mistake he could resolve by spending more time with Jean-Pierre and Natalie.

He turned to Carly. "Tell Gilles I'll ring when I'm heading back. I'm sure he'll have plenty for me to do."

Having let Carly say goodbye, he headed to the members' car park with the Duchesnes. Talk of the past was hard but inevitable, and the burden lifted—a fraction.

THIRTY-ONE

The mistakes worried Carly. Wanda kept going for the wrong stride, even though each fence came up just as her notes stressed. The oxer should be straightforward.

"The line's right—go for it girl."

But the mare tried to chip in an extra stride, clouting it hard. Wanda skewed, but the grip from the saddle and her long legs kept Carly on. The mare recovered without stumbling, picking up the pace again quickly—not unlucky thirteen.

Foot perfect through the first water complex, Carly was encouraged. Over halfway and the mare was finally locking onto her fences, but the time was ticking away too quickly. Or maybe the course felt longer? Were the twists and turns through the trees confusing her? Or was it the wind-flung sand?

She focused again for the upturned boat at the Ford, where the ground dropped away into the water. Wanda wanted to churn through. The crowds were jostling for a good view of the spectacle of a faller.

Carly tried to shut out the noise—a rising rumble.

She sensed the crowds were jeering. Was it because she was British and she was riding a horse that should be theirs?

The clouds were dark and low. The rain lashed like branches at Carly, stinging her skin. The wind whipped up waves that battered the hedge in Wanda's path. It loomed as they closed on it and Carly tried to find the right stride as the mare slid in the mud. Wanda leapt. Thorns tore into horse and rider as they crashed through the hedge.

As they fell, blood splattered the mare's coat and smeared Carly's face, blinding her. As they hit bottom, Wanda lost her footing. She crumpled, tossing her rider into the darkness. Voices screamed at her.

Carly floundered around, unable to reach the mare that had vanished into the mist. She was choking. Fingers were forcing her hands from her face, and the screams were hers.

She looked up into Gilles's eyes. He kissed her and held her tight. She shivered, and he wiped sweat from her face.

"You're okay, babe. It was a nightmare. You fell asleep doing your visualisation."

"But it was so real." She reached across to the shelf, knowing she had to test her levels. "I'm going to fall again, like at Burnham."

"No, you're not. Wanda can do this. Focus on it. We all believe in you—both of you."

"The mare okay, but..."

"Prove Roman wrong again—and me. The mare is no witch, but as you always say, she's magic."

Armand regained his breath after his dash towards the first water. He had glimpsed Carly and Wanda in the distance making nothing of 'La sablière', as he paused on a crowded slope. He jogged on and, as he casually glanced around at the clumps of people, he saw them. The vets from Burnham Market were heading in the same direction. He decided not to tail them, hoping he could find them later.

His concern was for Carly. After fence twelve, Les jardinières, the commentary had stopped talking about her.

Are my compatriots focusing on the home contenders? Or is the Oxer the culprit?

The loudspeakers refused to mention her name.

They came into view, full of running. Carly hardly checked, and the mare made nothing of the upright hedge-wall or the narrow brushes in and out of the water, resolving the demands without missing a stride.

Then, at the log table, Wanda took off too early. She banked the top, skewing slightly. Carly stayed with her, and the crowd applauded her stick-ability.

As they galloped out of sight up into the woods, he realised their talent would keep them going to the end. Gilles would watch the pair through the second water, although they were all sure the nightmare was just apprehension.

Armand noticed the vets again and made a snap decision—he had time to follow them. Gilles would head back to the finish and help Lina, and they wouldn't expect him until he stumbled back exhausted.

As he shadowed the vets, his doubts emerged.

Tailing them is ridiculous. Isn't this already a false lead? They behaved normally at Burnham, so why do they seem suspicious?

Because of Mick, among the crowd, watching.

The Vidarranj salesman conferred with the vets, handing them a metal briefcase, identical to the ones exchanged with Roman at Badminton, and to the one at Burnham.

The meeting dispersed in opposite directions, so Armand stuck with the vets. For the next hour, he saw horses over every fence on the course. The vets watched and made notes, probably on horses to test.

Are they were waiting for me to leave before they act?

"I keep telling you, Wanda will be sound in the morning, Vix. The vets weren't worried when you finished. It's just a knock. Let her sleep."

Carly paced up and down beside Wanda's stable, shaking her head.

"But she needs time to recover. I'm sure she won't pass."

Her worries kept needling her. She should have slowed down. If she show-jumped Wanda with a slight injury, it would get worse. Was this worth it? Carly wasn't ready to ruin someone else's horse. She kept telling herself they'd be up all night applying ice and the arnica-witch hazel gel. Then, the mare would still be spun.

"I'll withdraw her now, Gilles. Then you can all get to sleep. It's only fair."

"Don't be stupid—you're lying third. We've agreed to take turns to look in on her. Lina and Armand take over at midnight. Let the ground jury decide what's best tomorrow."

"But they don't know Wanda and—

"They're experienced. They'll know."

Before she could argue anymore, Gilles kissed her. His fingers unfastened her jeans, but there were too many people around, and Gilles was ignoring the muddy ground. She dragged him towards the shadows and supported herself against a tree. The risk aroused her, although they would avoid the prying eyes.

Gilles was being unreasonable. They had agreed on what to do about Wanda. Did he think she was getting at him for making love so openly? He had been as keen as her. He was so moody—she couldn't handle this drama.

"Damn you!" she said, hands clasped to his head. "Look, if I say we do her bandages again with more gel, we'll do it!"

"You did them an hour ago. They'll last till the others come—in fact, longer." He stared at her. "Check your sugar levels—please. Now."

"Don't change the subject. Get the..."

"You're sweating and confused. No food, stress and sex. I'm sorry..."

Wanda nosed Carly towards Gilles so he caught her as she collapsed.

He fumbled in her jeans and she struggled, then realised what he was doing.

"Hypostop—in my pouch."

It was always the same. As Armand and Lina sat and ate, they had chatted about life and discussed problems like Roman. Detecting reticence in Lina's words, Armand pulled back from sharing his past.

Wearing jackets to keep out the brisk night air, they headed through the ranks of horseboxes, where some people sat outside around tables drinking, reliving and releasing the excitement of the day amid the smell of charcoal smoke and grilled meat. The aromas would have been tempting, but the lingering taste of chocolate mousse, coffee, and brandy was satisfying Armand.

As they approached the second row of stables, Lina said, "Sneaky," pointing at the vets hovering around the end stalls. They were acting casual.

"They're the ones I saw at Burnham and earlier today. What are they up to then?"

"Obvious. That's one of the other leading horses. It must be a spot dope test. It looks like they've been taking mouth swabs." She gestured at the metal briefcase.

Then she hesitated uneasily and pulled Armand into the shadows.

"Is that allowed?" he asked. "I thought it was done officially at three-days. Don't they check urine still? Or blood?"

She watched them, hands on her face, eyes wide.

"Usually, but perhaps they hope to catch someone using something illegal. It happens."

This encounter was significant, especially as Roman and Mick were involved.

Should I ask Lina more? Should I tell her everything? She will know at once, as will Carly—merde.

He needed their scientific knowledge, but couldn't risk involving them.

I can trust the Duchesnes, whatever wrong I did them. That seems forgiven, or at least forgotten.

"Do you think we should warn people, Lina?"

"For now, I believe we have to tell Gilles and Carly.

Wanda is clean, but we have to protect her."

"Something is wrong, *chérie*."

"Why?" Lina looked worried.

"Because I saw those vets talking to Mick earlier. I think Roman is involved."

She cursed but said nothing, just kept walking. What did she know? Maybe he could glean more information later on.

They found Gilles sitting inside the stable with Carly resting against his shoulder.

She smiled up at them.

"I forgot to put my pump back on—or check my levels. Worrying too much about Wanda, but I'll be okay."

"Vix needs her last injection, and some food, then rest. The horse is good. Just do the ice once more before morning—the treatment's working, but you can walk her around if necessary too."

"Loup and I spotted some FEI vets doing spot dope testing. No need to worry—you and the mare are clean."

"Thanks, Wanda's cleaner than me," said Carly. "Insulin's only legal when you're like me—unsound."

THIRTY-TWO

A wall of colour and anticipation ringed the arena. Beneath the flags of the participating nations, faces were fixed on Carly and Wanda, following them over an upright and round into the treble.

"Ride the turn," said Gilles out loud. "Remember everything your Mom taught you."

She set Wanda up, and normally the mare would have been foot perfect over all three elements, even with the electric atmosphere and testing course, but her front hooves rapped the last one. Everyone groaned as the top pole rolled in its cups—but it stayed.

"*Mierda*—I pray she doesn't feel that knock."

"They can still do it, believe in them," said Armand rapping his fingers on the railings.

I'm as excited as the others. They must be jumping every fence with Carly and Wanda.

"Don't lose it now. Hold it together, please," said Gilles with just two more left.

With the clock ticking down, she had to be clear inside the time.

Carly cut the corner and set Wanda up for the final line.

"They can't do it," said Gilles but the poles stayed up.

They cheered as she competed clear and the final turn had ensured no time faults. Armand realised she would finish third—unless one of the top two blew it.

Carly hugged Wanda as she came out, but then jumped off and checked the mare's legs, while Lina held the horse.

"Cool move cutting the corner, Vix—another Ardingly," said Gilles. "You did great to get her round."

"She's the most exceptional horse—ever. A brill team effort."

"It's down to your hard work and determination."

"And hers. I must thank the Duchesnes for breeding her. Are they here, Loup?"

He pointed across to the Members area. "Yes. They'll want to congratulate the rider."

He had spent time with them so knew what they would say. The situation was easier after his absence abroad. They were concerned about the vets; they had their theory too and feared the consequences if they were correct. They would liaise with the other Zoos, and they promised to contact him with more information.

It's right that the comrades I abandoned are involved.

Family never walk away, but we need to know what we face.

A gasp from the crowd interrupted his thoughts.

The French rider, who was less than a fence above Carly, was taking it carefully. His sweeping turns between fences were drawing groans as the clock ticked.

Gilles chewed his lip, arm around Carly. Lina clung to the rails, halter rope over her shoulder. Only Wanda was calm and above all this.

The stallion didn't have the mare's sharp reactions and got under the first part of the treble. They scrambled over, but their striding was out. The rider tried to correct for the second and fortune favoured the home side—still clear. But his luck ran out at the last element as the stallion's hind legs dropped a rail. The crowd groaned but mustered up some applause when he cleared the final line.

Carly and Wanda moved into second.

As yet, nobody seemed to have realised that Carly was part French and Wanda was one hundred percent French-bred—not even the commentators.

The overnight leader was one of Britain's top riders on one of her second-string horses, so not yet a team prospect; but the gelding was ready to claim its first title.

This rider wasn't going to let time catch her out and chose a steady pace, keeping momentum and balance as she negotiated the course. The horse was clearing the fences with ease, and victory looked inevitable.

"She can afford two fences down and still beat us," said Gilles.

"Second spot is okay by me," said Carly. "I'd never have expected as much."

"Actually, she can have just one fence down," said Armand, "plus only three time penalties."

He was trying not to jinx the other rider. Earlier, he had feared Mick and his cohorts might be planning to stop Wanda. Now he hoped they weren't going to interfere to ensure a Boissard win, except the mare now belonged to Vecheech and Gilles. Natalie and Jean-Pierre had reassured him that it was impossible to intervene at this stage, barring a rider or horse collapsing with some mysterious ailment.

The crowd drew breath in unison as the plank on the double slipped off.

Now, the clock seemed to be running faster.

The rider was experienced and accustomed to pressure as a serial three-day-event winner. She had judged her round to perfection and was unfazed. She ignored Carly's cheeky turn to the final line. Perfect stride and momentum. The first fence cleared with plenty of air between horse and pole; the second fence jumped cleanly; and then the third.

The gelding was rising to the challenge, sensing victory as the murmur of the crowd grew. As the rider went clear, she relaxed, punching the air in triumph.

But time had run out.

Silence. People were unsure who had won.

Not Armand. He leapt into the air and embraced Carly, Lina, Wanda and everyone around him, inspiring jubilation.

Then the scoreboard confirmed Armand's celebration. A Hazelmead win by one point.

The crowd had rooted for a French win all weekend, and when the commentator emphasised that Sorcière des Saules was a pure French Anglo-Arab, bred at Compiègne, they were euphoric.

Well-wishers surrounded Carly and the Duchesnes, feting them as the breeders. Through all this, Wanda held her head high, knowing when to rise to the occasion, from her beautiful dressage to her moment at the mounted prize-giving.

"Mademoiselle Tanner, in many ways you are crediting the mare with this win, so it's a French victory then."

The comment was loaded. The press had avoided discussing Carly's nationality up to now, but the patriotism of Armand's countrymen couldn't be suppressed.

The reporter continued, "Sadly, top French breeding stock like Sorcière des Saules is lost to American money and foreign riders."

"Correction: we sold her to a French-Canadian stud," said Jean-Pierre, adding, "and we have the sire and the dam as well as other successful offspring."

But the journalist was persistent.

"Still, we lose prime bloodstock abroad. If selected, who will this mare be ridden for, at say the next championships?"

Armand wondered whom the journalist was criticising, the Duchesnes or the Boissards or even Vecheech? Had Patrick Harfang's reputation spread this far?

Carly fielded the question and diverted the journalist. "It's up to the owners of course, and it depends if I keep the ride. I would compete for Great Britain as I did as a Young Rider, but the Selectors have other more qualified and more experienced riders to choose from. Those riders are more suitable than a rider without their credentials."

A British journalist asked, "After your thirteenth at Badminton with Sylvan Torc, haven't you improved your chances of selection today—if not this year, then next year?"

Before Carly could answer, a voice from the back said, "Didn't you want to ride for France then?"

Armand turned and glimpsed a familiar face, but not a journalist.

"Thanks, Mick. Yes, my mother was from Brittany, and I approached the French Federation about riding as French—it was her final wish."

A murmur swept through the press conference, but she stemmed it by saying, "It's for her. I don't exactly qualify to ride for *La France* at senior level. As with Britain, there are others better suited—like those beside me." She smiled at the French rider who had taken third.

"So, if we discount any team ambitions, what are your plans for the season now?" asked another journalist.

"To give Wanda a well-deserved holiday, and then do another three-star. Or, even move a step up and do the four star at Burghley—but of course, that's also up to the owners."

The Duchesnes embraced her warmly.

"You have a real gift, a sensitive understanding of Sorcière... of Wanda that is precious." Natalie smiled. Glancing at Armand, she continued, "We bred her for... someone like you, someone special, so we're very pleased."

Blushing, she said, "That means so much, thank you."

Jean-Pierre waved over another man with a cavalry bearing, even in a suit rather than a black uniform. He was younger, about Armand's age.

Introduced as Captain Blavet, he said, "Congratulations, very well ridden. You have talent, and with training, we can use you."

She raised her eyebrows, wondering if by 'we' he meant the Cadre Noir.

"Mademoiselle Tanner, you said your mother was French, so I presume you have dual nationality. If so, we could help, if you want to ride for La France." That 'we' again. Who was he? "I gather that you have applied to the FFE for acceptance as a French rider. It's a slow process, but there are ways to expedite the procedure. Would you and Sorcière des Saules's owners consider doing an international three star in June?"

Carly swallowed. Was this stranger asking her to ride at an international event? Except, if he was a friend of the breeders then he might be able to help her realise her mother's dream.

"I don't have plans, so probably—if it would help. Of course, it depends on the approval of the owners and British Eventing, but I'll try to be there."

"Let us know what you decide to do. We will then ask the right people and see what we can do."

He bowed and shook her hand.

"It has been charming to meet you."

He smiled at the Duchesnes before saluting Jean-Pierre and walked over to Armand, whom he led to one side.

If Captain Blavet was Cadre Noir, Armand could have served with them, but on a horse, he didn't look cavalry trained. So, what was he?

From everything that Lina had said, he was a victim of gang warfare and an intellectual recluse, but now he was talking with an army officer that had saluted Jean-Pierre Duchesne. Carly tried to tie up all the contradictions. Maybe it was as simple as Armand working for the Duchesnes, to escape from a troubled background. It made sense and even explained the shoulder wound.

Did she dare ask the Duchesnes, or was she digging up the past Armand wanted to keep buried? It could wait.

For now, she needed to spend some time with her father before work pulled him away again.

THIRTY-THREE

With her eyes closed, Lina sat in the horsebox, her fingers twisting her hair, foot tapping on the dash-board. She was anxious about what awaited them.

"Roman won't want to provoke Vecheech," said Armand. "The equipment will be intact, chérie."

Lina opened one eye. "*Madre de Dios,* I hope you're right. I fear the worst after Saumur. He'll blame me because they won when they're meant to be useless."

"What can he do without annoying Harfang?"

"Destroy my research material. Roman will be pissed with Harfang and say the guy's a thief."

"What do you know about Patrick Harfang?" asked Armand, digging.

"Not much. He's shadowy—hard to approach. Gilles used to joke about him back in Canada..."

"I vaguely remember," said Armand, recollecting one fancy dress party when Gilles had attended as an obese ogre, Baron Harfang, which had irritated Roman.

"But he's rumoured to be a tough operator."

"And Roman claims he's a friend?"

"They belong to the same golf club near Bromont," said Lina. "The hellhound played golf with him, once, so thought they were friends—no longer, I expect."

They turned into Fenburgh, up the long drive.

Fewer horses grazed the fields, but there was activity. The sun glinted off the fences and the roofs, and the security cameras. He began counting them as he parked the horsebox behind the lab building. Was Lina doing the same security check? She seemed to be inspecting the place in detail—unless she was assessing to see if the stud had changed.

The rear doors were closed, so Lina reached over and tapped in her pass code. It was no use; Roman had changed it, forcing a frontal entry.

As they walked into the office, with Mistico adding his intimidating presence, they found Roman waiting with Mick.

"So, you've the impudence to come back. Haven't you stolen enough from me?"

Lina replied, "You were paid for everything. We're here for the rest of what Vecheech bought."

"Cheats," said Mick. "The mare alone was worth ten times what Vecheech paid us."

Armand noted the salesman's use of 'us'. Vidarranj must be a partner in Boissard Équestre.

"Hog shit," said Lina. "You never rated Wanda, until Carly won on her."

"*La salope* deceived us," said Roman. "Someone

has to pay, now."

Mick intervened, although his words didn't convince Armand it was out of friendship to Carly.

"It was not the rider's fault. Her employer should have provided a proper assessment based on what she reported and of course, Miss Jardero's research."

He pointed to the desk and a metal briefcase, which Lina checked.

"You found my research notes. I thought I'd lost them."

Does this explain her anger at Badminton and alarm at Saumur?

She glanced from Roman to Mick.

"*Carajo*, you took this and passed it to... the Vidarranj bastards."

"Why not? You did the work here, Jardero," said Roman, "so this is Boissard Équestre property. Mine to use and–"

Lina thrust her finger towards Roman. "You value nothing, shit face, horses least of all."

"Hear Pin was useless as a stallion, thanks to you. So, Mr Boissard had to take a knife to him—cut his nuts off." Mick gestured, slicing a finger across his neck. "Never forget that."

Armand resisted saying something, but Lina shifted position and took up an aggressive stance; Mistico bared his teeth.

"Shut up Mick, unless you want someone to do

that to you, pervert."

Mick responded by crouching and raising one defensive palm, but he said nothing.

Observing the stand-off, Armand wondered if either would attack. The martial arts stances were familiar.

Lina picked up the briefcase. Mick moved to stop her, but she shot out a warning leg; the side kick feint stopped short of the salesman's chin, freezing him.

Spinning on her heels, Lina strode towards the lab.

"I hope the equipment is ready. I'm not wasting more time here."

"Jardero, halt." Roman was on his feet. Pushing past Armand, he joined Mick. "You're not going anywhere until I get paid in full."

"Monsieur Boissard," Armand pulled out a sheaf of papers that Gilles had entrusted to him, "this includes a complete list of what we paid for, and you've signed it."

Roman grabbed the papers and threw them into the wastepaper bin.

"They're worthless now. My lawyers will deal with this so you can leave."

Lina turned on him. "No way, idiot, you will so lose. Better to give me the key now, or I will drive the truck through the damn doors."

Lina was resolute, and Armand was ready to help.

"You don't need the equipment, sir. You have us,

one hundred and ten percent. I assure you I have what we both want, or can obtain it, our way."

Roman punched his code in the lock and led Lina inside the lab.

Armand retrieved the contract from the bin and followed, noting Mick's assurance. Was the salesman reminding them of his earlier threat?

As they drove away from the stud, Armand asked, "That kick, did you know Mick would do nothing?"

"He was bluffing. The stance was a pose. Carly says he's a phoney and easily conned."

Armand wasn't so sure but guessed Carly knew her ex. If only he knew more about Lina.

"Your move was impressive. Where did you learn the side snap kick?"

She hesitated before replying.

"I needed to learn ju-jitsu. My father was... beating Mama and us kids... I left home to prove myself, make my own life."

"*Merde,* I'm so sorry, I never realised your childhood was that rough."

"No one does. Well, I told Carly a bit, but reliving those years is too painful."

"I'm here for you, if you need a friend." He was ready to talk about himself, although some details would have to remain hidden.

As he pulled onto the A11, she said, "I had to

handle cruelty and prejudice. And violence, like your shoulder, poor Loup. Looks like a gunshot wound."

What does she know?

"You recognise one? How?"

She closed her eyes and shook her head.

Is she like me? Have I finally found an ally? Impossible. I need someone to trust. But is that Lina?

"*Si,* sometimes I had to fight to protect myself and anything I valued."

THIRTY-FOUR

"We would like to invite you to join the Elite training squad, for those who we feel might be team prospects."

The official's words had left Carly stunned by the recognition. They favoured Wanda over the more experienced Torc, but maybe they were looking for future potential, so the results for both mares on their return to competition would now be under scrutiny.

Thinking back over the phone call, "team prospects" must mean next year or more likely later, but she was amazed the selectors would consider an unknown rider with no track record beyond a brief stint with the Young Riders team. Her health had to be a liability, and when they made the final choices next spring, or in the future, there would be others more suitable. This invitation was just to encourage her, and to ensure she stayed a British rider. However, competing with Wanda at an international one-day for the French Federation, as Captain Blavet had requested, might be misunderstood by British Eventing.

There was no urgency for now, but she should be doing something—there must be horses to exercise. She didn't need the afternoon off, even if Gilles had insisted she relax in front of the TV with Guinness while he dealt with the horses. He had claimed all the paperwork was up to date, but she checked anyway.

Gilles had done everything from the accounts to the entries. He had even made the travel booking for the Spanish three-star international, even though Pin might be fit sooner and able to do the three-star at Bramham in Yorkshire.

Checking through the paperwork, it seemed Vecheech had unleashed the Business & Economics graduate in Gilles—at last. He had also entered Wanda into the international one-day at Bramham. Had he intentionally ignored her French application, or was the entry a logistical decision? Whatever his motive, a good result there might satisfy both British and French Federations, without forcing Carly to make a premature decision over her nationality. She did love the Yorkshire venue, so it was tempting to ride Wanda there.

Relaxation beckoned, and Guinness looked at her, wanting her to share the sofa or at least let him warm her toes; but a nagging concern kept her online.

Odette Fédon. Gilles had said so little about Odette after the funeral, but Carly still needed to know more. So she searched and found three online newspaper articles. The first was a report of the funeral, confirming what she knew, but the second story, from the Montreal Gazette, disturbed her.

PREGNANT GROOM KILLED
According to forensic sources, the autopsy of Odette Fédon, 26, of Les-Trois-Ponts, has revealed that she was pregnant when she died in December while exercising a horse for her employers, Du Noroît Stud near Bromont.
A spokeswoman for the Québec Provincial Police says, "Mademoiselle Fédon was three weeks pregnant, but we are still treating her death as misadventure. All our evidence indicates that Fédon was knocked off her horse by a tree branch during a blizzard."
However, the police have interviewed several people, including her former employer Gilles Boissard, who now lives in England.

Did they suspect Gilles of being the father? Was that why he went alone to Québec? Did he fear that the police and the Fédon family would ask questions? She kept reading.

The Boissard family have denied any relationship between Gilles Boissard and Odette Fédon beyond her employment. However, the Fédon family have demanded a paternity test and expect an acknowledgement along with a financial apology.

The discovery was hard to absorb. She needed a strong black tea.

Odette's pregnancy must have been ill-timed when she was alive, given this Boissard reaction after her death. How did Gilles react? Odette had spent enough time alone with Gilles for the relationship to be well developed. Had Roman killed Odette, or paid to have her killed to stop her marrying his son and claiming a share of the Boissard fortune? There had to be other less extreme options, like attempting to pay Odette to renounce any claim. So, why pay a killer?

She had to read the next article and hoped that it brought closure. Instead, it stated that after the DNA tests, Gilles was determined to have been the father of Odette's unborn child. The Boissard family's lawyers would contest the Fédon family's financial claim, of course.

Despite that news, she was relieved the police had closed the case as misadventure. She didn't want Gilles caught up in a murder investigation, even if he had lied to her about his relationship with Odette.

Familiar sounds outside drifted into the room, birds singing, horses neighing and a tractor chugging. Everything seemed so normal.

She stood up and gazed out of the window.

Why hadn't Gilles told her? Again, he had been minimal with the truth. She had to challenge him about Odette.

Back at the computer desk, she bent down and stroked Guinness, kissing his head, comforted by her faithful companion.

Odette—what was Armand to her? Could he have killed her because he was jealous of Gilles's relationship? Was he hiding from that memory? She had to learn more about Armand Sabatier to be able to prove him innocent.

The search indicated that the Sabatiers came from the south, or Massif Central area of France; unless he was one of the knife makers from Thiers, which made her shudder. She found no living Armand Sabatier, but she recognised the limitations of the Internet. Why should someone be there unless they were famous or wanted to publicise themselves? That was not Armand, the lone wolf.

At Saumur, he had contacts, so the Duchesnes's stud website might throw up some clues. She blushed at the latest stud news item, which stated that Sorcière des Saules, the Saumur winner, was bred by them and praised the contribution of her classy Anglo-French rider with sympathetic hands.

The website impressed her, and among the photos of the stunning horses bred at Des Saules, she found Wanda's parents Phénix and Lune, who both had excelled in their careers. There were also details of their parentages. She was tempted to explore more, but resisted, saving the link for later.

How did Armand know them? She found the link to the family and clicked on it. Both Duchesnes were from equestrian backgrounds and Jean-Pierre's father, Maurice had started the stud. Jean-Pierre and Natalie had expanded the stud after they left the army, but there was no clue as to what regiment, only a brief mention of their commitment to breeding the best Anglo-Arabs in France.

Were the Cadre classed as the army? She remembered some French riders doing their National Service with them. Did Armand do that? But he was not a natural horseman and no Cadre Noir, although he was sensitive around horses. Maybe he had done his National Service with Jean-Pierre's son—except there was no sign of any Duchesne son. Was Captain Blavet a cousin perhaps? He seemed to be the right age to have served with Armand, and they clearly knew each other. Armand had even driven back from Saumur with a military-looking jeep.

She stared at the page, desperate for a clue. Guinness put his head on her knee, comforting her. She clicked through the stud's photo archives for inspiration and then froze.

The mare was staring at her: Lune des Saules with her filly Sorcière and the Duchesnes, as well as a groom. No, not a groom, but their daughter who was holding Wanda close. The "someone special" whom

Natalie and Jean-Pierre had bred the mare for. Odette Duchesne. Around her neck was a pendant so similar in style to Armand's that Carly had to check it. She saved the photo and then zoomed in with her photo software.

It was a bird—a swan, like Armand's tattoo.

THIRTY-FIVE

Carly was lying in Gilles's arms, but she wasn't ready for what he wanted. There was too much to deal with, and only he could resolve this, or else it was over.

"Did you ever meet the Duchesne daughter?"

"Didn't know they had one, Vix—so no, never."

"She's called Odette."

Gilles stared at her, mouth wide open. "What? Like...?"

"Yes, like your groom in Canada."

"*Maudit*—that explains why Armand has been acting so weird."

"And how he knew the parents. You never noticed the ring with the pendant around his neck? So, he never said he was married? Or why he didn't want to go back to France?"

She stared hard at Gilles, searching for any signs of evasion, but there was just confusion.

"Never, he's always been mysterious."

She breathed slowly, containing her anger.

"When were you going to tell me Odette Fédon was pregnant when she disappeared?"

He closed his eyes and tears formed, softening her mood.

"It's okay, honey, I would have understood," she said. "Even knowing you were the father."

"Babe, I'm sorry... I never wanted to... hurt you, but there was too much... too sudden."

He grasped her hands tightly and looked down.

Carly held his face and kissed him. Odette wasn't a rival; if he could stop living in the past.

"Please. Did Odette mean a lot to you?"

"At the time, everything, but Papa would never have accepted her. He didn't even accept her opinion on the horses, so we kept it quiet."

She could sympathise.

"And Loup and Lina, they're your friends?"

He shook his head, eyes closed.

"Yes, but I didn't want to... burden them with it."

"So, nobody suspected anything?"

"Never, although Papa always suspects something. Look at the way he is with us—he behaves as if we're all plotting—which is crazy."

"Poor Gilles, you must have been devastated when Odette went missing."

For a moment, there was only the sound of the wind, hooting owls and Guinness's snores.

"I was... utterly devastated. I didn't know anything. Had she been killed? Or had she disappeared? I thought the baby would make everything possible."

Carly could see Odette's dilemma and the way that she would have tackled the problem, with support.

"She sounds like someone who would have stood up to your father—your family."

"She did when she could, but it was difficult not to let our relationship slip out."

"Was her death really an accident?" Carly braved the question, "Could your father…?"

Gilles closed his eyes and held his head, then said, "Câlice, that's my nightmare still. If only I had gone with her, but I had a stupid meeting with him—with Papa."

"With Roman, so it was just an accident."

She tried to sound reassuring, but Roman could have ordered Odette killed.

Gilles had tears in his eyes again.

"It wasn't meant to happen in that way. We had plans, and the baby was a bonus."

Carly put her arms around him.

"I will try to be as... true as her."

"You are as special as her. She would have liked you. Happy and free is the way she would have wanted me to be—although it hurts."

He clasped her firmly and began kissing her. His hands were like butterflies again, exploring her body. The silk pyjamas that he had bought her were eased off, and his right hand inched downwards.

"Where do you think you're going?"

"You want a surprise, or shall I tell you? It's my favourite place."

"Hmm, I'm all anticipation... and all yours."

He eased the quilt down exposing her to the moonlight sneaking through the window.

"Well, you have to head across the prairies..." His fingers began walking across her stomach. "... towards the beautiful peaks...tracing a winding route upwards...seeking out the pass between them." He kept tracing patterns on her body as the words flowed. "The trail winds up and around them, then plunges down and across a high plateau... to a hidden sanctuary in a beautiful grove of red maples..."

Her body arched to meet him, and she pulled him closer in her desperation. She so wanted this dream he offered.

THIRTY-SIX

It should have been Carly, but she had refused to go, even with Gilles. Fortunately, Lina had talked to Mick, and Armand was glad the salesman had been taken in by her feigned enthusiasm.

Now they were getting a tour of Vidarranj's headquarters near Gatwick. If Mick thought there was a chance of getting them back in the fold, he acted his most amenable and slick—salesman Mick at full throttle.

"We don't manufacture any of the supplements here in the UK, just overseas where our farmers harvest the ingredients —it's best fresh."

"Where do you grow the produce?" asked Lina, "America?"

"No, our growers in Brazil are the very best."

"And it's just supplements to enhance our horses' performance and fertility?"

Mick smiled back at her, rising to her interest.

"For now. Our researchers are always looking for new ways to help our clients..."

"*Exactamente,* we are all trying to breed for the best performers."

It was hard to square this Mick with Roman's sly and vicious sidekick. It was as if that had never happened, and even Lina appeared relaxed and friendly. If Mick didn't suspect her of playing a game, then he was a gullible salesman, despite his hired muscle demeanour at Fenburgh.

Armand made good use of the distracting conversation to note the layout and the security. He might have to come back, and it would be easier hacking into their system from inside Vidarranj. Except, Mick was watching him intently, studying him as if he suspected at least one unwelcome visitor of having a hidden agenda.

Does he suspect me? Would it be better if I found an alternative access point? But where? This would be the best server to access.

"I see you've been looking at the photos of our grateful clients. We have them in everything—from the Olympic disciplines to polo and racing."

He was relieved Mick misunderstood his curiosity, although Armand had noted the photos.

He was also grateful when Lina continued her probing, asking, "What about recreational riders?"

"We service a handful, but this is cutting-edge science. We're talking about the elite, like you. Another top eventing yard like Hazelmead would be in good company."

At least Mick had now made it clear why he had

invited them into the den.

"If you come this way to my office, I can get you some samples. The new range of course, just released to great acclaim. Can I get you some tea or coffee?"

"So, after all that, what do you feel? Are those vets we saw at Saumur involved?"

Lina was sitting next to Armand at the kitchen table, and she furrowed her brow.

She closed her eyes before saying, "Probably..." She ran her fingers through her hair then picked up the samples that Mick had given her, at Vidarranj and Badminton. "Vidarranj's supplements have all changed in the last month. Maybe they were checking for traces of something...illegal."

Armand sensed her tension. She was holding back, or maybe she wasn't sure. Natalie and Jean-Pierre had their theory. It was a gamble, but he had to trust Lina, time was running out.

"It's crazy, but could they have been taking DNA samples as well?"

She sat up, staring straight ahead.

"Not for drug testing but... to make personalised antiserums... like I tried at Fenburgh as part of my research."

"What for?"

"General use, mainly to counteract common toxins, but poisons can be confusing. I tried making some for allergies too, like mine to plant sap. But the success rate is too low—without the proper lab."

"Wrong sort of facilities or not sufficiently sophisticated?"

"High-tech enough for the horses. These trials were more...more a personal diversion...for fun. Human drugs like Carly's insulin, now that's front-line research. Best leave that to experts."

Armand found Lina's explanation more mundane than the Duchesnes's conclusion, which had been disturbing in its implications.

THIRTY-SEVEN

As the horse approached the fence, Carly counted the strides to the first element of the Oasis combination. Clear, one stride into the water and then out.

She pressed 'send' on the radio and told control, "Number two-sixty-nine, neat and clear over 16A, and safely through the water at B," while Armand wrote down the details and checkpoint time on the fence scoring sheet.

It was less intense fence judging than competing, even though she found herself riding the jumps mentally each time. With the responsibility, as well, it would be a long tiring day, although it made her value the regular volunteers. Whether riding or helping, she enjoyed this undulating parkland with its mature trees and country house backdrop.

Guinness was stretched out on the grass beside the jeep. He growled as a familiar voice said, "Found you guys at last, though I didn't recognise this old jeep—should have known from those foreign plates, though."

Mick stood behind them, his approach masked by

another group of spectators enjoying their day out at Borde Hill. Carly ignored his remark about Loup's French acquisition, even if it did look like it had been through a war.

"I dropped by Hazelmead, and the place seemed deserted. I found a girl who told me you were here, so I came to congratulate you again, Vix, on your brilliance at Saumur. And to think, everyone thought Wanda was useless."

"Not everyone, we believed in her. 314 clear at 16A, heading fast through water at B."

"Slumming it now, I see."

"Not really, I usually volunteer here..."

"To ensure you get late entries—an easy trick. You all do it... not that I blame you."

"No way, we do it because our sport wouldn't survive without helpers. You should lend a hand, Mick."

Volunteering had also eased her late entry for Pin in the Open Novice, although it was not the main reason for helping. Anyway, Pin needed two runs before his delayed three-day outing, and she didn't want him to do an Intermediate at Eridge without an easier opener.

"Well, I might do something," said Mick, "now I'm back on my patch. Glad to escape the aggro of East Anglia."

Carly envisaged him dropping by too often,

although getting him away from Suffolk and Fenburgh might help.

Guinness was on his feet. The next horse refused, and he barked, just before Carly told the rider, "First refusal." He lay down again, and the horse went clear.

"Two-seven-one refused log at 16A. Clear at the second attempt and slowly through the water."

"How the hell does he do that?" asked Mick. "Or is he the reason why they refuse?"

"Nope, he knows from way out they'll refuse. At least half I can tell too, wrong speed, wrong angle, bad stride or no impulsion—no energy left, sometimes bad riding. And I've been there—"

"I call that outside assistance of a sort then—for the second attempt."

"Well, it ensures the horse goes clear unless the rider blows it. Again, I've done that and gotten the t-shirt."

She laughed, glad Guinness's party trick had lightened the mood, but Mick asked, "Gilles given up riding then? Leaving it to our favourite professional? Saumur must have been tough—especially as he found the mare."

"He has plenty to compete—not just Drac and Pin."

"But this is an excellent local event and the right sort of education," Mick said, then asked, "So, why isn't he here?"

"He and Lina went to check out new embryo transfer arrangements for the mares in Gloucestershire."

"Aah, transfers are one way to keep them competing."

She was making sense of his words when Guinness stood up. Armand pointed at a fast-approaching rider—out of control and on the wrong line for the water.

The rider and horse fought for supremacy and stumbled over the log, before plunging through the water. They missed the route out, and the horse tried jumping the bushes, but swerved at the last minute, dumping the rider into the undergrowth. The judges on the other bank ran to help, and the horse headed back through the water. Mick sidestepped and caught the horse.

"At least you haven't lost your touch, Mick. Thanks."

He led the horse across to the rider, who was now standing, then came back to pester them some more.

Carly concentrated on radioing control. "Three-one-six clear at 16A but fell in water at B. Rider walking off course with horse."

When an official arrived to check what had happened, Carly gave her report.

Then her mobile beeped; text message. "frndly warning. thnk G & L r 2 close—seem lik lovrs." Cryptic, and yet all she feared. Why did they need to be together so much? Was this weekend away just work? Was the anonymous sender a friend, or a fellow rider? After the next horse, she checked. No number she recognised. She rang it, but it was an anonymous message box.

"Who's that, Vix?" Loup asked. "Lina? Gilles?"

She wondered if she should tell him, in front of Mick, or would Loup guess? It was best to wait for a better moment.

"Not exactly... show you the text later."

"Think you guys might have a problem," said Mick. "If I was you, be careful who you trust. Sorry Armand, but one can't rely on some people—I know that from personal experience."

"You mean like you," said Carly.

"Only trying to help, Vix. You know me; I get to see a lot in my job but ignore me as always, just have to find out for yourself. Good luck tomorrow, *ciao*." With those remarks, he wandered off, leaving her confused.

"*Merde* that guy is so double-faced, I never know whose side he is on."

"Mick's on his own side, for his personal gain—never anyone else's. He's just a slick salesman after his next deal."

Vidarranj or Roman? Who is Mick actually working for? Whose support furthers his ambitions?

Mick could have been paid to kill Odette; if Armand could prove Mick had the skills.

Before he searched online for more on the salesman, Armand checked that the girls had put the chickens back in their secure shed. Something had disturbed them, but there was no sign or smell of a fox.

Angry barking—Guinness.

He ran back to the yard. The flatcoat stood, hackles raised, growling; defending Carly. Two masked figures in black sprinted across the fields.

"Guinness disturbed those guys attempting to break into the tack room, unsuccessfully, thank God."

"You okay, Vix? That's my concern."

"Yes, shaken a bit. The burglars heard Guinness and ran, knowing I had the best defender."

"Don't worry, we'll get them. You ring the police, and I'll try and see where those thieves are going."

"Don't be crazy, Loup. What happens if they turn on you?"

THIRTY-EIGHT

Armand opened the Peugeot P4's boot and grabbed a knapsack, with equipment that Natalie had supplied when she gave him back his keys and welcomed him back to the Zoos.

She knew I was ready to fight again. Reclaim your power, my therapist said. Now I can, and will.

"I'll be careful, just tell the police."

He pulled out a torch and swept the beam across the fields, picking out the cowering intruders. They stood up and turned, disappearing into a copse.

He turned to Carly. "Seems they were waiting to get back to the track, so they must have a car nearby. I'll let you know."

He jumped over the gate and followed them.

The torch gave away his position, so he switched it off. Reaching into the haversack, he took out some night vision goggles and slipped them on. Now he had the advantage as he tracked the intruders, using an infrared photon flashlight to expose the path. These guys weren't amateurs, but they left a trail and Armand could hear them. Thinking their pursuer had lost them, one guy switched on a small torch; a beacon for Armand.

Am I overstepping the law on the right to defend property? If I don't use a weapon, or attack them, then I should be okay.

As it was, one against two was risky if they were armed. For now, he had to know if these intruders were tack thieves or somehow connected to Mick. It was convenient that Armand and Carly had been fence judging, although not so convenient that the last class had finished early, nor that Armand and Carly passed on an end-of-day drink.

The figures headed away from Hazelmead, but they were bearing towards the main road.

If they have their vehicle there, I'll lose them unless I cut them off.

There were a few parking places nearby, maybe one of those. Armand could risk heading back to the farm and checking in his jeep. If he found a suspicious vehicle, then he could wait for the intruders.

Or will I risk losing them entirely?

Near the farm outbuildings, he phoned Carly, but it didn't sound as though the police were coming.

"... it seems Vix as if disturbing the thieves was enough for them. *Merde*."

He reached the Peugeot and climbed in.

"I'm going to get a license plate," he said to Carly. He was hoping to get more, but he wasn't ready to feed Carly's fears.

Why is she so worried about me? It's nice to have her caring about me.

He drove up the lane watching for the intruders or their vehicle.

Lina. He could imagine her helping, peering into the shadows. This skulking around fitted her image.

Am I missing the camaraderie of the Zoos? Could I even trust Lina now? Or are those malicious rumours about her and Gilles? Rumours that fit with the evidence. Why spend so much time with Gilles?

Right out of the drive, he continued looking—nothing. He turned down the hill to Highbrook and noticed a grey Transit parked in a gateway. It could be them, so he wrote down the number plate and found an unobtrusive place to watch from. Lights off and using infrared, he waited.

The strategy paid off six minutes later. The two intruders jumped over the gate and glanced around, but never registered the camouflaged jeep. Still in black balaclavas, they climbed into the van and drove north. Armand followed with lights off, so they didn't notice him pull out. Once they reached the outskirts of Ardingly, he switched on the side and then the headlights.

Their route branched off onto a country lane. With the headlights on dim, he trailed them from a distance for a while. After three minutes, he reached for the goggles and cut the lights, accelerating to close on the van. He would take his chance with other cars, and the police.

Five minutes later, the intruders, unaware of their tail, turned into a walled property, with floodlights displaying the building's elegance to anyone trapped in the glare.

Time to overstep the law—I have to do this.

Only after he had given Carly the Transit's registration details and reassured her did he move forward.

"I'll give the police that number, Loup. Don't do anything stupid, please."

"*Bien sur,* I'll just see who they are. It may take some time, so don't wait up."

"Ring when you're coming back anyway. Good luck and take care, please."

His conscience told him he should be at Hazelmead with Carly, especially if the two guys left again. She had Guinness, but would they return there?

Unlikely, as they don't know I'm following. I need to discover more. This could be the chance to access their base of operations.

He followed the course of the stone barrier around shrouded grounds. A drive on the far side was closed, with a lodge defending the seclusion. He continued looking for a vulnerable point of entry. Where the road left the wall, he drove further and found a forest track to hide his jeep along.

He slipped on his camouflage jacket, darkened his face, and clipped some items to his webbing belt. His black chinos would do. It had been years since the adrenaline had impelled him, but he was ready.

Is this what the doctors meant by Exposure Therapy? Facing the root of my trauma?

If his mind remained centred, the nightmare would stay buried.

He hiked back along the three and a half metre obstacle into the forest and, where the undergrowth reached nearest to the house, he climbed over and melted into the night.

Carly had tried a DVD, then some music, but her fears kept plaguing her. The noises she could identify, but it was the not knowing that made her worry.

What was Gilles really doing? Why hadn't he come home? Why hadn't either of them returned?

On the fifth attempt, she reached Gilles who said, "I feel so alone, Vix, without you. Look forward to getting home tomorrow. Tell you all the news then."

"Missing you too, honey, it's much easier when we're together. I need you here—"

"Tomorrow. Surely you can wait—just a few hours."

She wanted to mention the burglars, but Gilles sounded so far away, unable to help, and pre-occupied. Distracted? By who?

"Where's Lina?" she asked.

The answer was too immediate.

"Not sure... we've spoken, and I'm giving her a lift back tomorrow afternoon."

Was she there with him? Was that noise Lina? She wanted to trust them, to believe Gilles and not the idle gossip. "So want you home. Love you always."

She wanted to dismiss the fear. Had it had been her imagination before, at Burnham, or were they using the horses as a cover, again? The text message was more than a jealous acquaintance causing problems. It was what her heart had kept telling her. Even Mick suspected something, although he was trouble.

Should she discuss the rumours with Armand? But she knew she had to tell him about her concerns when he was back from playing at being the tough guy. Why was he being so stupid over a failed tack theft? Following the thieves could get nasty if he tried to bypass the law. Who did he think he was, pretending to be heroic? Maybe he wanted to be Gilles.

Armand moved in the shadows, choosing his route to evade detection, letting the sound of his passage merge with the night.

Beneath an oak, he took out his night-vision binoculars and scanned the approaches. The drive at the front was immaculate in the floodlights, which glinted off the SUV near the steps of the stone-railed terrace, a silver Jeep with a distinctive license plate.

There were people inside, and Mick must be one of them. Three silhouettes were behind the curtains, backlit by chandeliers given the height and spread.

No sign of the Transit, which must be around the back entrance.

Armand moved beside another oak from where he could see both entryways and all the vehicles. He studied the building for a way through the security cameras. There was one, but another obstacle strode into the glare; two grey shapes like wolves, although these were not Czech Wolfdogs. He had to stay downwind of them and out of sight until he was ready. Whoever lived here had something to protect, or hide. He suspected it must be Mick, but, with no proof, he needed grounds to investigate further. Was the meeting between the vets and Mick at Saumur reason enough to act?

He glanced at his watch, 22:04. He couldn't leave Carly alone this long. *Merde,* if only Gilles hadn't decided to go off to Gloucestershire with Lina. They'd been so evasive about their exact itinerary.

Maybe the rumours are true.

Two men walked out of the back entrance. The blonde one was carrying a metal briefcase. They climbed into the van, the dark-haired man taking the driver's seat, and they drove off.

The third man must have stayed indoors. It would

be impossible to investigate if he remained. The lights dimmed inside, and the man came out the front, turning to call the dogs. Having given the dogs some food, Mick climbed into his Jeep and left.

The house seemed empty, but Armand feared for Carly. Although he could have found his alternative access point, the incursion would have to wait.

He retraced his way back to the car, keeping downwind and out of sight of the dogs. They were some Shepherd-Wolf cross, like Mistico, so not reputed to be unduly aggressive, but not dogs to misjudge, either.

He was sitting in the P4 about to leave when the phone rang on silent. The number flashed: Carly.

"There may be a problem, Loup."

Armand prayed Mick, or his minions, hadn't returned.

THIRTY-NINE

Carly glowered at Lina and resisted hitting her for ruining what had been a good day, with rosettes for both Pin and Huginn at Borde Hill. Shutting out her suspicions all day, Carly was ready to challenge Lina when she showed her face at Hazelmead. Carly wasn't willing to let the two-timer win anything, especially now that Lina continued manipulating Gilles, the way she must have been doing for months.

"She has to go," said Lina jabbing her finger, "this stud doesn't need her, as I keep saying."

"No way, I've a job here. You only pretend to have one and order me around."

"Anybody can do your job. Gilles was riding every horse, until you scared him."

Lina deserved the riding crop for sleeping with Gilles, and now she was after total control of Hazelmead, but only if Carly abandoned the fight.

"You're a snake. Why did I see you as a friend? Saumur proved who I need—Wanda."

"*Puta,* without me the mare would still be a loser."

"Oh great, forget the real work—exercising her,

whatever the weather, mucking out, grooming her—and while you waste my time."

She headed to the tack room as a torrent of Spanish abuse hurtled by, punctuated by the phrase, "I know who Gilles will choose."

Gilles chewed his lip and paced across the workshop, scuffing his shoes.

"I don't know what to say, Loup. I'm sorry... I'm confused..."

Armand resisted hitting him. Gilles wasn't worth tackling, not when there were other priorities.

"Damn you, I feel betrayed, but Carly's the one you've wounded."

"You don't understand; I love them both—in different ways."

Armand tried to relate to those feelings. Lina and Carly were both friends, but only Carly deserved his support.

And Lina? Can I ever defend her? How deep is her betrayal? Does she genuinely care about Gilles?

He wasn't ready to let his Canadian friend evade responsibility either.

"Okay, but Carly is the one you've given up everything for—you've committed everything to her."

His faithless friend stopped and looked out of the window towards the yard.

"I know, and I need her. Without Carly, this makes

no sense. It's her fire that drives me, and her determination to help the horses achieve, especially Wanda."

"Then you must tell Lina it's over. Now."

"But I need her too. For... her knowledge, what she does for the breeding, for the horses, their feed."

"*Merde,* you're out of order, Gilles. You can't use people like this. Where's your commitment?"

But Lina had been part of the team in Canada. This betrayal wasn't some sudden affair.

Is this what ended the relationship with Odette? Is that why she died? Jealousy?

Gilles stared at him as if the guilt forced him to answer.

"I admit we flirted, in Québec... but that's just my way... never meant anything."

"You want me to accept that it was never serious before?" he said, gauging whether Odette had discovered something about Gilles and Lina. Answers were one death too late, but he had to ask, "Can you give Lina up? And work with her? Will she accept your decision? It might be better if you got her to leave."

"I have to end our affair... for Carly. But Lina must stay at Hazelmead, at least as staff. Lina knows we must be a team again. Vecheech demands that–"

"What do they want?"

"They need us all. Lina is the key to the science, Carly is the only one who clicks with the horses."

Armand wanted to ensure his devious friend

delivered on his promises—before the past repeated.

Did Gilles or Lina kill Odette? Is Carly safe? I must protect her whoever I face.

He grasped Gilles by his shoulders. "Then you need to tell Lina now before it's too late."

Gilles continued pacing and chewing his lip. "Okay. Lina keeps her job, and I make a commitment to Carly. Thanks for helping me sort out the mess in my head."

"If Lina stays, then I'm leaving—today." Despite the threat, Carly remained on the farmhouse steps.

"Don't you understand, babe, we can make this work again. Vecheech needs the whole team, otherwise Papa wins, like he always does."

"It's time to choose, Gilles. We can't both stay," said Carly. "How do I know you won't still be fucking the slut?"

"*Madre de Dios*. You're *la puta*, throwing yourself at him to get a job when you had nothing. Make her go, Gilles. The horses need me. You can ride again, and win."

The two women were standing outside the farmhouse, both spitting venom. Gilles's attempt at ending his affair with Lina was pointless now. When Gilles had gone to see her, Armand had hoped that he would resolve the conflict.

But the Frenchman had known compromise was

impossible when Carly said, "I can do her job. Gilles forgets I have an Equine BSc. Anyway, who else can ride Wanda? We don't need her, Loup, she betrayed both of us."

As he studied both women now and analysed their roles, Armand knew Carly was right.

I can't trust Lina anymore. Nor Gilles. I've let this happen. I've been distracted by my suspicions over Roman and Mick yet this is now clouding their illegal activities.

"You're not helping, either of you," said Gilles. "*Batêche,* I know what Vecheech needs, and this isn't it. I'm tempted to let you both go, and start again."

Lina slithered forward. "Forget what's happened. Just remember what we share. I've known what you want ever since university."

Carly's face was red, and Armand realised she was fighting to control herself.

"Don't listen to her, Gilles. She had her chance before you offered me the job. If you can survive without me, it's time I left. I've been moved out of Hazelmead before."

She turned and walked to the door of the farmhouse.

"Please Vix, you know I can't let you go. If you go, Vecheech will still want you to compete on Wanda, as I do. You're a winning combination."

"*Carajo,* Wanda's crucial to my research. Don't let her take the mare. Armand, support me... you know what's happening out there."

Was she trying to win his support by suggesting she could help against Vidarranj? However, the Duchesnes had already told him that someone, probably Vidarranj, was gathering the DNA from successful horses whenever they could access it. Lina had implied she knew what they wanted, but how much Boissard Équestre DNA had she supplied to Vidarranj? Was obtaining Wanda's her next objective or was there another motive?

I should never have trusted Lina. Nor should Gilles.

"*Madre de Dios,* Gilles. You've already sent her foals somewhere else. Not this as well, it makes no sense, please."

"I'm sorry, Lina. You've helped a lot, but I'm not losing Carly. Hazelmead needs her and Wanda. You no longer fit with that strategy, so it's time you went. Thanks for everything, but goodbye."

"Loup, don't let him. I need to be here. I can help you. I know the truth."

"Too late, I can't ever trust you. You failed everyone. Just leave, please. It's best."

Armand knew he had a chance to prise more information from her, but the lies would bury the truth if there were any.

"*Bastardo*. You don't understand real love. What did you want with that Odette *puta*? Does Gilles know you were sleeping with her?"

"Stop blaming Loup. His Odette is someone

else," said Carly, stepping alongside him. "You're so stupid—she's Odette Duchesne."

Carly looked at Armand and mouthed her apology for exposing him to the past, but its resurrection was inevitable.

"Please Lina, let's try and remain friends. Stay rightful," said Gilles.

"I will, it's my call, and I know where to go. You'll all regret this, and this *puta* will get nothing. I never lose when I know what I want. *Venganza*—revenge."

As she spun on her heels then strode towards the bungalow, Armand prayed that revenge was not why Odette Fédon had died.

Do I have to eliminate Lina? Can I kill again?

FORTY

Armand had heard a wolf howling, and now it was licking his face.

It must be Mistico. Lina's found me. Does she know about Odette? Has Lina been nearby watching? Is that why she's here now? To murder my cousin?

Armand forced his eyes open and saw Guinness, and he looked up at Carly. The worry in her eyes touched him, and he wanted to hold her, but this was his friend's girl; he couldn't fall in love with her. Except with the light framing her, the sound of the stream and the birds, and the smell of grass and apricots, he was captivated.

It's too late. Or is it just my need to defend Carly? My desire for someone to love?

"What happened, Loup? You look terrible. Can I get you something?"

"Thanks, I'm okay... just resting," he explained as he pulled himself up. "I was repairing the old shed, so the horses had some shelter."

Was she studying him? He leant on the rail looking at the water and said, "This feels like a special place, quiet. A place to come to be alone."

Carly dismounted and walked to where he was standing.

"Yes. I find peace here, with my memories. It helps me."

"It reminds me of where... they think Odette Fédon drowned."

"At Du Noroît, the Canadian stud?"

"Yes. But there was snow, and the trees were closer."

He fought to ignore the ruined shed that reminded him of another death. He had to forget, but he had struggled with the memories earlier.

I need to face the past. Fight for my life.

"Do you think it was an accident, Loup?"

The past was approaching too fast, and he didn't want to involve her, but yet he had nobody to share anything with.

"I'm not sure. It was convenient for some people, like Roman."

"Because she was pregnant?"

It was too late; she seemed to have worked out too much.

"How much did Gilles tell you, Vix?"

"Enough to realise Roman was opposed to them. But Gilles and Roman were together in a meeting when she disappeared."

The list of suspects was still too long, and even his

name remained prominent.

"He could still have found someone else to do it, Vix. If only I'd..."

"Don't torture yourself, Loup. There's nothing we can do. If there were a murder, the police would have found the evidence."

"Absolutely, you're right," he said, accepting the release.

Lina had been there, and Odette's position at Du Noroît threatened her. Lina, who had been implicated in Vidarranj's breeding plans and threatening to protect her interests. It might not stop at just Odette Fédon's murder.

Does she want to kill Carly now? Will Lina do that to regain the reins of Wanda, the key to the breeding and the cloning? What will she do to get Gilles back, or has she set her sights higher? She said she knew where to go. Patrick Harfang?

"Loup, please just stop worrying."

She hitched the horse and put her arms around him. The mix of horse and apricot comforted his churning mind. He clung to her, although she was Gilles's partner. His friend didn't deserve her loyalty.

Would Gilles remain with Carly, or would he cheat on her again? Armand could never cheat on someone as special as her.

"This place is so peaceful," he said, wanting to linger.

"I come here a lot, Loup... to remember my mother. Although she died at our farm, from a heart attack... collapsed face down in the mud."

As the tears flowed, he held her tightly, not wanting her to leave.

"The stream was her favourite place on our farm, quiet, like this..." She paused and gazed into the distance, searching for something. "Here, there's a vixen that comes and somehow reminds me of our time together."

"I understand. Life throws out random reminders of the past, even if it's painful, it can help us remember, and help us to stand firm. We have to face those old scars."

Am I saying too much? But it all feels like a release. It's time to confront all our demons, with a partner who understands.

She grasped his hand. Her touch was firm but comforting; like holding her in his arms.

"You were brave going back to France. I know."

"Yes, seeing the Duchesnes was hard, but when Gilles bought Wanda, I knew it would happen."

"Their daughter? You were...very close and..."

"I loved Odette more than anyone. She is part of me forever."

The urge to say more was becoming a necessity.

"Can I ask what happened? I feel she's your loss and–"

Her phone rang.

"Hi, Gilles... I'm with Loup. He needed to talk, but we're coming back. Bye, honey."

She kissed Armand on both cheeks and gazed deeply into his eyes.

"We can talk going back or whenever you feel ready, Loup."

He returned her kisses, but he no longer felt he could talk about Odette.

"Soon, when the time is right. Thank you, Vix. You're special."

Most of the windows of the farmhouse were open, letting in a breeze that cooled some of the anger churning through Carly, who was ready for an early night. She pushed the office chair back, having noted that the diary was blank—no appointments.

Gilles was stretched out on the sofa in the den, but he would hear.

"Why do you need to go back to Fenburgh? Can't Vecheech's lawyer handle this without you?"

"I'm sorry, babe. I'm their equestrian manager over here, plus I have a share in Drac and Wanda."

"Make Roman come here. He castrated Pin and had Odette killed. Don't go, please. We can't trust him."

"Her death was just an accident; the autopsy proved that. A lot of Papa's anger is a bluff."

She slammed the office door shut and strode into the snug, dropping onto the sofa where Gilles was.

"If he's so concerned about the horses then he can come to Hazelmead and see that the horses are better off here."

"That will only make him demand a greater share—again."

"He's the one that undervalued Wanda and Drac, not us."

"Yes. Anyway, I need my junk at Fenburgh, like the rest of the research material that Vecheech bought... plus Boissard bloodline info."

Carly put her arms around him.

"Okay, then I'll come with you. You don't want to be alone at the beach hut, and we had a great time there..."

"Tempting, except we have six horses to get ready for the Eridge event at the weekend. I don't think Loup can do everything on his own."

"Then we go to Fenburgh and get home in time to win. Simple." Easier, as Carly would prefer to avoid a repeat of their last wild night at the hut—skinny-dipping had lost its appeal. Nightmares about Gilles and Lina had replaced the fantasies.

"You need rest, not a long tiring day dealing with Papa."

And another thing still niggled about the Vecheech deal.

"I will when I know what happened to Wanda's foals. They disappeared on Sunday, while I was competing at Borde Hill. Was that why you came home, and Lina was so angry?"

His hand began exploring, trying to distract her.

"Umm—can't this wait? I've a better idea." She pinched him, and he said, "Okay, the foals have gone to one of Vecheech's Canadian studs, far away from Papa."

"Yes, but where?"

His fingers were straying into her silk pyjamas, exploring beneath the last reminder of luxury; soon to be discarded if Gilles had his way again.

"Well, you remember our journey across the plains... into the mountains... down to a beautiful forested haven..."

She pushed him away and stood up.

"Evasive as ever. You'll have to do better than that. I'm going to bed. When you're finally ready to confess everything, about Lina, Vecheech, your plans... well, I might let you back then. Sleep well on the couch."

FORTY-ONE

The two Wolfdogs were the same build and size as Mistico. Would they behave the same way? Mistico had been well trained, as Lina had devoted a lot of time and patience. Armand catapulted out the drugged meat more in hope than expectation.

Staying downwind in the shadows, he moved farther round the house, to a spot opposite the most overgrown corner, close to a balcony.

The dogs were either well trained or well fed as they ignored the meat and locked onto Armand. Their loping run and low howls might have scared a casual intruder, but Armand reached into his haversack.

The lead animal was ten metres away and circled, so its partner would catch him first. She closed to within three metres and was about to pounce when he pressed the button on his electronic dog repeller. It emitted a high frequency, accompanied by an LED flashing strobe. The female crawled away confused and blinded, but the male held its ground.

Training and aggression overrode discomfort and blindness. It prepared to attack, scissor teeth bared.

Armand adjusted his stance, and as the dog leapt, he thrust his pack towards the animal. Its teeth clamped onto the fabric. Armand's right foot swung towards its chest, while his flattened left palm sliced at its head.

Stunned by this counter-attack, the dog failed to stop Armand's gloved hands grasping its neck. His thumbs pressed the carotid arteries depriving the dog of blood and therefore oxygen. Within seconds the animal went limp, and Armand let it fall before it was dead. Hopefully, he had deterred it from attacking again when it awoke, and he returned, as would the female.

Lax security was not one of Mick's failings, so Armand checked for sensors as he approached the house and placed an electronic decoy in the bushes. It would imitate a dog's heat signature and distract the nearest sensors from him; the rest were focused farther away.

Using a grapnel launcher, he attached a line to the balcony. He scaled the wall and swung onto the ledge of a window, which was ajar, so he eased it open. Inside was a corridor with a light at one end, possibly a stairwell.

Edging towards the glow, he watched for signs of internal cameras or sensors, especially on and above the flight of wooden stairs that led down to another corridor. With his infrared laser, he blinded the micro-camera covering the stairwell before disabling the sensors across his path.

Downstairs, he moved towards the front of the house, searching for a study or office. A brass lock and a keypad on an oak door were as good as a name-plate. He scanned for the passcode with his modified smartphone and punched it in, unlocking the bolts. The brass lock was pure show.

Inside, any sensors, motion detectors or cameras had been de-activated when he entered the code. Dark panelling, roll-top bureau and a Chesterfield contrasted with the computer array in the bay window—the anticipated access to Vidarranj.

He linked the smartphone into the network, bypassing the firewalls and security codes using the Hareng Rouge software that Natalie had given him at Saumur. The smartphone was set to access the files and copy them, via Mick's wireless setup, to the Zoos' external data store in France. A glance at the files showed he might have the evidence to link some of his suspects, although references to a breeding project would need careful study at home.

He left the smartphone downloading while he searched the rest of the room. The bureau opened easily, exposing a box file. It was the research material that Lina had mislaid and contained labelled CDs for every horse in her care at Fenburgh, including Wanda, and a CD about Carly. There was no sign of any samples, although he suspected Vidarranj had what they needed from Boissard Équestre.

Intentionally or not, Lina's a major player in this breeding project.

Time was now against him, as Mick should be home in half an hour. Armand checked the bureau's drawers and found a hidden compartment. Stashed away were dozens of mobile phone SIM cards and a device he recognised. Mick had the means to send delayed text messages from multiple mobiles; perfect for sending cryptic and misleading messages to Carly or anyone else.

Once the software had loaded its Trojan onto Mick's computer, he disconnected the smartphone. He suspected not all the files were on this hard drive and Vidarranj's mainframe. He might need to follow up on this night's work, but without entering any premises.

I pray Hareng Rouge will unlock the right doors as Natalie intended when she created it.

In the files downloaded, he had proof Mick was involved in an illegal horse cloning operation in which Lina had a significant role. However, whatever Vecheech had acquired was incomplete so that she could hold the key.

How far has Lina betrayed us all? What more can she do and when? If Odette stumbled on her involvement with the cloning, that would be another reason for Lina to kill my poor cousin.

FORTY-TWO

Carly was pacing across the kitchen, shaking her head.

"Damn Gilles. Why the hell does he do this to me?"

"Because his priority is himself. Be strong, like I know you can."

"What if Roman or Mick did something, after the meeting?"

It was a possibility. The files from Mick's office indicated thousands of dollars invested in the bio-tech-driven breeding project that confirmed the Duchesnes's suspicions. The creation of super horses for select clients through advanced techniques was cutting edge animal science. However, he needed to reassure Carly.

"Unlikely, after they made threats demanding the horses back or compensation in front of Vecheech's lawyer."

"Except that it's been ten hours since he rang, and he hadn't recovered the missing sections of Lina's damn research. He could have gone back."

Armand poured two more mugs of coffee.

"He knows Vecheech can get them—unless Lina lied."

"Typical, the cow's two-faced. Lina will do anything to get him back. It's a trap—she set him up. I bet there are no missing files..."

Should Armand tell her what he had discovered? The hacked data had proved that Mick or Roman had returned the originals, probably in the briefcase he had seen at Fenburgh. But that still left enough time for Mick to make copies, and Gilles would want those if he couldn't access the original research.

Carly continued with her accusations.

"Shit, it had to be her and that serpent Mick. She pretends to dislike him while using me."

"Slow down, Vix, are you suggesting—"

"—that they did something to Gilles? Totally. Mick has a sadistic streak and is as manipulative as she is."

He took a mouthful of his coffee, realising this might fit. Carly sounded dramatic, but he needed to profile Mick.

"Sadistic enough to do what?"

"Weird shit... in bed... with whips and handcuffs... real embarrassing when it got out of hand."

He didn't know whether to laugh, so he shook his head instead. Not a killer, except in bed.

"Bastard nearly destroyed me. I dumped Mick when I discovered that he was with another woman—a slut willing to do anything."

"Makes it easier to dismiss a guy like that. Although, he could still be dangerous."

"The horses never liked him, nor did Guinness. The only dogs who adored him were his damn wolf-dogs and Mistico."

"Do you think Lina already knew Mick?" he asked, although unwilling to make them conspirators because of their canine choices.

But then, Lina is a manipulator, and Carly knows that.

"The snake must have known him, and before Fenburgh perhaps. Maybe he somehow visited Canada—and Du Noroît."

If Mick was in Québec, he could have murdered Odette, and Gilles might be in danger.

As he picked up the phone, he asked Carly, "When did you last try Gilles?"

"Before you came over. Do you think Lina and Mick... murdered him?"

"Lost his mobile more likely," said Armand although aware of the possibility. "You said he was going jet skiing when he reached the beach hut, and there's no landline."

Armand put an arm around her, but he failed to quell the fear undermining their reason.

"He could have crashed the jet ski," said Carly.

"Not Gilles, he's too good—"

"—yes, but another idiot could have hit him. Please, Loup, ring the police. He could be injured...

or even dead."

He held her face and her stare, still reaching for an explanation that didn't entail murder.

"In the morning, if he hasn't rung. It's midnight and he could be out celebrating after standing up to Roman and Mick."

"So, you don't think he's dead? Instead the witch Lina has found him and caused more problems. Shit, that's her revenge."

FORTY-THREE

At least the horses were some distraction, but Carly was still distraught. Armand recognised the symptoms, having lived with them for so long. Carly kept dwelling on what could have happened.

Five hours earlier, Vecheech's lawyer had not heard or seen from Gilles since the meeting. Nobody else at Vecheech had spoken to him for days.

Roman had been unhelpful, saying, "The ungrateful boy was way out of order yesterday. Maybe he annoyed my friend Harfang, so he dealt with him."

With that, he had put the phone down.

Armand needed Carly to concentrate on the positives, like the horses, so he had only told her Roman was merely abusive and unhelpful.

She had insisted he ask the police to visit the beach hut and they had agreed to check, officially, as Gilles was now missing.

With the horses exercised, Armand had cooked omelettes for lunch, and Carly had fallen asleep beside him on the sofa.

The phone rang, and he answered it before it woke Carly.

"Mr Sabatier. This is Constable Goodwin, Wells-next-the-Sea, we checked Mr Boissard's hut. There were signs he had been there, but he is not there now."

"And the car, his Subaru Outback?"

"No sign of that, but it should be nearby as we found a jet ski that could be his. It was washed up nearby, possibly crashed, as there were signs of a fire, although there was nothing to show that anybody was injured. The coastguard is checking—routine."

"I'll come up to the beach and see. Tell me where to find you please, Constable."

When the policeman ended the call, Armand was uneasy. Had Gilles been killed? Another convenient accident?

His body and 4x4 will turn up, but I must act. Who'll be next? Carly?

In his mind, he saw a silver shaft flash towards the Jet Ski; a thermite charge exploded, throwing Gilles into the sea.

Carly had insisted on going. Gilles was her partner; she had to be there, whatever they discovered. Her heart needed him alive, despite his affair with Lina.

On the speakerphone in the car, the lawyer was saying, "He gave me a sealed envelope, for me to open in case of his death."

She stared at the cold sea. The envelope seemed too calculated to be Gilles.

"We don't know he's dead."

"Of course not, then I will postpone opening it. Keep me informed. I will update Monsieur Harfang as instructed."

"By whom? By Gilles?"

"Yes, Monsieur Boissard instructed me to ensure Monsieur Harfang was apprised of everything since I represent Vecheech Enterprises in these affairs."

Carly said goodbye. Gilles trusted Patrick Harfang, so someone else had made him disappear. He had to be alive. Was that a gut feeling, or because she needed him?

"Loup, where do you think Gilles is? Is he hiding... from Roman?"

Armand's eyes were focused on the road, as they closed on their destination near Wells-next-the-Sea. He said nothing, but she noted his drawn face and the tears glazing his eyes.

"You think he's dead, don't you? Who did it? Roman? Or that snake Lina?"

"I don't know. Gilles could be alive still."

It was a glimmer of comfort, like the evening sun sparkling on the sea. But why wasn't he contacting her then? He could send her a message at least; especially now when she needed to focus on the horses. Torc and Wanda were back in work, which meant commitment and priorities, including Bramham in only nine days.

She needed Gilles, and he needed her—simple. Or maybe he didn't—maybe Lina had stolen him again.

The sun stained the 4x4 and its trailer red. Even the sand bled the hue, which coloured Carly's fears, and the policeman's words.

"Everything matches the descriptions you gave us. Mr Boissard seems to have left the hut and driven here with the Jet Ski, and then he launched it over there. We just need to establish where the Jet Ski crashed."

Armand pointed back along the beach. "But, there must be more fingerprints in the hut or the car? Was he alone?"

"There is no evidence to justify the expense of a detailed investigation. Our resources must be strictly allocated. Funds are always tight and..."

Carly's thoughts echoed Armand as she said, "Surely if a man goes missing then..."

"...we wait, but the coastguards are looking. Mr Boissard may have been swept out to sea by the undertow here. He could still turn up, in a hospital perhaps. This has happened before. Some people even fake their death to–"

"Not Gilles, I know him. No way he would."

"Mr Roman Boissard thinks otherwise, and suggested his son was running away from his business failures."

"Damn him. Roman is the one that caused all the problems. Did he tell you what he did to one of the stallions? Probably not."

The constable stared at her.

"No, but he was very helpful and concerned about his son's health."

"That's a bloody first. Roman always put Gilles down and treated him like an idiot. And I was called even worse, nothing but foul-mouthed insults."

She guessed that Roman had misrepresented or ignored the claim over the values of the horses, and the scandal over Odette's pregnancy. As Armand questioned the constable, she walked to one side and tried to lose herself in the landscape.

It still evoked the precious time spent with Gilles, the breakaway from Fenburgh. The memories were alive, riding along Holkham Beach, leaping over the surf and rolling in the waves. Watching skeins of geese flying, listening to songbirds singing, wrapped in each other's arms as the sun set in a panoramic display of reds, oranges, purples and blues. So natural and so unique that Gilles couldn't name a place to rival it.

"What evidence have you for those allegations, Mr. Sabatier? A burglary in Sussex, and an accident in

Canada? Nothing proves they are related. It's all circumstantial, like this damaged Jet Ski. There's nothing to work on."

As with their Québec counterparts, the local authorities were quick to take the misadventure route. Was this Roman's interference again, or just their interpretation? Armand could tell at a glance that the dents and burns were from a thermite charge.

How do I explain why I know about thermite charges without implicating myself? Let the forensics reveal that evidence.

He ignored the sunset and kept the snow at bay, but a storm was gathering within his head.

"Isn't it suspicious that Gilles's groom in Canada dies in unusual circumstances, and now he disappears after another accident? Aren't there too many coincidences?"

The policeman looked carefully at the damaged machine.

"Possibly, but as I said, this incident could mean Gilles Boissard is in hiding or has committed suicide. But that is mere supposition without evidence."

"But who gains?" asked Armand. "His father? Or perhaps the owner of Vecheech, who now has the best of the Boissard horses?"

"First, we must confirm that he is missing. It's only been twenty-nine hours since you spoke to him and the search found nothing but the Jet Ski and the car. I won't close the case, so I may be able to do something..." Armand didn't feel hopeful but let the constable continue. "...the coastguard needs the jet ski—for an accident report. The beach hut will remain sealed, and we can check the car."

"If I hear anything, Constable Goodwin, I will contact you."

"Thank you, please trust us. We want this resolved. We will talk very soon. Goodbye."

Is it too late to admit what I saw in Québec? But this is the wrong police force, and I've already broken British laws to uncover the truth.

He looked over towards Carly, who had taken off her boots and socks to stand in the sea. She was the one needing his help now. This was not the time to speculate on what might have happened. If the pattern emerging played out, then Carly could be the next victim; unless he forced his suspects to make an error that the police would act upon—a mistake that didn't risk Carly's life.

FORTY-FOUR

Carly tried hard to distract herself. Perhaps looking for some crisps or something stupid might act as a block. But the tears and the choking couldn't be controlled, and Armand must have noticed.

"It's okay, Vix. Let it out. Cry. I know, it's the best way."

"I'm not... hungry," she choked, "I'll ride."

"Not yet. You need to eat regularly, please."

He was right; the insulin and food were inseparable—like her and Gilles. She cursed to herself, asking why he had left her. Lina had tried but failed, but then there had been a twist. Gilles was dead according to the authorities, who had accepted a suicide note sent to Roman as genuine.

She kept asking, why would he send the note to his father and not to his partner? And why take that way out?

The memories were alive and hurt. Maybe going outside and riding Torc would help. Forget lunch and the post. Or maybe hack Wanda as there were so few days left before she would be going to Canada.

Vecheech had dealt the day's first devastation when she had opened the email to her:

From: Patrick Harfang

Re: Hazelmead

Due to the financial downturn, Vecheech Enterprises Inc has to consolidate its operations. Therefore, Hazelmead has become surplus to requirements and Vecheech will be selling the property. All eight of our horses will be shipped to our facilities in Canada. We have effected all the arrangements with our agents, but please confirm. Our thanks for your services and those of Armand Sabatier.

Please note that your contracts will expire in three months, with the usual remuneration.

Kind regards,

Patrick Harfang, CEO Vercheech Enterprises Inc

"Life makes no bloody sense, Loup. Gilles is dead, and now I'm losing the ride on Wanda, just when I have a chance. Why?"

"Patrick Harfang's timing is appalling, and we get evicted before the season ends, *merde*."

"Damn Lina. She threatened to have her revenge on us all, so she went straight to Patrick Harfang, damn her to hell! She had Gilles killed and now gets Wanda. Devious cow."

"I can't believe she persuaded Harfang, even with all her credentials," said Armand. "Unless she already had access to Vecheech, or perhaps offered him her Boissard research. Is it just coincidence that the two companies share the same initial?"

"It's simpler—she persuaded him Wanda was ideal for the Canadian equestrian team. So I've lost Gilles, Wanda, my job—everything."

"We have each other. And you still have Torc. I'll back you both all the way, whatever happens."

The lake shimmered as the afternoon sunlight flickered on its calm. Carly trotted Torc along the cinder track and turned up the hill, following Guinness's lead. The air smelt fresh from the shower, but it wasn't enough. The dry weather was making the going firm, just when the horses needed runs. Maybe she should just do the dressage or show-jumping shows.

It was gutting to have lost the other horses, although she still had Torc and Dido; and everything Gilles had taught her. Still, she had to focus.

She encouraged Torc up the shaded slope, where the trees reached limbs towards them. Guinness loped beside her. The sun filled the air with fingers of light in which insects spiralled and hummed. Everything was still alive, though drowsy.

Alongside the road, winding past the church, cottages nestled. Glancing at the church clock as it struck the hour, she checked her watch—four p.m. Even though Wanda had been amazing, Carly was glad to be on Torc. She would always be special as Carly's first star ride.

Whatever she had achieved with them, Wanda, Pin, Muninn, even clumsy Huginn, they would remain with her, in her memories; and she had learnt from all of them. Especially Wanda, but she had to fight the regret and look forward as there were still two mares to compete, and she had gained the recognition of Elite training. Or was that with Wanda, as she had been the one with potential? Torc had impressed at Badminton, proving her mare had more to give as well. Sad then, that Dido was not turning out to be a jumper like her dam. Maybe selecting an Arab sire for extra stamina had been a mistake.

As the main road came into view, she eased Torc to a slow walk and stopped at the junction, Guinness sitting patiently on the verge. They waited as a few cars worked their way past a grey van whose driver was poring over a map. She turned right out of Horsted Keynes, glancing back towards the village green and The Green Man, her favourite pub and a reminder of better days. There were some cherished memories, but not ones to distract her while hacking along a busy road.

Guinness chose the short route home, towards the Bluebell Railway. Carly enjoyed going back across the fields or through the woods, and Torc never heeded the train when it went past, chuffing and tooting. The mare slid on the tarmac, damp under the canopy over the road. It was darker here, and the roots rose from the bank like snakes.

Riding out into the sunlight towards the barn, she heard a mechanical roar behind her, the van. She moved onto the grass edge of the road, slowing to let him pass. At first, he seemed to skid, but then he accelerated towards her. Grey metal loomed. Steep banks and trees hemmed them in.

Adrenaline and panic spurred her and Torc on; the track was reachable to their right, but then the van careered towards them blocking their route. She pulled away across the bridge over the stream. The gateway was too far. The hedge between was too high—unless she gave Torc room to jump. She set up the mare for the first length of hedge. Impassable blackthorn, designed to deter animals. Jumpable, if it wasn't for the slippery road and a narrow take-off.

The van mounted the grass, scraping along the thorn barrier. With metal inches away, the mare jumped out of the killer's path.

Torc crashed through the hedge, thorns slicing them both as the sound of the van disappeared into the distance.

On an advanced course, she would be clear. Instead, the mare crumpled on landing, sliding across the water meadow on her side, before slipping over the bank into the stream. Carly stayed with her, one leg trapped. The mare struggled to get out of the water. Through a red haze, Carly kept clear of lashing hooves. She pulled her leg free as Torc straddled the stream upside down, trapped between the banks.

If she crawled out, the mare's head would drop underwater. She had to stay and support her until help came.

Guinness whimpered on the bank, unsure how he could help, except by licking off her sweat.

Despite the fall, her mobile was still strapped to her crash hat, but would it work here? She adjusted her position, resting Torc on her shoulder as her right hand reached the phone. It flipped open with one signal bar. She dialled Armand, and it rang, but no answer.

"Damn, just when we needed him, girl—frick."

All she could do was leave a message and hope he found it in time.

She was cold, wet and shaky. Dizziness wasn't good either. The fall had ripped off the insulin pump, plus her bum bag with the sugar boosts. Her immediate concern was, Torc mustn't give up. There was too much blood, and the mare was no longer attempting to turn upright. Her breathing was shallow, like Carly's own.

FORTY-FIVE

The flight details were confirmed, although nobody could say who would meet the eight Vecheech horses when they landed in Calgary. Someone from the company wasn't good enough. Armand wanted to know more, but the ultimate destination was confidential. Vecheech had not even given the bloodstock agents in England the information, just the essentials of where to collect the horses and which airport Vecheech wanted them flown to. Putting a transmitter in one of the saddle trunks was tempting.

He had noticed Carly ringing on the other line as he was closing his call to the agents. She had left a message, so he rang straight back.

The mobile kept ringing, and he expected a re-route to the home line. She must be negotiating traffic. Or the signal was weak. Or it was everything he feared.

On the eighth ring, she answered.

He realised the crisis as soon as she said, "Van made Torc fall—she's hurt badly." He told her he was coming with help.

Merde, *she sounds distressed and weak. I fear a hypo or*

worse. Everything's against her.

As he ran outside, he rang the emergency line and asked for the fire department. They had another Animal Rescue emergency, but their special unit would come as soon as it was free. They would notify a vet.

He ensured all his emergency gear was in the jeep, and then sped up the drive and turned right. He negotiated the lanes, juggling urgency and safety. The hoot of the Bluebell faded as the trees closed in on him, roots crawling out of the earth. His stomach churned as beyond the tunnel of trees he saw the black barn. He fought to ignore the image of another ruin, black and menacing in the snow.

Glimpsing Guinness pacing beside the stream, he skidded onto the grass kerb and jumped over the gate, carrying his knapsack. The dog barked towards what could be Torc. Sunshine glinted on water like on snow. He ignored it, although he could see white flecked with blood. There were lives in danger, so he forced himself forward.

Then the shot came.

His shoulder burst with pain, and he threw himself to the ground, knowing the sniper would fire again.

Cygne was lying in the snow, motionless. Blood oozed out of her head, from beneath the shattered helmet.

No that's the past—resist, for Carly. She's watching me, her eyes pleading. I can hear Torc's helpless snorts.

The crows fleeing overhead explained the loud report, a bird scare cannon. The sound wasn't a gun; that was in his head.

He forced himself to stand, and he assessed the carnage ahead: Torc on her side, head in Carly's arms, blood everywhere, speckling the mare's whiteness.

Focus. Breathe.

Torc was not only trapped just centimetres above the water, but she was also bleeding from a gash in her chest and others across her legs. Blood spurted from an artery near the left cannon bone. Her nose was haemorrhaging; hopefully, it was only a sinus bleed and not an injured skull.

"Help is coming, Vix. I'll do what I can."

"Thanks, Loup." The reply spurred him on, as she added, "I need to eat... my bag... lost..."

Armand forced his eyes along the glistening trail of the crash: blood on the barbed wire and thorns, blood in the pools of mud, and then the waist bag and the crucial medicine. He recovered it and smeared some hypo-stop on Carly's lips.

"Good, but I think this will taste better." He passed her two fruit-cereal bars. She tried to say something, but he said, "Quiet, *chérie*. Eat."

He checked her for other injuries.

He took the weight of Torc's body, and Carly

pulled herself onto the bank. She checked her sugar levels.

The mare jerked violently and snorted again, her eyes staring.

"We need something to support her," said Armand. "I have to get her out, when I've sedated her."

"That was a spasm—she's not struggling to get up anymore."

Rescuing them would test him, but he couldn't fail again. There were two lives this time. They were in the precious golden hour of survival. He must save them both.

FORTY-SIX

The transformation of Armand from mild-mannered helper to an ant on speed amazed Carly. Holding Torc's head, he unfastened the girth and eased off the saddle. Then, he took off his jacket and used it to blindfold the mare, while keeping it loose enough to slip off when she rose. She prayed Torc would stand again. The mare was all that she had left. The dream was now dead, but life couldn't end here—in the mud again.

Armand used some snags and his belt to build a support under Torc's head. He ripped off his shirt and wedged it over the worst wound, stemming the bleeding.

As he ran to the jeep, he shouted, "Those should hold long enough. She needs some blankets, and then you're next."

She kept an eye on Torc as Armand negotiated the water meadow with the jeep.

Once he had parked, Carly forced herself to lift the tailgate open. She found some rugs to throw over the mare before the cold caused more damage.

"Okay, Vix. Thanks. I want you to change into the dry clothes, on the front seat, now, please."

She changed as he disappeared into the stream carrying a coiled strap. In control, Armand's manner eased Carly's fears. He wasn't playing at being emergency services—he had become them. No, she told herself, this Loup had always been there, hiding in the shadows. Prepared for an emergency, with the equipment to respond, but not ready to act—until now.

"Hey, Vix, are you changed? I need your help."

"Coming, just say what you need, Loup."

He could cope, but he was getting her moving and motivated; so she didn't collapse. He must have seen the shakes and sweat. She was exhausted and ready to curl up, but she knew that she must not fall asleep.

"Put this loop around the hitch, while I secure it around Torc. Oh, and find the med kit in my sack."

As he scrambled back and tightened the ratchet on the jeep end of the strap, she searched for the med kit. It was fully equipped with bandages, needles, hypostop, spare blood meter, and insulin pump, as well as tail bandages, swabs, drugs and more. All designed for emergency field use and in a khaki case.

It now made sense. Loup had not been Cadre Noir, but with a rescue service, which explained the jeep.

"Okay, this is temporary. I can't lift Torc yet, but I need to stem the bleeding."

"The vet's not coming?" she asked as her breathing quickened. She couldn't lose Torc, not in this way.

"He's probably held up. I'm sorry and if you don't want to..."

"She's my girl; I'll help."

It would distract from exhaustion and the pain, especially in her shoulder; and stop her from thinking about her life unravelling.

They climbed down into the stream, and he removed his blood-soaked shirt while she reassured the mare. Despite their bond, Torc would struggle; especially when they moved her.

She hoped Torc did respond, otherwise they were too late.

"*Merde,* this gash has left a flap of skin. I'll leave the vet to operate, but lifting her could tear it more if it catches. I need to cover it."

He scanned the med kit, so she asked, "Clean it and stitch it you mean?"

"I can't do it properly—although I've the equipment. I'll clean what I can and tape it closed."

Loup took a phial of an anti-inflammatory drug, shook it and with a veterinary needle injected air into the bottle. Then he withdrew the same amount of drug, and after thumping it with the heel of his hand, he swabbed the injection site. He inserted the needle and pushed it in. Torc winced, to Carly's relief.

Then they wrapped another rug around the artery,

fastening it with tail bandages and duct tape.

"Okay let's try and get her out."

He climbed out of the stream and pulled a large box from the jeep. It was a portable winch, for lifting tree trunks, or horses.

Normally, this would need three or four experienced people, except Armand had to do this alone, until the fire brigade arrived.

He was worried about Carly and so was Guinness, who kept whimpering or growling whenever her eyes closed. She showed all the danger signs, and he feared it was not only the diabetes, but also an injured shoulder; maybe he had to choose.

"If you're worrying about me, Loup, don't. Just get Torc out, then I'll be okay."

"It's just, you're more..."

"No, I'm not. Torc is here because of me. That van was after me. Anyway, I can treat myself, thanks to the gear you brought."

There wasn't time to debate this. Carly was already checking her levels again. Aware of her priority, Armand threw a rope hawser over the overhanging branch that he had assessed was strong enough as a hoist point. He had considered building a tripod frame, but time was against them. With the setting sun and dropping temperature, both horse and rider were vulnerable.

He attached the rope to a sling that he fastened around Torc, ensuring it was not compressing any vital organs or stressing the severest wounds. He tightened the rig, letting the branch and the winch chained to the P4 take the strain. Torc thrashed, but she was weak, and Carly was nearby reassuring her as the jacket fell from her eyes.

The branch creaked under the weight of six hundred kilograms of horse. Armand prayed he had judged all of this correctly. The green wood held and Torc was eased up and free of the stream.

With a rope attached to the harness, Armand pulled the mare towards the bank. They lowered her to the ground, dripping blood and water. She struggled to stand, and to their relief, like a foal, she found her legs.

It was then that the fire brigade and the vet arrived.

It came as no surprise when they berated Armand and Carly for risking everything in a reckless rescue.

"You could have killed the horse or even yourselves. Are you crazy?"

"No way, Loup knows exactly what he's doing. He saved her, officer."

Torc was checked over and treated by the vet, while the fire brigade assessed Armand's work.

"Not bad, you show promise, but don't do this again, please. That's our job, we're the professionals."

"Of course, I won't."

Armand might have said the same thing once, in the past.

It was a relief when the paramedics insisted on giving Carly a thorough check-up, but Armand had to say, "She has diabetes, so as you know, there could be a greater risk of infection."

"Good to have that info. Don't worry, she'll be okay."

Having helped the vet load Torc into the horse ambulance, Armand was told they would be kept informed of her progress.

He walked up the road to the skid marks from the van's tyres, following them for clues down to the hedge. He dialled the emergency line, asking for the police, who took the details of what he insisted was a deliberate hit and run.

"Please don't concern yourself, sir. We're already in contact with the fire crew that were called out. They know everything."

"Except that Miss Tanner's partner Gilles Boissard disappeared in Norfolk—the Wells-next-the-Sea police are investigating that accident. And what about the break-in at our stud ten days ago?"

"Thank you, sir. I'm sure this is a coincidence, but we will look into everything. Miss Tanner will need to give a statement of course. Ring again tomorrow."

Can they do anything? Will they? Merde, *if only I was in France, I could put pressure on them.*

He traced Torc and Carly's trail across the mud and grass. The setting sun still flickered off the pools of water and flecks of blood. Angrily but focused, he made a final call, to Jean-Pierre.

"Faucon, Loup. As discussed, our fears are real, and the hostiles are ruthless."

"Vidarranj?"

"Others may be involved, but they have made their last mistake. Someone tried to kill Vix. We need to stop them, and on our terms."

"Understood. I'll contact the other Zoos and see who can volunteer. For us, they'll take time off."

"This is for Vix, and Cygne. I'll devise a plan, and then call in five hours. Use only the secure channels."

FORTY-SEVEN

The ringing persisted. Carly wanted to sleep as every part of her ached, especially the shoulder, but the klaxon was now in her ears, urgent and persistent. She tried turning over and burying herself into the pillows, but the pain in her right arm stabbed into her.

Armand's hand touched her forehead.

"You're sweating. I checked your levels before you went to sleep. *Merde,* guess I tested them wrong. I should have used the pump. Sorry, *chérie*."

"Don't worry, Loup. It's my body. It's really screwed up now." Her head as well, she wanted to say but noticed she was in bed. "How did I get in here?"

"I carried you. You'd fallen asleep in the jeep."

He busied himself with the blood meter.

Realising he was embarrassed, she teased, asking, "Did you undress me?"

"I'm sorry, but you were still wet. I had to... no choice."

She kissed him on the cheek.

"Forgiven, I understand."

As he rolled up her nightshirt, she scrabbled for her watch. He re-inserted the tube to her pump then attached everything, so gentle, not like the macho action man he was.

"Christ. It's five a.m. I thought it was still evening. I've slept for hours. Going to have to get up and..."

A firm hand held her down.

"No, you're taking it easy. I know you didn't have a hypo, but you were stressed and injured. I want you to have another check-up. I'm worried."

"I'm okay. You know me, I bounce back."

"Nobody does. You fooled the paramedics, again, but not me, I know you too well."

Carly couldn't help but think that it was crazy. Armand was a better friend than Gilles had ever been: more thoughtful, concerned, helpful, and he was around more. She didn't want to argue, just listen. His voice was soothing.

"I was watching. You fought hard, but I fear you were... unconscious, briefly. That's serious; you might have been concussed."

"No way am I quitting the competition. I'm not getting bloody suspended. I've commitments and–"

"No, this has gone too far. We're both disappearing, somewhere safer. With Dido, so you can compete her when you're fit."

"So, you agree that the van tried to kill me, and

Torc." She had wanted it to be a random accident, but his words had ended that illusion. "But you can protect us..."

"I will, but not here."

She wanted to sleep, but only after some questions. "I have to ask, Loup..."

"Later. There will be time."

"No, now. First, did the vet ring?"

"An hour ago, yes."

He said nothing else and she feared the news.

"And?"

"He operated on Torc, and she should recover, but it will take time..." Armand hesitated before he said, "the chest wound, the cuts, the fall and getting stuck. It was a major shock to her system."

"But we had to move her. Damn. Take time means months."

"She will recover and you can..."

"In that damn ditch, I knew my dream was over. Roman, Mick, Lina – they've won."

"No, the vet said we'd probably saved her. Torc will recover so they haven't won. You're both survivors."

"For what? They've taken everything. Gilles, then Wanda, and Hazelmead. Without Torc the future is dead. That's it."

"Don't forget Dido, the next generation. And I won't abandon you, ever—wherever we go."

She hugged him to draw on the strength that

had emerged, and that she still saw in his eyes. His warmth was genuine, and she had to kiss him. She was grateful he had saved them both. There was more; her body ached as it shouldn't. She should be mourning Gilles, and yet Armand's dedication felt stronger. His passion was evident.

But first, she had to know how he had saved them.

"Don't pretend, Loup. That was the real you, but... who...what are you? You became a different person—determined, focused. I need to know, please, tell me?"

He stayed silent. Staring into his bloodshot eyes, Carly sensed a maelstrom spiralling inside. He wasn't exhausted, but torturing himself, churning around thoughts that she had no right to force out. He wasn't ready, even if she needed to know.

"Okay, let's sleep on this, Loup. But please, when I wake..."

"I'll tell you. I promise—after you've slept."

He kissed her, on her lips. Long enough to resolve her confusion over Gilles, the man of empty gestures and false dreams.

FORTY-EIGHT

Armand had not slept. The same clothes and his unshaven face betrayed him. There was urgency in his actions, a determination to leave. Carly remembered that he had mentioned going somewhere safe, but where? First, she had to uncover his mysterious identity.

He held his face in his hands and leant on the kitchen table. He breathed deeply, took a mouthful of black coffee and then looked at Carly. "You're right. To begin with, thank you, because, without you, it might never have happened."

"Why? What did I do?"

She was confused. He had seemed so in control.

"You saved me in a way, but it's a long story. I've tried to forget, except I can't. Yesterday was everything I feared, everything I tried to avoid by being nobody and saying nothing."

He had delved into the pain, focusing on it again. He was about to confess something that she feared could unhinge him, yet she had to probe to help.

"You can tell me. It's time. I know it involves

Odette Duchesne in some... oh, sorry."

He stared at her, and she feared she had said the wrong thing and now he wouldn't be able to confide in her.

But he nodded and said, "Yes. Odette was my wife and... we served together—"

"—in the Cadre Noir?" She suspected so much but knew so little. "Sorry, I'll let you talk."

"I can see why you think that. Natalie was Cadre and a lot of their friends, but not us." He closed his eyes and the tears formed. "I enlisted in the army in '98... aged twenty. When I joined the Chasseurs, Jean-Pierre Duchesne was my commanding officer."

"Chasseurs? Hunters? Is that a regiment? Cavalry?"

"Chasseurs Alpins are mountain troops. Les Diables Bleus."

She realised the depth of everyone's misconception.

"My God, and Gilles thought you couldn't ski. That's so... crazy."

"Not really. I was sick and had problems that nobody was meant to know about, except Odette Fédon."

"She realised? Why her? And you say sick, were you wounded?"

"Odette Fédon was my cousin, but she's another story. I need to tell this as it happened. It's easier."

Suppressing the questions swirling through her head, she put her hand on his and left it there.

"Sorry, Loup."

"I didn't know Jean-Pierre's daughter was also a Chasseur, until a party. Valentine's Day 2004, when we fell in love." He choked back the tears; the memories were breaking free. "A year later we were married. We shared so much, and had great plans."

He closed his eyes, but his lashes still glistened.

The situation was familiar. Gilles and Carly had shared dreams, but now he was gone, leaving only memories that should have sent shivers through her body. But those feelings had been eroded by his affair with Lina, leaving too little.

Armand poured more coffee for them both, then continued, "We had a staunch group of comrades, nicknamed the Zoos, but then..."

He shook his head and put his face in his hands again. Carly's hand stroked his hair to help him continue.

"After three precious years, we were sent to Afghanistan, as part of NATO's security force. My troop, all friends, comrades remained together, but the reality was so much worse... you can't prepare—even though we were trained."

"I've seen the news, but I can't imagine what it's really like. If you don't want to say..."

"I need to finish. It was worse for your British troops and the civilian population." He stared straight ahead. "Nine months into our tour we were on an intelligence gathering patrol in a supposedly friendly village."

He stopped and stood up.

She couldn't let him go on; it was too hard for him. She had to hold him. Knowing was no longer important, and she feared the inevitable. But he had to let it out after so long.

"The insurgents—guerrillas—knew the area and where to ambush us. The snow was deep but passable, which should have helped us. It was our terrain, but I made mistakes..."

Armand paced, his fists opening and closing.

"Were you in command?"

"As Capitaine, yes. I was too relaxed. Odette, as our intelligence officer, should have... been safe in the VMB—the armoured carrier. Not in the open with me..."

"From the little I hear, nowhere is safe. Indiscriminate attacks, roadside bombs..."

Armand sighed and sat down.

"Not this time. There was a ruined building I should have cleared... a sniper was hiding there... but there were no tracks, no sign of anyone."

He grabbed her hand and clasped it.

"Then shots." He winced, his shoulder jerking. "The sniper has targeted ones he thinks are important..." Armand closed his eyes as he said, "...me first... and then..." His eyes stayed closed, and his grip tightened, "...Odette. I'm just wounded, but she's shot in the head... a bullet shatters her helmet. I drop beside her. Our blood covers my hands, and I can do nothing. Blood oozes across her face and onto the snow. She is dying in my arms—I've killed her. I keep seeing it repeated—even yesterday and even now—and I can do nothing."

Carly remembered him on his knees clutching his shoulder, staring at the ground. Now she understood. She held him to soothe his pain, but she was unable to help. Could anyone ease his conscience and bury the memories?

"Le sang vert, c'est pour la France."

"Green blood?"

"Red is the colour of the lips of my beloved. Never blood. Chasseurs have green blood, which Odette paid with. That was all I could say to Natalie and Jean-Pierre... when we buried her... knowing she would have lived if I had secured the area. I failed her and them, so I quit the Chasseurs. I ran away, like a coward."

She held his head and looked into his soul.

"No, it was war. It could have been anyone. I feel Odette's parents have forgiven you."

"Perhaps, but it should have been me, not my precious Cygne. And the flashbacks, day and night, reminding me. I lived with the guilt and the memories. The triggers kept firing—until yesterday."

"The accident? How?" She stared at him.

"You gave me another chance, Vix. I had to save you and Torc. It all came back by the stream, my nightmares. I couldn't let you die too."

She understood, from the tattoo for Cygne, swan in French, to the trauma of her death tormenting and driving him. But there was more when she stared into his eyes. Why was he in Canada? Who was the other Odette, his cousin?

"I want to love you, Loup. I feel a bond that is growing. I just need—"

"—time to mourn Gilles. I understand."

"But you've always been there for me. I'm not Odette, your Cygne, and never can be, but I'll share your pain—if you'll let me."

"Forever, if you'll accept me. Never again will I fail someone—someone I now realise means so much to me. You are special."

They held each other. Carly caressed his face as he kissed her. Even though her body and heart still ached, she didn't want him to go, not now. They needed each other.

First, they had to confront whoever tried to kill Torc and her—whoever killed Armand's cousin.

FORTY-NINE

On an ordinary day, the morning feed was routine, but it would never be again. In six hours, the yard would feel empty as the shippers were coming mid-afternoon for Vecheech's horses. She cursed Harfang. Was there any point to three months' notice if she had nothing to ride, except Dido? Lina had taken everything as she had threatened.

Carly closed her eyes and turned away from the kitchen window. With her injuries, she shouldn't hack out Wanda one last time, although the mare needed it before her journey to Canada. But she really wanted to ride Wanda. Should she let someone else get the pleasure? All hers had died with Gilles. She should forgive him for everything, and she craved to hold him in her arms again, but his mad fling with Lina had hurt too much.

Her tears betrayed her to Armand, who said, "You will always find reminders, I still do. But it's good to cry for Gilles, whatever he did when he was alive. I should've cried more, perhaps."

"Thank you. I have to move on."

She had to let Loup guide her, to help her handle the memories as he had managed.

"I think you should read this, Vix. It's not all bad."

Staring out of the window was better than reading some depressing legal papers.

"I'm not interested in what his family get."

"Roman gets nothing, Gilles's niece gets everything else, except minor bequests, and the horses."

"Don't tell me, the snake, Lina, has fixed that..."

She put her jacket on and walked towards the kitchen door. Armand could read the document, she told herself. If she couldn't ride, at least she could walk.

"Wait. The will doesn't mention Lina. You get Wanda."

She turned wanting to believe him. "You're not serious. That's so untrue. Please don't tease me, not today." She grabbed the letter and scanned its summary of the will, feeling her heart beating and a warm tingling up her back. "And you get the Outback."

After reading the letter again, she realised there was a second buff envelope. It contained a new horse passport with Carly Tanner as the mare's owner. A covering note said the other updated documents, like studbook and freeze mark registration, would follow.

It didn't feel right to Carly.

"Weird. This document has been too well worked

out," said Carly. "Gilles ensured, whatever happens, all the bequests are inevitable. It's like a seamless transfer of assets, not a will. Somebody helped devise this."

Armand studied the letter.

"I think I see what you mean. I suspect Gilles made sure nobody could challenge this will. He guessed he was a target, so he needed to move his assets to safety – to people he trusted."

"But will that stop them? Did somebody know yesterday, when that van tried to kill me? Will they try again before Bramham? Time is against us."

"That's why we're leaving as planned, but with Wanda as well. I want to ensure you're both ready if you have to do Bramham, but only if we can neutralise the threats."

Armand had been desperate to get Carly somewhere that he could protect her. Hazelmead wasn't Fenburgh with its wide, open approaches and ultra-high-tech security. Although he had persuaded Vecheech to invest in sophisticated protection for some of its property, it hadn't included personnel. Making arrangements to move safely had taken a few hours, but his fellow Zoos and their connections had helped.

Carly had made her own helpful suggestions, although she was finding it hard to forget Gilles. It would take time. Armand let her talk about her feelings, as it was better than silence. He had taken that route hoping the memories would vanish, but they only became distorted. At least they had each other, and the growing feelings for each other were their strength.

As the plan evolved, there had been one crucial stage. "We have to get you checked up properly as soon as we can," Armand had said, hoping Carly would concede.

"To be honest, my whole right side aches and my head. Bit dizzy, but my levels are okay, so I should be fine."

"*Merde*, hopefully, the medicine will support you until tonight. You can't ride feeling that way, and risk concussion."

Armand had known the hospital wouldn't want her in after the paramedics had checked her over. They were too busy and their resources were too stretched to deal with someone injured during their recreation. Anyway, she needed to be somewhere safe.

They both needed this time away. It was a chance to rebuild. The tragedy of Cygne would continue hurting, but he had buried the trauma and his fears of returning home. Perhaps time there with just themselves and the horses was healing enough.

But not when there was a killer out there.

He heard Carly dialling the phone, and listened as

she mapped out just enough of their plan to a journalist with the right contacts. Carly said this friend could be trusted.

"Yes, I hope our five days in Ireland are a chance to recover and avoid any stupid suspension while keeping the girls fit... just two horses left in work, so Wanda and Dido will come to Ireland. Sadly, the others are all going back to Canada as Vecheech have pulled out and they're closing everything down."

He put his arm around her as she answered another question from the journalist.

"Yes. We're staying with a friend near Stroud tonight and taking the midday ferry tomorrow." She smiled at him and winked. "...Torc was severely injured. I'm really concerned about her. She's at the vet's recovering, and it could be some months."

Armand gestured at the farm buildings where the part-time grooms were mucking out with their headphones on.

"The liveries and grooms will keep Hazelmead ticking over, although it's being closed down in three months. There are a few horses left here, just liveries." He motioned at his watch. "Oh, I need to make sure we have everything. We're leaving in four hours."

She nodded at Armand as she listened to a final question.

"...Yes, we plan to be back on the seventh, for Bramham, if they let me ride in the CIC. I want to build on Saumur, prove our potential. I trust you to say what is necessary. Bye, and many thanks."

As Carly put the phone down, Armand prayed the journalist would use everything in the right way. The timing of the story's release on equestrian internet sites was crucial for the deception to work. They didn't need anyone tracking them down too quickly, not if the real intent of the hit and run van had been murder. Armand hoped the police could trace the van and connect Mick to it.

He may be too crafty and evade us. I want to blame Lina, but she wouldn't want a horse to die, even Torc.

To: Carly Tanner
From: Roman Boissard
Not intelligent enough. You won't have the mare for long. I'm not letting you sell her and profit at my expense. The family will fight MY son's will. He was unstable and not sane enough to sign a legal document.
Major Roman Boissard, Rtd.,
Director Boissard Équestre.

However threatening the email was meant to be, Armand was sure the assignment would be difficult to challenge; even the minor bequests were watertight, like the token bestowal to Odette Fédon's family.

"He can't do this. Vecheech will oppose him, and

they are too powerful, I think."

Armand glanced at the list of other emails that Carly had been sent. Bills, spam, and scattered among them what looked like offers for her mares, which he let her read.

"Wow, someone here's offering me ninety thousand pounds for Wanda, crazy money. So tempting, but she's too important ever to sell. Although I could buy youngsters instead and then..."

"Sure, but Wanda is your chance to prove you're a top rider, hopefully as part of a team, whether British or French."

"Unlikely, but I suppose yes. Wanda is capable of winning another three-day."

"You've both more than enough talent."

He glanced at the email and noted the offer was from an American stud. When Carly opened the next one, it was German.

"Strange, all these buyers, how did they all know?"

"Odd," she said. "This one even reminds me that the mare will be out of work if I breed from her. Even says they want to help riders like me, bloody cheek."

As he listened to the rain outside, he let her check the emails, but the speed of the offers concerned him. The report was not up on any sites, so someone else had leaked the news about Wanda.

"If I keep saying no, will they raise the price to say, one hundred thousand?"

"If they forget you have enough talent to keep winning."

"Am I being stupid, Loup? A valuable horse today could get a serious injury and be worthless. I've known it happen, and it's tragic."

"Are you thinking of selling?"

"No way, I'd never sell Wanda. Anyway, that's not why. Gilles left her to me, and this email confirms the terms."

"Terms?" said Armand, sensing that was suspicious. "An assignment with terms?"

"Well, Vecheech had to agree to waive their share and..."

She shook her head and sat back, hand on her mouth.

He read the offending words.

'In the event that you decide to sell or retire Sorcière des Saules or choose to retire from competition yourself, then the mare must be offered to Vecheech Enterprises Inc.

By making this assignment of their share in Sorcière des Saules, the company hereby retains the first option to re-acquire her at her full value...'

Vecheech was ensuring they were in a win-win arrangement. They had Wanda's foals and probably her DNA. Carly, as the mare's best rider, could add value to the mare and her progeny. In the final analysis, Wanda would still be theirs. For Carly, this was little more than a loan until retirement, but Armand couldn't help thinking, what does retirement mean?

FIFTY

Carly watched the raptor soaring on the thermals high above the limestone cliffs of the gorge. A griffon vulture, Loup had said when she noticed the first one earlier. Was it an ill omen, or a warning to any pursuers? The bird was majestic, surveying its domain of towering rocks and tumbling waters.

She glanced to her left across the horsebox cab at Armand. "If it's much further, we should rest the horses again."

"We should be there in an hour, so we'll stop beyond the town. There's a good place."

With every kilometre, the confidence in his face made her feel safer, even though their adversaries needed to discover their haven. Mick's determination was etched on her memory, as was Lina's persistence. How long had she worked with him? Lina had taken the DNA for Vidarranj when she was at Fenburgh, but where was she now? What more would she do?

When Armand had explained about the cloning and Vidarranj's super-horse project, it made total sense, although she had been oblivious to the clues at the time. If only she had bothered to apply what the university degree had taught her, she might have been more aware of their plans. At least she could now share her knowledge and observations with Armand. Tragically, Gilles had died without revealing what he knew.

She had to ask the question again.

"Loup, were Gilles's death and the accident connected?"

"I'm not sure. I think Mick is involved, even if the police trace on the van was—"

"—a dead end, because a C M Tanner rented it—the witch used my card. Stole my details and now wants me to blame Mick, because, as my ex, he could have known the PIN."

Armand shook his head.

"That online booking, on the day before the attack was made with a credit card that could have been one of his scams. Maybe we're meant to suspect her."

"If he turns up over here. Sorry, my gut feeling is Lina. She has reasons to do everything. Shit, it's like she's saying my actions are responsible."

"But if you were injured, who would ride Wanda for her? Mick knows riders. And she has no obvious skills, although she's fit. We can't rule either of them out, or even Roman, but we'll know soon."

Armand turned into a busy town with stone houses perched along a stream spanned by narrow bridges.

For Carly, it was a refreshing new world. Could it be a real haven? Could they escape and build something new—a home? "If they make a larger offer, then we can end this. Or is that giving in?"

He said nothing, just pretended to concentrate on his driving, but that must be his worry, she thought.

"You think there won't be another offer. Vidarranj doesn't need the mare anymore. I'm an inconvenience now, like Gilles. That's why they tried to kill me." The fear of what lay ahead welled up. She was putting Loup's life at risk as well as the Zoos.

"No. First, I'll never abandon you, Vix – I'll always be here for you. Second, if Vidarranj doesn't need the mare, it means they have live clones, which are healthy. And third, Wanda alive with you riding will always increase the value of any clones."

"...or any foal. Vecheech has those. Damn. Retire could mean kill. Then they get Wanda. Is that what Lina wants?"

"If she's working for Vecheech and not for Vidarranj. Whatever happens, you're safe here. This area is my territory."

She clutched Armand's knee with her left hand. Guinness leant his head on her lap.

Armand's smile staved off any darker thoughts.

From the vantage of the horsebox, she glimpsed flowers everywhere, in flowerbeds, hanging baskets, window boxes and throughout the bustling market, with its stalls strung and spread with produce and goods. The colours promised a wealth of scents.

"It would be great to explore this properly one day, Loup."

"One day, yes. But there are remote tracks we can safely explore. Nobody will notice two more riders along the *drailles*—the old sheep trails."

"Disappear into the landscape, sounds cool. Thanks, Loup."

They turned out of the town with the afternoon sun glinting off the roofs. A wooded hill led them up into rolling farmland with remote buildings and flocks of grazing sheep. Armand pulled onto a lay-by with a wide grass verge.

"This must do as a short break for the horses. Half an hour, then we must leave."

They unloaded and tethered their precious cargo on the grass. Armand put his arm around Carly as she savoured the scenery.

"Welcome to my home."

He pointed across the fields to the crags and forested mantle, their sanctuary.

She had worried about making the long journey when they had arrived in Gloucestershire. Although Armand had explained his plans to spirit Wanda and Dido away, she was surprised to see Armand and herself on their arrival inside the farmhouse at the equestrian centre. At a glance, it should do, but she had second thoughts about her double's wig, even though it matched her hair colour.

"*Chérie*, meet Oreillard and Furet. If this doesn't work out too well, they can defend themselves. We served together in the Chasseurs. They're good friends, but we tend to use our call sign names—from Zoo creatures—mine being Loup."

As their stand-ins drove off in the Hazelmead horsebox to catch the night ferry to Ireland, the reality of the situation had hit her, and she hoped their deception would work. The false press information, a couple fitting their description driving the Hazelmead box to Ireland, a chestnut and a grey on board. Not Dido and Wanda, but horses brought from France and switched amidst the evening bustle of the yard.

The recollection stirred her conscience.

"It's crazy, Loup. I still worry. We may not be risking your friends for more than a few days, but the horses are like...like tethered goats."

"Oreillard and Furet will see anyone following first; they're our best, trust me. They still work in security, freelance. Mick, or whoever, will want to confirm the target and by then it'll be too late."

He had already tried to convince her that the Zoos could deal with any malicious tail. He had unearthed Roman's military record, and his only active use of a firearm had been in a shooting team. The Zoos classed him as skilled, but not a sniper, even if he could have learnt to use a crossbow for hunting in Canada and liked sneaking around his Du Noroît domain.

However, that still left Mick as a possible culprit, and she had ransacked her memories of him for any ability he had betrayed that indicated he could have killed Gilles and Odette. Armand had suggested survival training, and she recollected Mick mentioning trips to Wales with some cadet or TA group before they met. Not surprisingly, Mick hadn't stuck it out, but in combination with Roman the skills were there and posed a threat. Lina was an unknown quantity beyond her vindictive and athletic persona, but she was involved.

At least a welcoming reception was being arranged for any pursuers that unravelled the deception and traced the genuine Armand and Carly, who had slipped over to France via the Plymouth-Roscoff ferry, disguised as Oreillard and Furet.

Would their pursuers take the bait? Or were they already following Carly and Armand?

Smelling the grass and feeling Armand's secure and loving arms wrap firmly around her dismissed any uncertainties.

"You can feel safe here," he said. "My comrades and I have the advantage. Some of us even grew up here, living off the land."

She gazed out across the pastures up towards the

forests of the Cevennes. Guinness bounded over bursting with reassurance. Her eyes swept back to the road, which curved around a craggy bend like a proud gateway. Beyond, she glimpsed a grove of tended chestnut trees leading onwards.

"There is a tradition of resistance here. Our grandparents were in the Maquis de Vabres—it's in our blood. Our adversaries are the interlopers. The Cevennes is your home as well now. I would do anything for you."

She turned and kissed him. She could move her life on here; Loup was offering her the chance. "You already have, rescuing me and bringing me to your home."

"A new beginning—for both of us." He wrapped his arms around her again. "Later, I'll show you some of my favourite haunts, since the doctor at Stroud gave the go-ahead for you to ride."

FIFTY-ONE

Carly slipped into bed and switched off the side-light. She curved her body around Loup, who was as soundly asleep as Guinness curled up by the door.

Armand must have been exhausted. Having driven from England, he then insisted that a night hike into the valley was needed to test the defences. He had remained undetected until mid-morning when a black fur-ball had pounced and then licked his face, while Carly straddled and tickled him.

Amazingly, after suggesting improvements to the security, he had insisted on riding with her. That might change over the next few days, but the precautions were crucial, and all these preparations were for her and the horses. Loup was devoting himself to her, and she felt his energy invigorating her. Her apprehension about the danger was buried deep below the warmth now, as were any residual feelings for Gilles. She had to move on to survive. Loup's love was genuine, and her heart was his.

She watched the moonlight flickering through the mulberry trees and listened to the contented breathing of her two men. There were memories to sustain her while confined to the protected area, like riding under the vast expanse of the trees along the nearby sheep trails, through scenery her mother would have loved. Chestnut, holm oak, beech, larch, she would have tested Carly on them all and been fascinated by the restoration of the Cevennes's green mantle that was spreading once again. It was so different from Vidarranj's approach to manipulating nature. Why interfere so drastically when the roots were already there? Torc had proved that with Dido—even if the youngster didn't seem to be an eventer.

Then there were the Przewalski horses on the Causse Méjean, being bred for reintroduction back into Mongolia. Riding with Loup on the remote plateau, seeing those wild horses galloping alongside them had inspired her. As had the scenery, so remote and vast, arid with dramatic limestone outcrops and the only signs of life, the occasional bird of prey, the Przewalski and hundreds of sheep—a contrast to the lush beauty beyond.

She had vaguely thought it might be another chance to find out how Odette Fédon was related, but the opportunity never emerged.

The Cevennes was so magical that a part of her wished she could stay. This time away was just an enforced break, while she recovered, except this place drew her to its heart. It was special, so precious that she wanted to explore this world. Was a new home here another option?

Loup had even tempted her by saying, "You know you said Dido had incredible stamina like her dad, so how about trying Endurance with her?"

"What are you getting at?"

"Well, there's a major race up here, Les 24 Heures de Florac."

"Sounds like you want to move back."

"Why not? Our jobs at Hazelmead end in three months, and the *mas*—the farm—belonged to my parents. When they retired, my siblings and I just rented it out for grazing."

She was now as confused as when the chance to ride for France had become a reality. Her mother would approve, and for her, France had always been her first home. But Carly was an eventer, and England had been home all her life and it was where her father was—if he was ever at the farm. But still, France was an eventing force that rivalled Great Britain.

However, despite the idyllic surroundings of the *mas* and the Cevennes, she couldn't stop remembering that whoever wanted her dead was being lured to the valley, and she was the bait.

FIFTY-TWO

As the early morning sun washed the valley, Carly reached the grass school that the Zoos had created from the pasture, clearing away any treacherous boulders and tussocks. Not a long stretch, but enough to keep the mares fit without risking her shoulder. Guinness was enjoying his change of scenery, exploring every corner and tracking every scent. She looked forward to schooling over the fences that the Zoos had built near the path through the chestnut grove.

Accustomed to a yard of horses to ride, Carly had found other chores around the *mas* to compensate. There was plenty to do on the land beyond securing it. From sheep that needed tending to repairs demanding attention, the Sabatier family home was as abandoned as Hazelmead had been when she had left—for a dream job, and Gilles.

Now, she had found someone that cherished her, and Armand had taught her some basic self-defence moves, which might have been useful if the intruders at Hazelmead had turned on her.

"Loup to Zoos, all systems working. Renarde in

manège; no sign of intruders."

Armand's voice in the headset that she had been given to wear reminded her of the weirdness of being watched by invisible eyes. She had accepted the call sign that the Zoos had given her, realising the need to use them. She had adapted to calling Natalie and Jean-Pierre by their names, Ouistiti and Faucon; and to speaking French all the time. The Zoos made her feel welcomed into their family, and it seemed the comrades had laid Odette to rest. However, she sometimes wondered whether she was being judged and compared with Odette. How much of the preparation was for Loup and Cygne—like the rebuilding of the *mas*?

This loyal handful of Loup's comrades had taken time off from their daily lives to help protect her. The Duchesnes had reasons, but why the others? They had moved on from the army, some into security like Oreillard and Furet, but what brought a sports therapist like the woman nicknamed Blanculet back? The camaraderie, or the adrenaline? The Zoos had become a unit again, an efficient team, rekindled like Loup rescuing her and Torc.

Loup's confidence grew once the narrow choke points into the secluded south-facing valley were being watched by both electronic and human eyes. However, the Zoos needed the advance warning from Ireland, but he had reassured her saying, "When anyone uninvited arrives, this secluded valley will appear to be a working *mas* and not a monitored trap."

Armand would never live down his fur-foiled attempt to pierce the defences, especially with his Zoo friend Mouflon around to embellish the tale. She could spot a lecturer anywhere, even when displaying his considerable shepherding skills. She realised why Loup knew Captain Blavet; Mouflon was his identical twin.

When they met on her first morning run up the valley, they had exchanged the usual greetings, and then Mouflon said, "What they've done to your mare is wrong, it's an insult. Rest assured we will ensure that your horse and you can compete again soon, maybe for La France."

"I would be honoured," said Carly, although as yet she had not abandoned the British alternative, even if Captain Blavet had implied he would push hard to get her French application accepted.

"This might be difficult to answer, but would you ever compete on a cloned horse, if it was allowed?" asked Mouflon.

"I couldn't, knowing the number of embryos it had probably taken. Even if it was perfected, the cost in lives would have been too high. I just know the natural way is best."

"I understand and agree. Sometimes I feel the

wastage of farm livestock is unacceptable, and then there are the defects."

Mouflon advised the Duchesnes on breeding advances, and like them, he was a firm advocate of the benefits of using embryo transfers. When Wanda's foals had been transferred into a surrogate dam to carry to term, Wanda had continued competing.

Would they ever be back competing? The dressage at Bramham was in three days, maybe four if she was lucky and her test was on the second day. She and Wanda would be fit and ready, but the window for departure was closing.

Even with the Zoos protecting her, and all the additional security measures, she was scared. Armand had given her a ballistic vest, and the mares had similar overlapping circular discs-like scale armour worked into their summer rugs. The Zoos had even attached steel plates to the stable doors. It didn't feel like it was enough, but Loup was confident that the stratagem would work.

Except Wanda and I are still the targets.

FIFTY-THREE

"So, Bête has found them, Loup?"

"From a well-laid trail and enough clues. Oreillard and Furet say he's easy to detect, too obvious. Not what I expected, Mouflon."

Armand was surprised after the lack of evidence when Odette Fédon and Gilles were the victims. The Zoos had given Mick the call sign Bête after the local wolf-creature of Gévaudan, although that beast had eluded people for years.

Am I right to assume Mick is the killer? Carly fears it may be Lina, which could be intuition—or jealousy.

"He's getting careless," he said to Mouflon, "the road accident was messy, but perhaps that's his weakness. Getting desperate and rushing into it, and yet he has been stealthy and invisible."

His friend sat beside him humming a shepherd's tune, happy to be tending sheep again.

If we hadn't joined the Chasseurs, would we have returned home and farmed? We always said we would, from those childhood days chasing through trees and splashing in the water, to dusty, sleepless nights on alert.

The sheep grazed along the brook that skittered down the pasture into the stream. Mouflon claimed he had no lectures to fret about while scanning the valley from the stone hut. The *cazelle* above the cliff gave him space and time for his thoughts, although he joined his comrades for meals and work details.

"Now Bête knows he's been tricked, he'll trace us here. Although he could backtrack to Stroud, I think he'll realise that we've headed over to France."

"Shame then, that you hid your past here, Loup. Did removing the name Sabatier from the land deeds ease your loss?"

"Looking back, no. I was running away, from anything that reminded me of Cygne."

"And now?"

"I know it was wrong, I hurt you all more, and you all wanted to help. Even after all that, Ouistiti and Faucon still ensured there were no clues on the stud pages."

"But you're home, and with your comrades again, which feels right. Even if we've all moved on, we're willing to put our lives as lecturers, horse breeders, farmers and builders aside to stand as Zoos again."

Armand smiled.

"Never again will I abandon you all. Anyway, Bête was at Saumur, so he'll fly to France and go straight to Des Saules, then be directed here. He should be in the valley by morning."

"We're warned and prepared, and my brother masks our identity."

"Blanculet to Zoos, Renarde leaving *mas* towards the *manège*."

Alerted on his headset by their latest volunteer, Armand watched the *mas* through his binoculars. Carly rode out of the farmstead, zigzagging through the chestnut trees to the grass school, Guinness loping along behind.

Am I right using Carly and Wanda to bait the trap?

"She's such a natural rider," said Mouflon. "And she's facing this bravely. Again, you've done well, my friend."

"She's learnt to live with adversity and risk," said Armand.

"She's stronger than she looks. Never thought she'd beat me at arm wrestling last night. Reminds me of..."

"Cygne. Don't worry. The memories are all good ones now—thanks to Vix. And for the arm wrestling, their trick is holding six hundred kilos of horse, at speed."

Judging from past observations of Loup, they would be alert in the morning, despite the cask of cider. At least they had eaten a meal to match, starting with his special variation on his mother's *aligot* recipe, followed by *truite aux crepes* with locally grown vegetables. The flavours that he had blended with care kept teasing her as she tried to identify the familiar tastes, like the intense garlic of the starter, to the subtle hints of wine in the sauce; but there was plenty to savour and remain mystified over.

She wondered if, under the laughter, the Zoos were as nervous as her about the arrival of the killer. Or was their adrenaline stirring? Wasn't this celebration premature? Or was this the eve of battle feast?

"You've surpassed yourself this time," called Faucon when Loup produced bowls of bilberries, grapes and chestnuts. "Or did you have some help from my wife?"

Loup put his arm around Carly and kissed her.

"Maybe it was someone else. Feeding you lot is a real chore. Be glad I'm not giving you army rations tonight, even if you work best hungry. From tomorrow, you'll be back to the usual lack of sleep and meals—comes with volunteering."

They laughed but then the boisterous mood switched to steely determination, as Loup drained his glass then put his elbows on the table and clasped his hands together.

"Mouflon, you're on guard tonight until Blanculet relieves you at 05:00. At 00:00, Oreillard and Furet return from Ireland—as of that time, we are on full alert. Our target could be here any time after 01:00, given the alert from Des Saules."

"Our friends locally should give us advance warning," said Faucon. "They are looking out for anyone asking all the correct questions."

Mouflon grinned.

"You mean about picturesque remote valleys to hike into, hunting licences and secluded riding centres. Or, maybe Bête's careless and will ask where Loup's family live by claiming to know him."

"Unlikely, Mick's reckless, but not stupid. What about someone sounding like a Spaniard?" asked Carly.

"You mean Lina, they know about her as well. We've told the *mairie* as much as they need to know, they're trusting us."

Ouistiti brought a pot of coffee from the stove and poured out six mugs.

"You've studied the profiles of our three main suspects," said Armand, "the Irish operation indicates that we should expect Mick Roper. All previous incidents suggest he acts alone without a spotter. But expect two infiltrators as he may change under pressure. According to our research, none have trained with an elite unit, but Bête can still be stealthy and invisible."

Faucon took over and pointed at a map of the farmstead, pinned to a wall where a rural landscape painting had hung.

"Bête will use the half-light to make his move,

probably at dusk when he's spied out the valley. We want him to find that the best and only line of fire is above the designated target area."

"He'll have to use the same route as me," said Armand, "west through the old larch plantation and along the ridge. He can get down the cliff. It's easier than it looks from below. How else do you think I made it down that drop?"

They laughed, and Faucon said, "Ouistiti has added a monitor up there. Remember, Bête is nervous of witnesses so once he's detected, we melt into the landscape. Then, we present him with a clear shot, before closing the net."

Carly winced knowing what the words meant to her and Wanda. She prayed the Zoos had all eventualities covered.

"Never forget that Bête may not be alone. We have to be prepared to neutralise other hostiles within the valley."

The Zoos nodded, then stood and raised their glasses.

"Fallen comrades."

Carly drank with them and saw the tears in their eyes. Were the tears just for Cygne or had other Zoos died? The Chasseurs had a distinguished service in the line of duty. After that fateful patrol, the Zoos had been in Afghanistan for the Battle of Alasay.

As one, they saluted, saying, *"Si vous avez des*

couilles, il faudra le montrer!"

This was camaraderie melded with the desire for justice. Moved, Carly tried to follow the words as they started singing.

FIFTY-FOUR

"Faucon to Ouistiti, any sign on the monitors? Bête should be out there. Watch for other hostiles too, over."

"Ouistiti to Faucon, nothing all night. He's lying low even if the gendarmerie spotted him around 01:13. As soon as he moves into the valley, the cameras will detect him. I'll keep watching on the screens in the barn, over."

"Faucon to Zoos, time to take up work stations before the sun's up. Just remember we're farm workers. I'll be by the woodshed. Confirm positions, over."

"Oreillard, working in the chestnut grove with Furet, within easy reach of the lower pastures, over."

"Loup, Blanculet and I are concealed on the cliff. We can tackle Bête once he has implicated himself, over."

"Mouflon, on ridge tending sheep, over."

"Merci Zoos. Bonne chasse."

Carly followed every word of the walkie-talkie exchange in French, and her stomach flipped with the apprehension over her role as the decoy for her hunters.

An hour after she had exercised Dido, a twisted sensation grew, and she failed to pretend it was pre-competition nerves; this dread wasn't the exhilarating adrenaline building before the cross-country.

As she untacked the mare, the warning echoed in her head mike. "Mouflon to Zoos, Bête entering outer zone, same route as Loup. Moving upstream onto south flank. Letting him recce for a position."

As he moved deeper into the valley, the other Zoos locked onto their quarry.

Ouistiti had picked up the masked figure on her monitors and was tracking the intruder. Carly looked over the shoulder of the gendarme beside her and studied the skulking figure. The dawn warmth trickling into the barn couldn't ease the feeling of something wrong, but putting words to her new fear was useless. Whatever lay ahead had to be confronted.

From his camouflaged vantage, Armand observed as Bête, clad in fatigues, sprouting twigs, leaves, and a green mask, moved along the escarpment studying the terrain. He must have checked out relief maps online, and the promotional material about local *drailles* that Ouistiti had ensured was on the town hall's website. This animal would use the implied route.

"Loup to Zoos, he's climbing down to my position—should be on the cliff monitor shortly. Time to start Renarde, over."

"Ouistiti to Zoos, Bête on upper left camera at eleven, but upper right twelve inactive. Will remain in sight down chute to cliff, over."

As the sun began climbing above the valley, Armand watched as horse and rider flickered through the trees, walking down to the arena.

I trust the troupe. This trap will work. The risk is justified to remove the threat.

A momentary shudder as the alternative flashed through his mind. Not this time, they were ready. The past was buried, even though this was the next test.

Bête clambered down the cliff onto the ledge overlooking the arena with unexpected difficulty, unlike Armand's careful hike to the same spot. The figure made a scrape position among the scree, shaded by scrubby plants. He unstrapped a mottled green rifle from his back and attached a telescopic sight.

Merde, *this isn't Mick. He's taller, less agile. I've been an idiot.*

"Loup to Zoos, quarry not Bête. Wrong suspect. Possible decoy. This bogie is either alone or has backup that may be Bête. Re-check for other incursions, over."

"Mouflon to Zoos, possible signs of alternate intrusion behind lead quarry. Investigating, over."

Armand studied the figure now lying down facing the arena and watching his target with binoculars. Roman. It was clear he knew about Ireland, so he was checking if this Carly was another double. A scan of the weapon told Armand that the rifle was a dart gun, yet Roman's lack of stealth didn't match the killer's modus operandi.

Where was Mick, Bête? Armand scanned the rocks and bushes around Roman. Nothing visible except for a swarm of midges around some foliage. Drawn by an animal or a person? A spotter or backup?

"Ouistiti to Loup, camera twelve is still out. It's interference, a jammer. Can still see key areas. No sign of other intruders, over."

The area that the camera covered was too far out. An intruder couldn't see the arena from there but could see the ledge.

"Loup to Zoos, presume we have three hostiles. Report other aberrations ASAP, over."

If the second intruder is Bête, who is the third? Not backup. A watcher? Like Lina? Merde. *She's invisible, like an elite, but what?*

He re-scoped Roman. The rifle was ready, once the ideal shot presented itself.

The pattern of dressage movements began again, and Roman raised the gun. Armand suppressed the pain at seeing Carly shot at; she would feel it more.

The first muffled thunk ran up the cliff, but the

recoil didn't register in his head or shoulder. The dart hit the grass just behind the horse at its extended canter, dust leaping into the air. Roman, frustrated and stung by his failure, fiddled with his sights.

His quarry just cantered across the diagonal, continuing a dressage test that the hunter must know.

"Loup to Ouistiti, I'll take him out after his second shot, if you've recorded the evidence footage? Over."

"Ouistiti to Loup, enough. Be quick. Renarde is not taking this too well, over."

Loup levelled his double-barrelled tranquiliser rifle on Roman, but there was no second thunk. Roman scrambled off the ledge, dropping his gun as he fell into the river. Renarde vanished among the trees.

Faucon ran across the arena.

"Faucon to Zoos, hold positions. Watch for the other intruders." He jumped into the water and waded to the prone figure. "He's conscious, but sweating badly."

"*Maudit*, wasps."

Armand heard the burst of Québécois as Faucon dragged Roman ashore.

Armand stepped onto the ledge. There was no sign of any insects, just scattered rocks and vegetation thrown aside as Roman had panicked. Perhaps some overhanging thorns spooked him. Except for a game hunter, that was unlikely. Checking over the area, he took his time, although he was aware of being watched, although it didn't feel like a threat, yet. A slender twig drew him, half-hidden by kidney vetch, and he palmed it before climbing down the cliff.

"Loup to Zoos, unknown intruder and Bête active. Secure area. Mouflon and Blanculet, cover ridge. Oreillard and Furet, hike east. Taking intruder into barn with Faucon, over."

Roman staggered as they steered him inside. His face was bleeding, and he was gasping. Red welts had appeared on his right arm.

Armand asked, "Did you intend to hit Carly, or were you aiming at the horse?"

"Just the horse. The slut means nothing. So, I hit it?"

"No, you missed."

Roman scowled and shook his head.

"We'll get her. A bookworm playing soldiers won't stop us."

"Blinded by the books. No wonder you remained a corporal if you can't recognise a Capitaine."

As Roman stared, the gendarme handcuffed him, and after reading him his rights, the gendarme led Roman away.

Armand put his arms around Carly. "How are you, Vix?"

"I'm okay, just shaken up watching myself being shot at by that bastard. Can't promise not to have nightmares, Ouistiti's holograms are realistic."

How do I admit that someone more dangerous is out there? Is it Lina? Has science blinded me? All I've done is reveal our capability to the real enemy.

Armand hugged Carly, hoping that she would not detect his apprehension. Her heart was already thumping against his chest, and he was unable to do more.

"Blanculet to Zoos. We spotted a shaking bush below the ridge, and Mouflon leapt on a cowering intruder. Bête de-activated, over."

"Mouflon to Zoos. Being back in action is good. Or maybe the Cevennes air has got to me again. Bringing Bête in. Over and out."

Carly's smile was a relief as she said, "Poor Mick, can't even sneak away unseen. Must have been waiting for nightfall."

FIFTY-FIVE

The evening light was dying and the night was encroaching as Carly tried to accept her tiredness was mental as well as physical. Loup's arm was around her, letting her head rest on his shoulder as they drank French coffee in the kitchen with the Zoos. Her mind was finding ease at last—until the phone rang.

Ouistiti took the call and then said, "It was the gendarmerie to say Roman died in his cell. The doctor says it was anaphylaxis, a severe allergic reaction to multiple wasp stings. But he said most people are not allergic to wasp stings to that degree. If Roman were allergic to wasps, he would have died sooner without treatment following such an intense level of attack."

"Unless they weren't wasps," said Loup as he placed a plain wooden box, about 16 centimetres long, onto the table.

He paused, then continued. "Someone wanted him dead. A cunning killer, the real Bête." He reached inside revealing some pieces of wood. Plain straight slithers without any foliage. He passed them to Ouistiti. "I found these on the ledge. As we suspected, someone else was out there."

"So, as we thought, we had a third intruder, the one that jammed the camera."

"Faucon said the Irish quarry was poorly trained, and Mouflon caught Mick sneaking away. He may be in jail, but the real killer used this. The pieces would have degraded like any bit of wood, just like the bolt that killed Odette Fédon..."

"So, Mick wasn't responsible for your cousin's murder," said Carly. "Lina killed her to get her hands on Gilles. Now she wants Wanda alive, but my life..."

"Supposition I'm afraid, though possible." Ouistiti was piecing the slivers together. "They're part of a dart. It's incomplete, but it carried a payload, like a MIRV. Sorry, Carly, that means a missile payload containing several warheads, each capable of hitting different targets. In this case, the dart had minuscule thorns perhaps—pseudo wasp stings."

Ouistiti passed the pieces to her husband, who studied them. "You're right. It's your assassin, Loup. A tranquilliser gun by this rifling. The stings were all down his right side. But, why kill Roman?"

Carly's hopes of competing again vanished. Wanda's life was still under threat. The Zoos and the refuge had been exposed.

Armand pulled down a whiteboard from the ceiling.

"I think we'll find the wasp venom was modified to react with Roman's system. Someone who had access to his DNA created the toxin. The dart was personalised."

"Had his name on it," said Furet. "Who could do that?"

"That snake Lina took mine!" said Carly. "She's totally responsible, that vindictive—"

"We don't know that yet."

"She knows all my weaknesses. She's the killer, and she's framing Mick."

"Women make excellent sportsmen and soldiers, but statistically, most female assassins are fanatics or terrorists," said Blanculet. "Would this Lina want Roman out of the way? What's her agenda?"

Carly resisted her gut response and let Armand write down all the incidents on the whiteboard: Odette Fédon's murder in Québec, Gilles's suicide in Norfolk, the attempt on Carly's life in Sussex, and now the assassination of Roman.

"We have to re-assess the evidence, for these four hits." Armand added the timings, the conditions and the victims.

I was nearly the fourth.

The others added details, many echoing the list that Loup had discussed with Carly.

"The MO for at least three is the same," said Faucon, highlighting the features before he looked around the gathered Zoos, then at Carly. "Sorry, Carly, what I mean is the modus operandi or the way in which the killer works is the same."

Addressing the Zoos again, he added, "With today's murder, we know that the killer is resourceful, furtive and well trained. He evaded our monitors and took one out without detection. Plus, skiing, rock-climbing, scuba diving—that's a familiar package."

"For an elite soldier," said Furet.

"But he let Roman shoot at Wanda and me. Why?"

"Because he saw the hologram flickering through the trees," said Ouistiti. "I felt that was a flaw, but I needed more time to perfect the image."

Loup put an arm around her. "No regrets. It worked. The assassin wanted Roman to squirm, to feel a failure, and he did."

"But Loup, which of your suspects fits?"

"Someone that wants Wanda alive. So, Mick and Lina—although they must have different agendas. Mick only acted concerned about Roman when you caught him, Mouflon."

"Yes, and he's saying nothing useful to the gendarmerie and the only thing they can charge him for is trespass."

"Oreillard and I scoped him in Ireland, where he wasn't too furtive. Can they hold him for that?"

They laughed as Armand said, "Sadly, lack of stealth is not a crime. Did he say anything once in custody, Ouistiti?"

"He claimed he was checking on Wanda's performance, as he's been doing at other places."

"Technically the law allows the gendarmerie to hold him for four days without charge. Up to four years once he's charged," said Mouflon.

"As I feared, somehow, we must pressure for the maximum so that we can concentrate on our furtive assassin."

"Poor Mick, he flunked cadet training and now this. He's everyone's scapegoat. Surely Lina's involvement with gangs gives her the right experience?"

"She told me about that as well," said Loup. "It means she should be capable of using a weapon."

Ouistiti pointed to the darts. "But these? I'd guess these were covert munitions. Who would have access to these?"

Armand pointed at one name. "A salesman with contacts, territorial army training alongside regular army, and a corporation backing him. Also, Mick had extensive technical expertise judging by everything I found at his house. Plus, he also ran the Vidarranj website and was capable of framing Lina for the hit and run."

Everything was pointing back to Mick, and despite Carly's character observations, Lina was slipping away when her guilt was so obvious.

"But Lina was a scientist," said Carly. "She took

the DNA and could have stolen blood, hairs or any material from Boissard Biotech when she was alone at Fenburgh. And she hated anyone standing in her way."

"Renarde is right," said Faucon, looking over his wife's shoulder as she switched on her laptop. "Ouistiti, did you find anything more on Vidarranj's website, to implicate her, or Mick?"

"There are two encrypted links to further details. Until Hareng Rouge finishes its task, all I can tell you is that the programme is classified, as Project Pegasus."

"Horses that can fly like the wind, clever but disturbing codename."

"They have to resolve the speed-anatomy dilemma," said Ouistiti and looking around at some confused faces added, "Carly's the practical scientist, she can explain."

"Well, unlike human athletes, horses' speeds are restricted by their anatomy. They're a near-perfect balance between lungs, heart and muscle. Stamina, however, can be improved, and their ability to handle stress too—using the illegal DNA and cloning, perhaps."

As the others talked about the implications, her mind sifted through scraps of classical knowledge. Could the password be the hero associated with Pegasus? But what was his name?

Faucon interrupted her thoughts by putting Roman's rifle onto the table.

"We need to find the dart from this gun. Whoever Roman meant by 'we' will probably use the same payload. Loup and I will locate the dart at first light. Oreillard and Furet, look for our third interloper's vantage, the angle of shot might be critical. Mouflon, back on sheep herding—watch out for strays."

Carly needed to sleep—if the nightmares didn't come. Guinness laid his head on her lap, and she stroked it, comforting them both.

"There is one other suspect, I'm afraid," said Faucon. "Loup, you were tracking the ex-Boissard horses, you said."

"The ones from Hazelmead that Vecheech bought returned via Calgary. I could only track them until a local agent arranged their onward journey to a ranch. But there hasn't been time to check the tracker inside the saddle and tack trunks."

"Do we know if this ranch was always a Vecheech one? Could it have been a Boissard one?"

Carly didn't want this to continue. Her gut instinct told her it wasn't what she needed to hear.

"Not sure. We only know it's somewhere in the Rockies."

"My God, the ranch Gilles dreamed of, but he's dead. You told me, Loup." Carly tried to hold back the tears. "Okay, he was a two-faced unfaithful bastard, but I knew his heart. So did you, Loup. He isn't a killer, please. Just leave him dead. That's bad enough."

"Relax, Renarde. I wasn't meaning Gilles."

"So, Faucon, who is this mystery suspect?"

"Patrick Harfang or someone he hired to help consolidate his takeover of Boissard Équestre. He may have given you his share of Wanda, but Vecheech owns the foals and some of her DNA. Plus, the terms favour Vecheech."

"But we know nothing about him," said Carly.

"Except that he has numerous enterprises, extensive contacts and as a recluse," said Armand. "That means he could be—"

"—An ex-soldier," said Faucon. "We need more about him."

Even as Armand agreed and Ouistiti continued her searches, Carly feared what might emerge. The assignments had been so neat and so planned that Gilles could be alive even if he hadn't contacted her. Why would Harfang kill Roman? Vecheech had everything of value that Boissard Équestre owned. How many killers were there still waiting for her outside?

Bramham and her dream of proving Wanda's real potential was now dead.

FIFTY-SIX

As morning trickled through the trees, Carly was sleeping soundly on Armand's shoulder. Tresses of hair tumbled onto his chest as she turned over.

Armand had slept fitfully, and for at least an hour he had been listening to the dawn approaching, waiting for these first glimmers of light. He watched Carly breathing deeply and gently and then reviewed his dilemma.

She wanted to be competing. She needed to be competing. It was her life. But there was still at least one killer out there, and another that the gendarmerie would release within four days—during Bramham, the event Carly insisted she had to compete at. Lina and Mick both fitted the modus operandi and in a twisted way had motives.

Carly stirred but only turned over. The birds were now in full song. Should he wake Carly so she could feed the horses, or let her sleep?

She's going to be stressed by the threat and wanting to compete. She needs to ride and work Wanda, at least.

It was good if she stuck to her routine. Five minutes,

then he would tease her awake. It was probably safe to school today, although she would want to explore another *draille,* they couldn't leave the secured area.

I want her back in her world. I need normality. I had abandoned army life, but now I've chosen to embrace everything I had rejected. It's what I needed.

Bramham—they needed at least twenty hours to get there.

It's too much of a gamble. No way can we leave tonight.

It would be safer for her to prepare for Gatcombe in five weeks. The selectors would understand if she delayed her return.

This was frustrating for horse and rider. Schooling indoors had its limitations; Wanda needed more hill work. Until the Zoos had neutralised all the suspects, this was the only option Armand could allow. Even though Blanculet had helped perfect the indoor rider workouts, Bramham on Thursday looked impossible.

Merde, I wanted them to have the chance. They're looking so good.

He watched as Carly finished her circuit on Wanda, then rode up and looked at him on the raised seating as she said, "So, you still say no then. It would mean everything to me."

"I don't want to lose you."

"With me as bait, we caught Roman and Mick. That worked."

"Not again. The... assassin is too smart. He or she has killed three times."

Carly dismounted, hitched Wanda to a railing and sat beside him. He poured her a mug of coffee from the flask.

"I'm not bait. I'm the next victim. Why? What do I have in common with Odette Fédon? Who was she?"

His eyes closed. Carly wanted him to remember. Visualise the past. Clever, find the missing jigsaw pieces.

"My second cousin. My father's mother was from Québec."

"You're part Québécois? My god, did Gilles know? Lina?"

"Never, only the Zoos, and now you."

He cupped her head in his hands and kissed her. She deserved to know everything since he wanted to share his soul with her.

"So, you were studying in Canada as you had family there. Did Odette introduce you to the others?"

"Québec was my escape from France, and yes, Odette knew about my wife. *Merde*, she talked about the grooming job at Du Noroît, before I did my PhD. She was ecstatic about the stud, at first."

Carly held him closer, stroking his head.

"So, neither of you knew anything about Roman and the problems?"

"Not until I moved there when Gilles and Lina

graduated. Odette and I kept our kinship secret. There was too much to explain, especially with Roman suspecting everything. He'd have fired her, or he'd have found out and..."

"No, you would have been killed as well. But the accident, what did you see? Feel it."

He concentrated and let his mind go, feeling safe as Carly was there if the trauma returned.

"A figure in white with a crossbow..." He rewound the memory to the moment before he left the cabin. "I told Lina where I was going, that I had to see someone."

"Odette? About what?"

"She needed to talk. She sounded worried, and I presumed it was about Roman as usual."

"Or it could have been about the baby."

"Or about the cloning. We have to tell the others, now."

FIFTY-SEVEN

Armand had added the words "Knew about Odette Meeting" to the whiteboard in the kitchen.

"Until now, the evidence has pointed at Mick as our killer, which was convenient for Lina. Now, she is my prime suspect and fits the profile. She has the motive, opportunity and skills: skiing, jogging, martial arts, technical proficiency and gang survival. She's more than a scientist. Prove me wrong."

The Zoos studied the data.

Carly prayed they endorsed her gut feeling.

"Oreillard and I found the second shooter site, a lone marksman," said Furet. "I'll let her explain. I need to relieve Mouflon on watch."

Armand shook his head. "*Merde,* three intruders and we spot one. We're getting old and incompetent. No wonder they retired us."

"Except you guys kept me alive. You flushed out and stopped Roman. Mick's in jail. So, one lonely viper left."

Armand smiled and then said, "Next time then, we take her and any other hostiles out. Oreillard, shooter profile, please."

"Light and tall, I'd say a woman. The range was at a dart gun's limit—one hundred thirty metres. She's good, in fact, a pro. Even game park vets don't shoot at that distance."

"My internet searches show she's married," said Ouistiti. "And this explains some of her motivation. Patrick Yudan Harfang married Doctor Velinda Luisa Maria Jardero on Thursday, May thirty-first, at Owlhead Stud, British Columbia in a private ceremony. The story was leaked to the media yesterday."

"Shit, perfect alibi while her driver tries to kill me. Damn her. She threatens to go to Harfang and then marries him. The evil snake is after everything."

"Or he is. I tracked the horses sent from Hazelmead—to Owlhead," said Ouistiti. "It's a remote mountain location, but the transmitter signal is now dead."

"Found or failed?" asked Armand. "They may have identified us."

"Other than the incursion into the valley, there have been no attempts to breach our security. My adaptations to our military spec make it hard to intercept our transmissions, but I'll keep monitoring all the suspects. Hareng Rouge is still active."

"So, we can still plant misleading information and decipher passwords—good," said Loup. "Shame I didn't infect Patrick Harfang with the Trojan."

"Bastard had Lina kill Gilles and then bought the ranch Gilles dreamed of."

"Owlhead must have been named after the place where Gilles skied, his favourite hill. Harfang is asset stripping Boissard Équestre, unless..."

Armand pointed at Gilles's name on the whiteboard.

Carly nodded. "I'm an idiot. Harfang was the castle in 'The Silver Chair', one of the Narnia books. The giants in the castle were as two-faced as Vecheech."

"And Harfang is the codename for a military drone," said Armand. "But more crucially, French for a snowy owl—the official bird of Québec."

"And Vecheech?" asked Carly.

"Search threw up a Slovakian town," said Ouistiti. "Meant to make us think that was the origin."

Armand punched his hand. "*Merde,* it's an anagram of Chevêche, the little owl."

"Gilles is alive, the bastard," said Carly clenching her fist then standing up, knocking her chair over. "He's a devious, manipulative... jerk! Does he think I feel nothing?"

She stomped over to the fridge and grabbed some milk, then strode back to the table, aware that everyone was watching. She drank the milk in one long gulp.

"Sorry, rant over—until I see the bastard, then he'll wish he had died. He never tried even once to contact me, not bloody once. What was he planning?"

Although, Gilles had given her Wanda and the strange will was really a transfer of ownership – with terms. Was that action a cryptic message? Or more likely, it was his guilt over destroying her dreams to be with Lina. Or was it another business manoeuvre?

Faucon nodded and held his hands up. "His manipulations have cost lives and complicated everything. He's fooled everyone. Never believe what you see, whether it's a bookworm, or a scientist, or a playboy..."

"A playboy who enjoyed extreme sports from skiing to the scuba diving that allowed him to escape his faked death. Gilles fits the profile, although he had the alibi of his meeting with Roman, when my cousin, Odette was killed."

Armand added red lines from all the incidents to Lina's name, but then wrote "Marksmanship—?" to one side "Prioritise any investigation that reveals Lina's past. All we know is that she graduated from high school, worked for various veterinary and supplement companies before getting straight As at McGill."

"Where she persuaded Gilles to hire her, bloody perfect. Now she's stalking me. I so want her dead."

"My cousin's killer might deserve death, but we can't resort to murder ourselves, whoever it is."

"Apologies, Renarde, he's right, there are other

ways," said Mouflon who had come off duty and walked into the room. "But we can't forget Bête, Mick Roper. The gendarmerie might have to let him go. A legal challenge by a Paris lawyer could nullify provincial law."

"Also, Loup and I found Roman's dart. Initial analysis showed traces of a drug—insulin," said Faucon.

"I was the bloody target. That's crazy. My pump would counteract an extra dose."

"No, this insulin seems to have been a modified hybrid tailored to you."

"The bastard lied—he wanted me dead."

Roman had always hated her, even before she won Saumur. He blamed her for Gilles destroying Boissard Équestre.

"The Hareng Rouge derived evidence shows Vidarranj had their scientists modify insulin," said Ouistiti, looking up from her laptop.

"So, could Lina, the witch, using Vecheech's resources."

"But she saved you and Sorcière. Mick was the one there backing up Roman, for Vidarranj," said Faucon. "They don't want you killed, but if they can aggravate your diabetes, Renarde, you might sell the mare, regardless of any agreement with Vecheech."

Carly wasn't sure that she would sell but feared that someone could persuade her, if her diabetes got complicated. The Zoos had to stop the threat before that occurred.

"I don't think Roman or Mick knew about the terms," said Loup. "Their plan was blackmail, probably with a financial inducement as well. I'm sorry, Vix, but they feel another rider can replace you. Vidarranj already deals with some top yards."

"You mean I'm expendable, which Lina said to my face."

"Replace doesn't mean they want to kill you. Anyway, we won't let them." Armand pulled down a second whiteboard and wrote, "Lina, Gilles/Harfang and Mick," each one at the head of a column, then continued, "We need to entice the first two into a trap, which will draw in Mick if he's released. We can't use this location; it's compromised."

"Okay, I've the perfect answer, we leave so I can compete at Bramham."

"Vix, no, I won't risk losing you. There has to be an alternative."

Nobody offered any, and the silence signified agreement with Carly.

"You hardly need to send invites. They'll come. I'm not going to hide until this has all blown over. You taught me, Loup, that we must face the past. They're all my past—Mick, Gilles and Lina. Gilles especially needs to explain himself. Why on earth give me Wanda when he's Harfang?"

"Because he needed the mare to have the best

rider. And you're right, hiding never works, as Loup knows," said Ouistiti, "and Project Pegasus must have a deadline. If not, why Roman's desperation? It's more than just anger at Carly's success."

Armand looked distraught, so Carly threw her arms around him and kissed him, knowing he had to agree. She had trapped him.

"Okay, I recognise your logic. Roman's irrational and reacts aggressively, but Mick was Vidarranj's henchman and controlled Roman. Mick's central to Project Pegasus, and it's the key."

"So, we go to Bramham."

"Yes. Just be glad we'll have more of the Zoos troupe available at the weekend. We must leave tonight, plus we still need to know who Lina is. Any more info, Ouistiti?"

"Nothing yet. US military is still searching under all her names. They had checked if she served in the Nicaraguan forces like her father, a major with the contras. But they found nothing."

FIFTY-EIGHT

Carly was relieved that they were going to Bramham, but angry that Lina was remaining elusive. That had to be more leads to her scheming. "Project Pegasus?" she asked. "Does that lead anywhere? The encrypted links?"

"I've tried variations on Perseus, Pegasus, and Medusa. I even tried a symmetric algorithm to bypass the firewall."

"Why not try Bellerophon? He rode Pegasus to kill the Chimaera," said Carly, her Classical memories surfacing.

A flurry of keystrokes later, a log progress bar started creeping up. Then, a new Vidarranj page appeared on her screen.

Armand turned to Ouistiti at her laptop.

"Are those the hidden pages?"

"Just the one showing that Pegasus has two phases—Pegasus and Chimaera. First, breeding super-horses... which seems to have floundered after the death of the clones..."

"So, they need Wanda to discover why they died?

Run tests on her?"

"That's what Vidarranj's experts think. They have instructed Mick Roper to acquire her in the next few days, by whatever means necessary—price no object."

"And Phase Two, Chimaera?"

"To market the contaminated GM feed," said Ouistiti. "To undermine those studs not connected to Vidarranj or their associates—that launches in exactly a week."

"The deadline you feared, so we have to act at Bramham," said Armand.

"Wait, there is another section. In which Mick Roper gives his CV."

"Weird-like but typical Mick," said Carly. "Self-obsessed."

"Says here that he was in the Parachute Regiment—2 Paras—before Vidarranj recruited him." Armand leant over Ouistiti's shoulder as she read the rest. "An expert marksman with mountain experience in Norway and Canada."

"That doesn't sound like the Mick who struggled with Outward Bound." This exposure reminded Carly of unwrapping Mick's present. Boxes within boxes, intended to confuse or hide the truth?

"But if this is genuine," said Faucon, "the British authorities will need concrete evidence before they arrest him."

"*Merde*, I should have guessed," said Armand.

"Pegasus is the magazine of The Paras because the British Airborne Troops in World War II had the insignia of that guy on Pegasus attacking something with a spear."

"That's the guy I mentioned, Bellerophon slaying the Chimaera."

"Apologies, Renarde, that wasn't the password. I hacked in with my algorithm, except it only opens one... this part of the site is strange..."

"How?" asked Faucon.

"Neither file is part of the main site. Either Mick ran this from his home location, not from Vidarranj's mainframe, or..."

"You mean like our system?" asked Faucon. "Decentralised to deter hackers and strengthen the network?"

"Yes. Or..."

"Lina planted the evidence. The viper invented this CV to deceive us. Mick's not paras, but she's Bellerophon."

"Renarde is right. The name means slayer with a projectile, dart, javelin, needle, arrow, or a bullet," said Mouflon and bowed to Carly, as his brother had done to her at Saumur. "As she said, deception. Chimaera is an impossible fantasy, like perhaps the super horse, although we know the GM rice bran has genetic side effects."

"Let the authorities decide if this is fact when we

give them all the files we have, plus the evidence to link it to either Mick or Lina," said Faucon. "Especially as Mick's itinerary shows that he was in Canada when Odette died; at a feed symposium, on behalf of Vidarranj, talking about rice bran."

As Ouistiti continued typing, Carly noticed her changing the language, after reading about Bellerophon.

The second file opened. "Ancient Greek spelling, Bellerophontes, and in Greek letters," said Ouistiti. "You were both right – Renarde, Mouflon." She scrolled down and then put a hand to her mouth. "*Mon Dieu,* Lina was an expert marksman in the US Marines, and trained others, before she was discharged for assaulting a superior officer. Then she took a private sniper course before enrolling at McGill. From there she joined Boissard Équestre."

"*Merde,* the two-faced scorpion. Does Gilles know? Is that why he's with her, as Harfang?"

"He knows, Loup. This document is a copy of her Vecheech profile," said Ouistiti. "It looks as though Harfang's planning a hostile take-over of Vidarranj, the company his father tried to side with."

"If Project Pegasus threatens Vecheech's research, the simple solution is to undermine and discredit them, then buy their assets. Lina made that possible. As did Roman's pride, thinking he was friends with Harfang. Idiot never recognised his son in disguise."

"Or the shark he had created," said Faucon. "But Gilles, or perhaps we need to call him Harfang, took the family rivalry to another level."

"By recruiting Lina. The US Marines will confirm her profile in detail. Latest info received says she was in a Marine Junior Reserve Officers' Training Corps course for three years, while at High School, as Luisa Jardero. The Marines will give us access to her records."

Carly wondered if she was ready to die for a horse. If Mick didn't kill her, Lina would. There was an easy way out, retire and give Wanda back to Vecheech. That was what Gilles wanted, once Carly had made her valuable. Her retirement would thwart him. Or would Lina only accept death as her revenge?

FIFTY-NINE

The familiar surroundings of Bramham Park made Carly pleased to be back at her favourite British three-day-event, despite needing her invisible protection. The arena edged by busy trade stands on two sides, the views onto the cross-country winding through mature stands of trees, and the grand house, all welcomed her back. The crowd was growing, drawn by this majestic setting for four days of equestrian sport that culminated with the eventing finale and some pure show-jumping. It was a venue that would inspire anyone, and this time the challenging course was not the only test for her.

Carly longed for a cool breeze. Neither her skin nor the ground was handling the heat wave well. The shade that the awning attached to their lorry provided was welcoming, as she sat on a folding chair.

At least she would soon be back in action again, even if it were with only two horses, but all the worries were re-emerging about the real challenge. She faced a strong field, and all of them had probably prepared better for this competition.

She was grateful that the organisers had agreed to let her do her dressage test late on Friday, the second day. After arriving at six p.m. following a nineteen-hour journey, Wanda would benefit from the brief rest.

A black shape bounded over, dragging Loup behind him, who looked relaxed hiding behind his shades. Guinness sat down beside her, pink tongue hanging out.

"So, you gave him a good run—hope he wasn't chasing the deer? Dogs are meant to be on leads, at all times." He winked as she asked, "Are they coming? Or did you hit them?"

"Model of English manners, even if I was ready to kill them both. Lina said in five minutes. We need to get ready."

Everything around them had seemed normal. Horses were being tacked up, washed down, lunged and groomed. And riders were fretting, enthusing, eating burgers and drinking coffee. Carly wanted to look forward to the evening gatherings by the boxes, barbeques, buffets and wine. The Zoos deserved the reward; once she was free of the cloud blowing back over her life. Then there would be time to socialise, learn about Loup's friends. It was beginning with some, like Blanculet. She felt relaxed with the therapist; the older sister she'd never had. First though, they had to confront the betrayers.

As Lina and Gilles arrived, Carly smiled and greeted them as if they were still old friends. "Congratulations on the miraculous resurrection – and your marriage. Come inside."

Armand uncorked a bottle of Vin de Pays Cevennes and poured four glasses.

"Nothing special, but perfect for toasting your union. Life is more civilised with this."

Carly hoped it would also unlock some secrets as well. She just had to keep smiling at the devious couple that had cheated her.

"Surprised to get your email and learn you were coming, Vix. Brave return, or maybe foolish."

"For Vix, it was a necessity. *Santé et bonne chance*—to a successful event and a deserving winner."

"I may just be doing the CIC, but don't know if I'll be pushing Wanda, as I haven't worked her much. So this is your chance, Gilles. Is Drac ready for this?"

"He travelled well, yes. Might not be aiming for another four-star, but I'll be pleased when Wanda gets there. Right, Lina?"

Pleased, as when Wanda got there Vecheech would benefit through their foals. Lina must know that. But hopefully, she was confused at the welcoming reception, since she smiled and said, "That's why you invited us here. You need our help, again."

"You removed one threat—Roman—although you just had to stop him."

Gilles looked at Armand. "I may have hated my father but not enough to kill him; it was an accident..."

"The dart was meant to incapacitate him, but something went awry," said Lina.

"You didn't know he was allergic? You must have his DNA like everyone else's at Fenburgh."

"Why bother with his DNA? I needed to just monitor the ones that were at risk. I wanted to protect what was important, like Vix. So what happened to Mick then?"

"Our gendarmerie arrested him, and he's in jail but can't be charged. So he may be released by Saturday. Do you think we can deter him?"

"So, the Cadre needs my help. You cavalry guys are out of your depth, but I'll help. I can neutralise him, easy."

Armand poured more wine, hiding any amusement as the trap opened.

"What does Vecheech want for protecting Wanda?"

"We have her foals, so we just need her to win with the best rider for her. So, we have to give her that chance."

"Thanks, Gilles, but tomorrow you have a chance to beat me."

"Amiga, even now the rivalry. Is that all Gilles means?"

The Latina couldn't hold her venom back, but Armand had taught Carly aikido well—use the attack.

"Once, he meant more, but now I've moved on. I've a better deal. Can you say that? Have you got what you wanted?"

"Yes, it's all in Canada, or here beside me. I'm happy, Gilles needs me, and we share his vision—Owlhead, the horses, Vecheech. Could you do that or was your career the priority, Vix?"

"Both—sharing everything including the career. So, was Odette in the way?"

Lina went silent and threw a look at Gilles, who said, "Come on, Vix, you know I loved her. Okay it wasn't an accident, but who could have known Mick would kill her—just my father, as he ordered her removed."

"Why have Odette killed? Did she threaten the family by carrying your child?"

"I never told Papa or anyone about the baby. There was another reason."

"Odette made the mistake of asking too many questions about Project Pegasus after she stumbled over it," said Lina. "We tried to stop her talking to Roman. She wouldn't let Vecheech resolve the situation as planned."

"So, that was why you created Vecheech, to halt the Project?" said Armand.

"Vecheech was the only way to stop Papa destroying Boissard Équestre."

"And Vidarranj?"

"They controlled my father through that viper, Mick. Luckily, I had the basis of Vecheech in place at McGill, with the help of friends and lawyers disenchanted with Roman's incompetence."

"Why didn't you ask me? Or was it before we met?" asked Armand.

"I set Vecheech up before we met. You seemed to be troubled just by life. So, why involve you when it was under control?"

"Gilles has business flair. Nobody credited him with anything, with his pure ideals. Odette knew his plan but failed to understand what it meant. No imagination. The pregnancy made her dismissal inevitable. Poor Gilles."

Carly could see Armand read the confession in those words. Lina had dismissed Odette, with a crossbow.

Gilles ignored his wife's blunder and reached into his jacket, taking out a USB flash drive that he handed to Armand.

"This is Vecheech's research on Vidarranj, showing how they debased everything. It might help prosecute Mick. Just because Papa's died, Vidarranj will keep Mick on the case. Their future depends on it."

"You mean Project Pegasus? It's on the drive?"

"Everything, from the Du Noroît research to the latest problems. Wanda's DNA was the basis for the only two successful foals."

"Therefore, they don't need her anymore unless..."

"The foals have died, so they need to start again, with Wanda."

Gilles took another sip of wine.

"This isn't bad. Like old times." He drained his glass and stood up. "Lina and I need to go, but we are around if you require our help again. You know where our box is, au revoir."

"Then Lina should come to our briefing tomorrow. 06:00 by the start."

SIXTY

The morning light and the coffee fed their readiness, but the numbers of volunteers present indicated a weakness in Armand's strategy. At least it should to Lina, as he said, "I've divided the course into six sectors per the visibility and accessibility of the fences. Each of the Zoos is assigned one."

"We should work in pairs as a spotter and sniper would, but your Cadre friends are too few."

"I tried to get more volunteers, but our friends had priorities, like their horses."

"You guys don't understand the meaning of emergency, but I'll help point out the vulnerable positions. Some fences offer the optimal positions for Bête to strike from."

"Like the water, where some people are waiting for a fall—like the paparazzi," said Armand. "Crowds equal cover."

"Vantage points too, for a good sniper," said Lina, her face betraying nothing.

"What about weapons? How do we stop Bête?" asked Brochet, a Zoo who had taken off a long weekend from work as a truck mechanic.

"The British criminal law restricts us to using such force as is reasonable in the circumstances of preventing crime," said Loup, and concerned Lina would ignore these words, he added, "Bête attacking Renarde or the mare would suffice, but avoid undue force."

"*Jesus Cristo,* sounds like the cuffs are on us."

"You can also pick up something defensive, which the law calls 'instant arm'," continued Armand. "We can only use whatever force is needed to suppress the attack. Any further violence would constitute an assault. We don't need weapons to impede Bête or someone else."

Lina mimicked dodging in front and tripping him.

"Exactly, or just an arm to the chest can do enough."

"Unarmed combat, *perfecto.*"

She was proficient without weapons so she wouldn't be at a disadvantage, but Armand had to say, "Citizen's arrest is legal, but we must call the authorities as soon as we can, and no heroics."

He was about to progress the briefing, but Lina took the lead.

"Bête will be armed, but not with a regular dart rifle, crossbow or pistol. It may be a modified blow-pipe, something to deliver a dart to the right place. Any more suggestions?" She spun round and faced the Zoos with a fiery glare, and then laughed. "Anyone think they are as clever as me?"

Blanculet braved a reply. "Perhaps an umbrella or a walking stick?"

Her response encouraged Brochet. "Surely anything from a toy to a radio or cell-phone could be adapted."

"Impressive, but remember it has to be accurate against a moving horse."

Armand expected Lina to say a camera or even a flashlight, to conceal the CO2 cartridges, although the Zoos were aware of that already.

"Okay Loup, what do you feel? They're your friends, but you need to impress me."

"I'd choose something with a targeting device for accuracy, like a camera perhaps, still or video."

"Correct, anything suspicious might be a weapon. We might eventually make a real soldier of you, one day."

"The crucial thing," said Loup, amused at her misconception, "is that we are on the cross before first light and that we check every sector for anything suspicious. When Bête is spotted, we shut him down before he can act."

"Agreed. Let's walk on. This fence is too exposed, but the next one might be one Bête would choose. The tree increases the cover, and a rider must steady before the first element."

Lina's rising to the bait. She's relishing being back in

charge of her raw recruits.

Just six selected Zoos were required to attend the briefing. Armand had briefed the others on how to cover the gaps.

This deception must work. Using covert assets is vital. Lina believes we are ineffectual cavalry guys who need her assistance—good.

SIXTY-ONE

Standing beyond the water by a stone wall, Carly grinned at Gilles and said, "Giving me another perspective, to confuse me perhaps? I have to remember you're a rival and a Canadian who needs horses."

"Vecheech sponsors the Canadian Equestrian Team, so we could always use a horse like Wanda." He stared at her, then smiled and said, "Except she's yours."

"Until I retire, but I'm grateful for the ride for life; even with the strict terms. I'm surprised Vecheech didn't just loan her. You'd still have got the same results."

"I owed you, for wrecking your dreams. Plus, don't owner-riders give more, like passion and commitment?"

"We know what's best for the horse, yes. Another shrewd move."

"Anyway, those terms have one loophole I fear, my oversight. Any future embryo transfers are yours—unless you want to take a bet if I win?"

"Don't think Lina would approve. That's one of your bad habits, though it sounds tempting. Plus,

I know your team needs some help." She continued walking across the parkland towards the next complex.

Gilles responded to her taunt, saying, "*Tabernac,* we've won medals–"

"True, your lot won team silver at the recent championships, just behind our team, but—"

"We're getting competitive. Watch out Brits. A few more years and we'll be all over you, if not next time."

They both laughed, but it was true. With Vecheech putting their muscle and resources, including Lina's research, behind all the equestrian teams they would be a force.

She pointed at the taxi-shaped roll tops ahead and said, "This new complex poses a lot of questions."

"So which route do you favour, Vix?"

"No way, first you show me yours."

She let Gilles pace out the options through the mounds and trees, snaking from taxi shaped fence to fence. The sun filtering through the leaves threw shadows across the uneven ground, adding to the test.

Gilles relaxed back into eventing mode, and the tension between them dissolved. However, she was prepared and waiting for when the time was right to make her move.

He walked back to her, glancing at his notes. She watched another group of riders walking the combination.

"Well, I know what I'll do. I would just choose to take two alternatives on this course, depending on the conditions tomorrow."

"It's meant to be sun with light cloud," said Carly, hoping the British weather could be relied upon to deliver.

"Then the quick route here is jumpable if you can keep your balance through here with these mounds and roll tops."

"Should be fun for the spectators, seeing riders trying to keep their weight back, arm in the air."

"Totally true. It's aptly called Hailing A Cab. Anyway, we'll be okay, though in the wet it might be wiser to go longer. But it'll cost you time, and I might beat you again."

As he nodded his agreement, although perhaps not to another defeat, she smiled. Despite everything else, Gilles had always had the trainer's knack, if not the winning ways.

Half an hour later, they walked away from the finish down past the lorry park and stabling.

Carly thanked Gilles, saying, "That was so useful, and it helped, you knowing Wanda and me."

"I'm here if you need me. Just sorry about the past. Have you time for a coffee? Or do you need to work Wanda?"

"I've time for one at Charlie's, black of course. I've three hours before my test."

"Is your insulin pump working right now? If not, the company has the latest, and it meets the Olympic regs."

"I'm all right, and my pump is great, but thanks for offering."

Carly wasn't going to tell him about the modifications made by Ouistiti, so the pump delivered glucose as well. It would even combat a modified boost from Mick.

Watching the dressage from beside the stand, familiar from so many events, she could have so easily slipped back into old ways. Now was her moment.

"Are you still Gilles Boissard, or have you and Lina become Mr & Mrs Patrick Harfang? Just wondering if I'm sitting here with a celebrity?"

She grinned as he put his head down and glanced around.

"Not sure I'm that if I stay as Patrick Harfang, as I intend. More like a bête noire. And it's all cost me enough... dollars."

How many friends has he lost by stabbing them in the back?

Continuing to delve she said, "Poor Gilles. Your money—did you fund Vecheech and all of those horses?"

"My money, plus a bit from grand-père, as he

always supported my ventures, without Roman knowing."

"Your grandpa knew you were Patrick Harfang?"

"Totally, and it made him proud. Proud that I was a real entrepreneur, unlike his son who was a spendthrift that strutted around and bullied people. Grand-père laughed when I disguised myself to play golf with Roman, who never realised I was Harfang."

"That easily fooled. So, your grandpa agreed with your ventures?"

"He said I was ahead of my time when I invested in biotechnology, wherever appropriate."

Carly smiled as he added further fuel to Armand's surmise that Vecheech planned to take over Project Pegasus.

"But the ruthless image? Remember the Saumur press conference—that isn't the future. Harfang is surely a reaction to your father?"

"As ever, you're right. With the threat gone, I suppose I'm free."

"Gilles, the guy I fell in love with had positives to build on, like the talented trainer and the person who found Wanda and me. The man who made us a team, perhaps medal winners. And as a Canadian sponsor, you need a new image."

"What's the catch, Vix? With you, there's always one."

"How about doing an interview with French TV? A

chance for Patrick Harfang, competing at Bramham, one of Britain's stately homes, to show he's supporting eventing in so many ways: as a rider, a breeder, a sponsor, even ensuring a Brit gets her chance to ride a brilliant horse."

"And this is your idea or Loup's?"

"Mine. He just agreed. They're here doing a documentary on the Duchesnes."

Plus, they were extra eyes around the cross-country, especially with their cameras.

"First, we need more coffee for inspiration."

She hoped he wouldn't talk his way out when he returned with two more cups.

"So, you need the Canadian perspective, a walk-on part? Not sure then."

"No, your own piece, linked to Wanda. Director even muttered about you commentating on my round, crazy idea."

Brilliant if it kept Gilles occupied up in the control box.

"Tempting, it's hard hiding behind a false image. It's my chance to play the benevolent role, and it'll be an opportunity to make Vidarranj squirm at my humanity. Say hi to the new Vecheech."

She wondered if she had created a dangerous hybrid monster, with the charm of Gilles and the venom of Harfang. Would he just thrive in the spotlight while Mick used the distraction to strike?

SIXTY-TWO

"Wanda looks out for me on cross-country, and you're all watching as well. At the speed we'll be moving, there's a chance Mick will miss," said Carly grinning.

Is she too foolhardy? Brave more likely, and it's our duty to protect her. I don't want to lose her just for a team place in the future.

"I like your spirit, *amiga*. We'll ensure he doesn't try. I've these Zoos well-schooled, once they paid attention."

Armand hoped she was right, and they had found every vulnerable position along the four-kilometre track. The Zoo reinforcements, the cameras and the organiser's co-operation should give them total coverage. Bramham was a popular international event in the heart of an equestrian county, so there would be large crowds drawn by the warm weather as well as the action. Mick could easily disappear here.

Damn Vidarranj and their Paris lawyer. As Mouflon had warned, the gendarmerie had been unable to hold Mick for even four days. As Carly walked back to the horsebox, he waited with Lina by the Water complex as they continued to survey their sector.

"Have we assessed the Vidarranj risk correctly, Lina? Do they need Wanda alive?"

"Trust me, Loup. They need her alive and winning with Carly on board. They only need Mick to secure ownership, like Roman tried and failed."

"So, a simple agenda."

He had been relieved when the British Ministry of Defence had confirmed Mick was never in the Paras and had only trained with the Territorial Army one summer and then quit. As predicted, more Vecheech misinformation. The Canadian company's computer incursions had increased the security level of Vidarranj, although Hareng Rouge was bypassing their firewalls.

"Loup, did you ever trust me? Or your best friend, Gilles? Why not enough to tell us what you suspected, even if it was minimal? Perhaps if you had, we wouldn't be fighting Vidarranj now."

"I tried once, at Saumur, but you shut me out. We could have shared information then."

But then Armand would have been exposed, making himself a target.

"Hogwash, you only told me what I already knew. Why not say you were Cadre? Or did your riding let you down? Were you ever promoted? Sergeant? Corporal?"

He suppressed his amusement but wondered

if this was a bluff and that she had discovered his history with the Chasseurs. Was he her next victim?

"Maybe for the same reason you never mentioned the Marines. Why didn't you tell me that you served?"

"I couldn't say anything. Nobody ever understood, until Gilles. Nobody felt my torment, especially not *mi padre, hijo de puta*. He was only capable of abusing my mother when my brother Luis was killed, in a stupid accident."

The pain seemed genuine. Did her father wish she had died and not her brother? Armand let her continue.

"Some drunk driver, the police said. My father wanted me to be the son he lost, but he never gave me a chance. So, when I graduated from High School, I joined the army."

"Where you were driven to succeed at everything?"

"Yes. Everything the officers would allow me to do. My commander was okay, but there was a Captain; he gave me hell, demanded too much. Raped me, then ensured the army booted me, the victim. So, I was expected to live with that bastard's dishonour, but Gilles helped me bury my past and build a better life."

"*Merde*, I'm deeply sorry." However, her suffering was no justification for murder. "How much does Gilles know?"

"Everything, we trust each other. Like you and Carly."

"Your Marine skills? Did those help when you both faked his suicide?"

"I had the know-how..." She hesitated then said, "But that rat, Mick. He has to pay for all of this."

He tried to gauge if the venom was real, or if some of it was contrived.

She's had it tough. Abused, raped and now this, but can I forgive her? Would Odette?

"Can he be responsible for everything, Lina? I thought it was your darts that killed Roman."

"That was defensive, like now. Mick is your assassin, trust me."

Except he couldn't. Lina was the proverbial scorpion. It was in her nature; she was Bellerophon.

So he said, "And I promise we will neutralise the assassin today." She winced, but he pretended not to notice, continuing, "I need to check the other side."

"You're wasting your time, Loup. He'll strike from here or elsewhere."

"And if you're wrong, what happens?"

"Isn't Carly wearing body armour like ours?"

"Too heavy, so she has an adapted body protector."

He didn't admit she was wearing a hybrid textile the Zoos had access to, designed to be dart and needle resistant.

"And Wanda? She's even more vulnerable, a larger target area."

"That's why we have to stop Bête first. I'll be back."

He crossed the course to where a covert Zoo was watching near the lobster sculpture alternative. "Salut, Homard. Keep watching Bellerophon while I turn away."

He switched to the covert net.

"Loup to Ouistiti, ready to use the Euphorbia dart. Target unaware and confirmed. First, we need to find and fix Bête. Over."

When he returned, Lina was checking in with her recruits.

"No sightings."

Cross-country control confirmed the situation on the fence judges net, saying, "We're still waiting for number thirteen, Gevaudan Blood," before adding, "but we have our first starter in the box."

"Macabre name for a horse," said Lina, unaware of the coded message to the Zoos. "Why not Gevaudan Dalliance?"

"People are strange, as we know."

The horse cleared the first log-topped bank and dropped over the large hedge into the water—the quick route again. The going was making the time achievable, but dark clouds were gathering in the distance and threatening the sunshine.

The pace of the horse was just right, ideal for clearing the fence on the island mound. Perfect speed for a marksman's shot.

So, where's Mick—Bête?

Lina was scanning the crowd with image-stabilised binoculars.

"Another call for number thirteen, Gevaudan Blood. Please tell us if you intend to run."

"Ouistiti to Zoos, Renarde about to start, over."

He controlled his breathing and his fears.

We will stop Bête. He must be here.

"Ouistiti to Zoos, on the cross. Into zone one, over."

He glanced at his watch. Carly would enter this target zone in five, maybe six minutes. He prayed for protection, divine if necessary.

"Just started, Carly Tanner and Sorcière des Saules, winners of the Saumur three star, and a combination with great potential; we're sure, one to watch."

Gilles's commentary continued to track Carly and Wanda's measured passage around the first part of the course. She had made it over the walls and the narrow brush at five.

"Blanculet, clear zone two, over."

As she approached, the key points identified were secure. Lina had endorsed their decisions, but would Bête?

The sky darkened, and he saw people put on jackets against the impending storm. Instead of bright t-shirts and sweaters, there were now dark muted shades and the odd splash of colour. The conditions he dreaded, treacherous under hoof and foot with low visibility.

He spotted a movement, a flash on the slope into the zone—harsh sunlight on metal. A twinge of memory shot up his spine, and he was helpless. It was too far to run, and if false, he would be out of position. Why had he missed the threat, again?

The cameraman panned as Wanda sailed effortlessly over the triple hedges. No time wasted in the set-up. No time lost in the air. Spectators applauded.

She's the real flying horse.

Then, he saw an old man with a walking stick hovering beside Lina. Maybe an elderly diehard follower, or perhaps it was Bête in disguise? It was too far away to decide clearly. The animated exchange with Lina was inaudible against the crowd's excitement, but the gestures provoked Loup's auto response.

"Brochet, clear zone three, over."

Armand forced his way through the swell that was building in his path.

"Loup, intrusion, zone five. Homard track Renarde, over."

A swift thrust of Bête's arm. Lina's hand chopped towards his neck. He squirmed free as she flailed the air, then struck his departing heel.

Armand reached her as she sank to her knees. The blood seeped out from under Lina's jacket.

"Get him. I'll be okay."

He turned to where Bête dodged through the

crowd, no longer a sick old man. "Loup, in pursuit of Bête, over."

Her wound could be severe if the knife had struck under the armour, but as he left, someone else had reached down to help her. On the covert net, he alerted the others that she was injured, without Gilles hearing.

As he talked on the radio, Armand tried to close on Bête, who slithered through the crowd.

A couple blocked the path, pointing at the approaching horse.

"Homard, entering zone four. Loup pursuing Bête. Am assisting, over."

Wanda turned towards the water.

Armand closed on Bête. Too late. The assassin raised his hound-headed walking stick.

SIXTY-THREE

The water slowed the mare, but her momentum carried her forward. Carly asked for another leap and Wanda obliged. A sharp stab in her right thigh made Carly wince, but she tried to ignore it.

They were clearing the hedge without wasting any effort, but then Wanda tripped on landing.

Carly wondered if the stumble was the mare's leg. Bad timing—she'd been so sound.

The worry was fleeting as Wanda responded with another burst, plumes of water flying off as they sailed out over the second hedged bank and onwards.

She leant forward and patted the mare then glanced at her watch. They were slightly up on the time, which was good.

Except, now her thigh was aching and her face was wet. Sweat? Or the first signs of rain? She glanced at the darkening sky, as they galloped towards the let-up fence before the next complex. Thick clouds were closing in over the park.

She wiped her face, wet with perspiration before the rain hit.

Then, they were over the fence and curving left-handed towards Hailing The Cab. The skies unleashed their fury in sheets, and visibility closed down. Wanda slid on the slick ground, studs tearing at the grass as they fought for grip.

Should she choose time or safety? It needed to be a quick choice, and she made an instant change of route.

"In the wet, it might be wiser to go longer." Gilles's words echoed in her head. Time would cost less than a run-out, but she could hardly see the fences, let alone the treacherous undulations.

She glimpsed the first element in the gloom and rode for it. As Wanda cleared it, the decision was locked in. Having walked the fence enough times, Carly knew the correct striding, and the mare trusted her.

Wanda's abilities now came into play. They weaved through the complex, taxis looming in sequence, the mare precise each time.

Except now, Carly's head spun, her body ached, and she was soaked. The downpour continued to bite into her and Wanda. Was the mare slowing too much?

She glanced at her stopwatch. It had misted up. There was no choice; she had to guess and use a hunting pace suited to this track.

But there was something else. Usually, she would suspect a hypo, except she had double-checked her levels, and had calculated for the adrenaline surge. The wet and cold would be having an effect, but her dual pump should compensate. She was confused. She needed glucose fast, but nothing happened, and the next fence was upon them.

Thankfully, Wanda knew what was needed—or was she tiring too?

As they turned down the avenue of cedars towards the final group of fences, she remembered the stinging pain at the water. Had someone done something to her? A name hovered out of reach, somewhere in the driving storm.

She willed herself and Wanda on. *We must make it for Armand, and for Mum.* The hunger and the pain had to wait. The crowd of faces blurred into rain, leaves and deer.

Or were those deer sculptures?

Her focus had to be on the last three fences, not their embellishments. She was so nearly home. Except, her body just wanted to slip off, but she had to hold on.

The noise was deafening. It sounded like a dam bursting. She was being tossed upwards. Blinding light rushed by, a spectrum of colours as she was swept along. Balance failing, fighting to stay aboard, but she was sliding again.

The ground was so much more secure. The chaotic movement had stopped. Her eyes took in the horse looking down at her, the blue of the sky, the scudding clouds and the crows. Now she ached everywhere and realised the pounding was in her head and her chest.

Faces were peering at her as a voice said, "Her vital signs are erratic. We need to get her checked, urgently, or we may lose her."

SIXTY-FOUR

The torrential downpour made the pursuit difficult. At one point, Armand's quarry cut across the course just as a horse approached. Armand waited and then leapt over the ropes and ran down the slope. He managed to stay in sight for a while, despite the crafty feints and jinks, but the volume of the crowd was against him. He tried calling for backup from the other Zoos, but it was to no avail.

It was as if Bête had staked out a route and was using confederates—the people casually blocking the path—to keep him at bay. Like a nightmare, Armand never seemed to get any closer.

Then, he heard the loudspeakers. "Carly Tanner has cleared the last on Sorcière des Saules. It's been a brave round in these conditions. Wait... *maudit,* she just fell..."

A gust of blinding rain and the groan of the home crowd drowned out the rest. Clutching at the crazy comfort that everyone needed her to win, he sprinted for the finishing area.

The commentator had changed, supplying distinct,

but uninformative info about the other riders negotiating the course, but no news of Carly and Wanda.

Vengeance spurred him towards Bête, at last, hemmed in by the crowd, and Faucon.

Armand grabbed the arm as the stiletto slid towards him. His sidestep diverted the blow.

"Too late. The bitch will die."

Mick tried to wrestle free, rolling like a jockey and then lashing out with his knee.

Armand absorbed it and twisted it under him.

"I've done you a favour stopping the killer. Vix will live—if you give us the mare."

Faucon helped force him to stand. Mick relaxed and put his hands forward as if ready for Faucon to handcuff him. They slackened their grip, and he jumped over the ropes.

Armand plucked a bolas from his belt and swung its weighted cords. He released the weapon. The bolas spun through the air towards the fugitive. The cords entangled his legs, and he staggered.

The ambulance skidded to avoid Mick, but the paramedics were rushing to the finish and couldn't miss. Their vehicle hit him full on, the impetus throwing his body over the roof, and onto the ground, where he squirmed, clutching his stomach.

The driver leapt out.

"Jesus Christ, I was responding to a faller. Now we've got ourselves a goddamn suicide."

"Don't worry; he caused the fall. Just treat him, we'll send the police."

As Armand ran to the finish and tried to ignore the air ambulance approaching, he realised the driver had a Canadian accent.

"Loup to Ouistiti, Bête neutralised. Any news on Renarde? Over."

The crowd gathered at the finish concerned him.

"Ouistiti to Loup, down but conscious. They're checking her now, over."

He could see the crumpled figure on the grass with a doctor kneeling beside her. Ouistiti came over and reassured Armand.

"She'll be okay. She rode across the finish and then just slid off. Admitted she was exhausted. The conditions were horrendous. She was more concerned about Wanda."

They watched as a doctor helped Carly into a Range Rover.

As the sun returned and banished the last of the summer storm, he tried to remain positive.

"Perhaps Mick missed. This collapse was just the weather and the general pressure."

"*Câlice,* you dash after Mick and leave Lina bleeding."

He turned. Gilles was sitting on the tailgate of a paramedic ambulance.

Lina was inside and said, "Don't listen to him, Loup.

You did your best. It was me he caught unguarded, and the armour deflected the blow, so it's only a flesh wound. I'll live."

"*Maudit*, you said the wound was throbbing badly when I reached you. That's not like you."

"I've experienced worse. As I'm sure you have, Loup. We're both fighters, aren't we?"

"But some fight dirty. They use poison or worse. Or is that justified against vermin?"

Armand climbed inside, palming the dart as he knelt beside the killer. He leant over and kissed her on the cheek one last time, scratching her skin with the thorn.

"It's not my way, but my cousin Odette wanted flowers, Euphorbia."

SIXTY-FIVE

The last few hours had been a blur. All Armand wanted was to be with Carly, and instead, he was in the Peugeot heading for Fenburgh.

I never wanted it to end this way, but it's the way Gilles has chosen. So, he's headed to the only bolt-hole he has left in England.

Armand turned off the M11 knowing what the Canadian hoped to find there—the same thing that had led Mick to the stud—but they would never get the last piece to complete Project Pegasus.

"Loup to Blanculet, how's Carly doing? I'm about to contact Harfang. Just need to check positions. Over."

"Blanculet to Loup, she's still asleep. On schedule. Over and out."

"Loup to Ouistiti, what's our target's status? Over."

"Ouistiti to Loup, Harfang's contacts have reacted as expected. Confirm Vecheech paramedics took Bellerophon and Bête to Fenburgh. Arrest warrants have been issued, and there's an all-ports warning circulating to stop any of them leaving the country. Over."

"So, the Harfang jet was held at Stansted as requested? Over."

"Grounded due to a bomb alert. The airport authorities told Gilles the incident could delay his departure by 24 hours. Hareng Rouge is now working within the Vecheech and Vidarranj servers, so incursion on schedule. Over."

"But Vecheech's medical team were allowed in? Over."

"As arranged. Monitored communications indicate they have already set up a private intensive care facility at Fenburgh. Over and out."

Lina will face death, even with their specialists. The euphorbia sap will complicate Mick's deadly venom. Toxins are confusing. And if Hareng Rouge has crossed over, someone hacked into Mick's computer recently. Good, that will add to the confusion, as Gilles must be searching for the hidden secrets.

Armand wasn't ready to relax yet, but as every familiar landmark brought them closer, the trap was closing.

He called Faucon and asked when they would be in position.

"We'll be inside the stud by 00:30. The Inspector needs to know your location."

"Just past Shippea Hill on A1101. ETA at Fenburgh Stud is 00:35. Frontal arranged. Police co-operation appreciated. Over and out."

Armand auto-dialled Gilles's mobile.

"Hi, is Lina recovering okay? We can't lose them both."

"Praying for her, but she's worse. Mick won't talk, and the medics are mystified as it's no poison they know. They thought it was an anti-coagulant, but the symptoms are confused. She's conscious, but unable to speak, except she keeps trying. *Batêche*, the shaking, the burning rash..."

"Might have the toxin ID'd from the dagger we found at the site. We have an antidote, but it will cost you, friend."

"*Maudit*, it's for Lina for god's sake... okay, name your price."

"Simple. We need the antidote for Mick's dart. He either has it on him, or he's hidden it at Fenburgh."

Vecheech held the report that had made the dart feasible to produce, regardless of how they had explained the theft, and it was Lina's research throughout.

Another reason to let her die.

"Nothing on Mick, but we found a lot of antidotes here, and we're still looking. How is Vix? Any clue to the infection? What's the analysis? Tailor made?"

The search was primarily for the final Pegasus materials, but however hard the Vecheech team searched Fenburgh, they wouldn't find the illusory DNA goldmine that Hareng Rouge had created.

Armand reached the roundabout and turned onto the A10 heading north alongside the river.

"Vix is still in a diabetic coma. Our med team says it's chronic Somogyi rebound. Mick used a modified insulin analogue to trigger a hypo. Now she's fluctuating from hypo to hyper. Conventional treatment only exacerbates it. I need that antidote. Please."

"Don't panic, Loup. She has exceptional metabolism, all Lina's tests proved that. I'm sure we can find an antidote here, but please..." The tears sounded genuine, which was good. "Lina is dying and... just come; I'll turn the alarms off."

"Okay be there in ten, just after half past midnight. Be brave."

Armand smiled and turned onto the road across the fens to the stud. Lina was proving to be his weakness, even now, undermining his inflexible Harfang persona. But would he sacrifice everything for her?

At 00:30, the floodlights around the pseudo-Georgian mansion flickered as Gilles turned off the alarms.

"Loup to Zoos, going in. Maintain silence. Activate Hareng Rouge follow up. Over."

"Faucon to Loup, in position. Understood. The line will remain open. Over and out."

As he turned into Fenburgh's main drive, additional security lights came on, bathing the buildings and paddocks. His frontal approach would be on camera for Gilles to monitor from the main house, even if the alarms were silent.

In the floodlights, the avenue of trees threw etched silhouettes across the drive. Among the remaining shadows, he could detect crouched figures waiting. The moon was entering its last quarter, but its light was still another searchlight in the cloudless sky. Zoos had already climbed onto the roofs using grapnels and were ready to blind the CCTV cameras with random images, before the final act.

Pulling up to the front door, he noted that Gilles had never sold his Impreza; he had parked his precious car under the balustrades.

SIXTY-SIX

Armand could tell that the drip was doing nothing to stem the tremors or help Lina's mouth emit more than croaks. Even the straps failed to achieve their purpose. Her eyes flickered open and shut. It would not be long now.

As long as Lina hears what I need to say, then I have to be satisfied. How long did Odette suffer in that freezing water? I pray it was quick, unlike this sad necessity.

Fenburgh's master bedroom was doubling as intensive care unit and office, curtains shutting out the real view outside.

Instead of the stud's wealth or shadowy figures, the CCTV monitors infected by Hareng Rouge were flicking between random shots. A single laptop was idle but with a screensaver of flying horses.

Gilles was standing, his face accusing Armand of treachery.

"*Câlice,* I'm about to save Vix, and this is my reward. I know your toy soldiers and the pigs are outside somewhere. Your cheap tricks are so obvious, Loup. I'm losing my wife, and you're playing games with lives. Well, I can kill Carly too, unless you give me what Lina needs."

"She already has it, dying in the way that she decided others should die. Did you forget that Euphorbia were my cousin's favourite plants? Or did you never learn that when seducing her and getting her pregnant? And the Chasseurs Alpins never play games."

"Cousin? Odette? Alpine troops? You're crazy, Loup. Give me the antidote."

"It won't work. A hybrid dose of euphorbon could be interacting with Mick's warfarin dagger."

Gilles picked up a syringe, and it flew across the room, smashing against the wall, but leaving the needle embedded.

"Then Carly dies too. You can't access his files, and he won't talk, look next door."

Mick's body lay on another bed, not breathing, rigid. Beside him, there was some medical equipment including syringes and a defibrillator. Despite the lack of wounds, they had tortured the salesman to death for the secret of his knife, and for the missing parts of Project Pegasus.

Did I cause his death by playing for time? By playing games? Or would I have been too late? Why does the scapegoat get left to die? His death demands more revenge.

"Afraid it's just us left making this deal. We tried to save poor Mick, but his heart gave out. He was injured too badly in the accident."

"This was better than taking him to a hospital?"

"It was quicker to fly them both here. Best facilities, just too late. Ask the medics downstairs. Anyway, how's Wanda? Will she survive?"

"No sign of any virus and I don't think the mare's infected. It was a hoax designed by Vidarranj to force our hand. Like you, they wouldn't risk her long-term breeding or competition value."

"I'm pleased she's unharmed. If Carly's retiring, so to speak, then the mare's ours."

"You scheming bastard. Wanda's mine and you will never get her back. As you can see, I haven't retired."

Armand smiled as Gilles whirled to face Carly, who was standing in the doorway beside her new friend, Blanculet.

"Impossible. You said Carly was dying, Loup. And the paramedics said the doctor took her to hospital."

"An exaggeration, part of the subterfuge. Unlike her win with Wanda after you had run. You lost that bet too."

"But, why my Lina? You can save her. We've so much ahead, together."

Carly unleashed her anger. "Damn you Gilles Boissard. You're cruel and heartless. Patrick Harfang is not just a front. You've become him, ruthless. You want us to feel sorry for that murderess? She never grieved for Odette or Roman."

"Those were accidents, Vix, like yours."

"No way, you arranged them all. Even the accident that nearly killed me."

"That was Mick. She told me."

"After she framed him. You knew. And I thought you loved me. All those promises: the maple grove, the ranch, the new life—meant nothing. Why did I ever cry for you? I suffered for what? Were they the same false dreams that you offered Odette? Tell him, Loup."

"Karma is a pretty bad kickass, as you said. Lina's death and the end of the dream are yours. What has all your scheming gained you? All these deaths for Project Pegasus?"

Gilles sat on the bed by Lina, who stared at her executioner with bloodshot eyes, hearing but unable to snarl back.

"Everything's here, on my laptop. Just take it, give me back Lina."

"*Merde*, you had my cousin's love, but you had Lina kill her. You had Carly's heart, but your whore tried to destroy her. Now you're losing her, and you can't buy her life. It's too late."

"You never intended us to be together," said Carly. "You played with me, used me. And the suicide? You could've told me, but no. You're a cheap rat with his whore... sorry, your dying witch. Now it's your turn.

Goodbye."

Armand and Carly walked towards the master bedroom door as Blanculet waved the police inside.

"*Maudit,* you misunderstand me. I intended to take you to Canada, Vix. Originally, it was meant to be with you, but it all went shit wrong. I never knew what Lina was doing. I only wanted to be loved. She hated Odette and wanted her dead. She hired that van. She wanted everything. Project Pegasus, Vecheech. Believe me; I'm her victim too."

"Then learn how it feels, Canuck vermin, with her blood on your hands," said Carly, venom coating her words. "Time to end your flying changes with another corpse to your name."

Armand turned back to Gilles.

"Don't try and convince the Inspector that you're innocent. When you gave us that USB drive, it proved that Vecheech had hacked into Vidarranj's servers, on your orders, Harfang; and it proved that you planted the misinformation. The authorities here, as well as in Canada and France, will receive all the evidence needed to implicate you in Project Pegasus, plus the three murders, and the hit and run attempt. Every keystroke has incriminated you and exposed your schemes to the asset strippers."

As Armand put his arm around Carly, he was confident that the Inspector would ensure that he investigated this crime scene thoroughly.

Outside, they looked at the paddocks bathed by the moon and stars.

"Will he milk this? Can he use the TV to his advantage?" asked Carly.

"Not with the evidence growing every hour Hareng Rouge eats away at Vecheech. He will face a lot of questions, and charges before he ever dreams of seeing Owlhead again."

"And Lina? She deserved to die, but murder is too harsh, as we agreed."

"She deserved to die, but she'll suffer as the modified toxin puts her in a controlled coma. She'll recover consciousness in prison, facing three murder charges."

EPILOGUE

The chorus heralded the light. Mist swirled from the river and the clouds rippled in the water. Carly dismounted and hitched Wanda to the corner of the wooden bridge. Armand looped the reins of Dido to the other support.

She laid a rug on the ground and gestured for him to join her.

"This place is best. We must decide—and don't just say whatever I want. That's a cop out—and so is saying it might be a boy. This girl knows."

Armand grinned and kissed her. "I was going to say, Marguerite or Maggie, after your mum. She means so much."

"And so do others. What about Odette Marguerite Sabatier?"

"If you wish, but this might be premature. Are you really..."

She nodded, pointing to her stomach. "Absolutely."

"Should you be riding tomorrow at Ardingly?"

"It's just a one-day event, and better riders than me have done it at bigger competitions. Might even notch up a few more points in the South East Eventers League."

Wanda nickered, then lowered her head and nuzzled them.

"So, I have to take you to the Seahorse Ball?"

"For sure, I so like dances." She snuggled into his shoulder. "Anyway, now I need to ask."

"Of course, anything, chérie."

"Our daughter, where are we going to bring her up? Is she French or English?"

Armand held her hands. "Well, Peter has said we could stay at his place beyond the end of the season, it's your home."

"I won't let us impose on Dad for much longer. We need a home of our own."

"But you know we can't afford to buy a place. Hazelmead is way too expensive, even with the foreclosure. Anywhere else is..."

"Aren't I French now? Can you afford to let your family *mas* in the Cevennes run to waste? That's another option, although the memories?"

"At rest like your mum, just warm inspiration. We have to look to the next generation now, and I agree, home in France."

"Dad might even be tempted to re-design the abandoned buildings—if you want. He was sorry that he couldn't help at Hazelmead more."

"I know. I realise we weren't meant to stay there,

but in France, he'd be very welcome. There's still a lot to do."

"Your friends made a brilliant start," said Carly. "And I want to get to know them better."

"Not just call sign names, then? A friend called Blanculet would be odd."

"And Loup isn't?" Carly blew him a kiss and squeezed his knee. "Just joking, to me it's cute, and it's you. But Tamara suits our friend better than her call sign."

"Not Mademoiselle Chastain?" Loup grinned, then asked, "Have you thought about my crazy suggestion?"

"Endurance?" I wouldn't be the first eventer to try my hand but..."

"Well, Dido's part Arab so she might make an endurance horse, although..."

At the *mas*, she had checked Florac out and realised the extent of the challenge.

"You wonder if I can compete outside my comfort zone. It's another discipline completely, but at the same time tempting. Let's leave it at that."

"It's your decision, and I'll support you, whatever you decide."

"Whatever happens now, Mum would be proud, and she's where she belongs—deep in my heart—and within our child."

"And she lives on in your achievements," said

Armand putting his arms around her and kissing her.

They let the embrace envelop them, like the sunshine spreading its warm embrace over the water meadows.

They held each other and then there was an unmistakeable scent. Two foxes appeared through a hedge. Majestic in their coats and thick brushes with distinctive black hairs streaking the tips, they trotted across the bridge and melted into the dawn.

Carly and Armand tossed three bouquets into the water and watched them drift downstream.

THE END

Made in the USA
Columbia, SC
28 July 2017